HOW TO ACT LIKE A LADY

"From whom are you hiding, Eden?" he asked.

Heat rushed to her cheeks at the sound of Trevor's voice. "The crowd. Sometimes the attention overwhelms me," she responded.

"Perhaps if you controlled your impulses . . ."

"I've done nothing wrong this evening." Anger flashed through her. "Nobody told me I shouldn't play cards."

"That's not a bad idea. The next time you need advice, you may call on me." Trevor leaned back against the bench. She wanted to wipe that smug look off his face.

"Then please impart your wisdom, oh wise one."

"Sarcasm does not become a lady."

Eden stood. "Very well, tell me what else I need to know."

Trevor examined her until she grew uncomfortable. Then he rose and circled her. "You shouldn't be out here with a man."

"I wasn't. You joined *me*, remember?"

"That is irrelevant."

"Then perhaps I should leave." Eden pivoted on her heel and took a step forward. His arm reached out and held her back.

"Your dress. The color. It's too bold. And . . ." He stopped, frowned, and cleared his throat. "It draws the gaze. If you aren't careful, your actions will bring about consequences you don't care for."

"Such as?"

"Such as this."

Before she knew what happened, Trevor pulled her into his arms and captured her lips with his own. . . .

Dear Romance Reader,

In July, we launched the Ballad line with four new series, and each month we'll present both new and continuing stories set everywhere from medieval England to the American West—the kind of passionate, romantic stories you love best, written by the most gifted authors. At the back of each book, we'll tell you when you can find subsequent books in the series that have captured your heart.

This month dazzling new author Lynne Hayworth begins *The Clan Maclean* series, the passionate and dramatic stories of three brothers torn apart in the aftermath of Culloden. In **Summer's End,** one of these proud Scottish men must choose between fulfilling a debt of honor . . . and losing the woman he has come to cherish. Next, talented Cynthia Sterling completes the *Titled Texans* trilogy with **Runaway Ranch.** What happens when a reformed rogue and brand-new vicar finds himself at a shotgun wedding—where *he* is the groom?

New favorite Sylvia McDaniel continues the funny, sexy saga of *The Burnett Brides* when a man haunted by the Battle of Atlanta rescues a woman from stagecoach bandits. Soon enough, **The Outlaw Takes a Wife!** Last, rising star Gabriella Anderson offers the second book in the charming *Destiny Coin* series, in which taking a headstrong American girl's hand in marriage becomes **A Matter of Pride** for one rakish British bachelor. Enjoy!

Kate Duffy
Editorial Director

THE DESTINY COIN

A MATTER OF PRIDE

GABRIELLA ANDERSON

ZEBRA BOOKS
KENSINGTON PUBLISHING CORP.

http://www.zebrabooks.com

ZEBRA BOOKS are published by

Kensington Publishing Corp.
850 Third Avenue
New York, NY 10022

All Kensington titles, imprints and distributed lines are available at special quantity discounts for bulk purchases for sales promotion, premiums, fund raising, educational or institutional use.

Special book excerpts or customized printings can also be created to fit specific needs. For details, write or phone the office of the Kensington Special Sales Manager: Kensington Publishing Corp., 850 Third Avenue, New York, NY, 10022. Attn. Special Sales Department. Phone: 1-800-221-2647.

First Printing: January, 2001
10 9 8 7 6 5 4 3 2 1

Printed in the United States of America

To Jean Price and DeWanna Pace—
Thank you for believing in me.

PROLOGUE

Massachusetts
August, 1819

Corinna Grant brushed her hair at the dressing table. The short, quick strokes gave the only evidence of her irritation. That and the silence between husband and wife. These wood-paneled walls had seen their share of arguments and apologies in the past. The bust of the emperor Hadrian stared with vacant eyes from the corner as if he had seen them squabble so many times that he was bored. His comical expression assured Corinna that this dispute, too, would pass. Poor Hadrian. Since they had had the bust repaired, his mouth held the hint of a smile, and they never had found the tip of his nose. Corinna returned her attention to the looking glass.

Stuart Grant surrendered the battle of silence first. He

stared at his wife's reflection through narrowed eyelids. "You can't mean to give her the coin."

His stern expression didn't frighten Corinna. "I thought you didn't believe in it." She sighed. "It is time, my love. Let the coin work its magic. She's ready."

Stuart lifted the silver circle from the dressing table. "This coin is an ordinary token. And she's still a baby." He crossed to the display case and laid the coin in its velvet bed.

"She's older than I was when I married you."

"She's still a baby."

Corinna put her brush down and retrieved the coin from its place between a Roman necklace and the tiny figurine of an armless goddess. "Yes, my love, but 'baby' is ready to leave. She can take care of herself." She dropped the coin into her pocket.

With a soft chuckle, Stuart took her in his arms. "I remember when you claimed the same thing."

Corinna nuzzled her cheek against his chest. "And I was right, wasn't I?"

"That's not how I remember it."

Pulling his face to hers, Corinna kissed him. Her heart raced as he responded in the way she knew so well. After all these years, he still took her breath away. A shock of gray colored his temples, but he was still the most impressive man she knew.

"Woman, you won't get me to change my mind." His warm breath sent a familiar tingle skittering down her spine.

"I didn't expect to."

A knock at the door interrupted their discussion. Corinna stepped out of her husband's embrace. "Come in."

Eden breezed into the room. Her daughter's blond hair never failed to bring a smile to Corinna's face. Although brown streaked Eden's golden tresses, she was the only fair member of the family. Eden's twin, Nicholas, inherited their father's black hair, and Corinna's hair was auburn, well, before the touches of gray set in. But Eden was the only child to have her father's crystal-blue eyes.

"Our guests are asking after you two."

"They can wait." Corinna returned to the mirror to finish putting up her hair. Two identical sets of blue gazes focused on her reflection. Smiling, she pulled back the long auburn lengths and twisted them into a chignon.

With a shake of his head, Stuart turned to his daughter. "We were just discussing your trip."

"I suppose I am excited to see Europe. Think of all the wonderful music I shall hear. It's just too bad I have to go with Mrs. Roberts." Eden wrinkled her nose.

"Mrs. Roberts was a fine governess, and I can't think of anyone I'd trust more to guide you through Europe," said Stuart.

"But she's so proper."

"All the better reason to send her with you," countered Stuart.

"If I were a man, I wouldn't need a chaperone."

"Yes, you would," responded Corinna.

"Mother."

Only a daughter could make that word sound like an accusation.

"You will sing for me tonight?" Stuart tilted his daughter's chin and smiled down at her.

"For you, Daddy, anything. Besides, I'm leaving in two days. How much damage can it cause?" Eden grinned up at her father.

Corinna blinked away the tears that filled her eyes. "That reminds me. I have something for you." She reached into her pocket and pulled out the silver coin. She pressed it into Eden's hand. "A good-luck charm. My mother gave it to me, and now I'm giving it to you."

Eden turned the coin over in her hand. Venus stood on one side. Her symbol, Venus's mirror, rested on the goddess's outstretched hand. On the reverse a swan glided in a tarnished lake. Letters curled around the swan. "*Numquam tuas spes dedisce.* Never forget your dreams. Are you sure Daddy wouldn't rather have it? You know how he loves this old stuff."

"No, it's yours. Remind me to tell you of the time I lost it and your father found it." Corinna shot a glance at her husband out of the corner of her eye. "Keep it with you at all times. It will bring you luck."

"I never thought you believed in such things, Mother."

Not with most things. "It can't hurt." Corinna kissed her daughter's cheek. "Now go. Our guests are waiting."

Eden hurried out the door, putting the talisman in her pocket as she left.

The tears Corinna had been saving welled up again and trickled down her face.

Stuart wiped a drop off her cheek. "We don't have to let her go."

"Yes, we do. It's time." She drew a deep breath and managed to stop her crying. "I will miss her so."

"You sound as if she will never come back."

Corinna thought about the coin. *She won't.*

She raised her gaze to his face and smiled. "I'm ready. Let's go see our guests."

CHAPTER ONE

London
April, 1820

"Don't be such a donkey, Lily. This is our chance to see Edmund Kean at Drury Lane." Eden Grant gazed at her friend. "What could go wrong?"

Lily Baylor shot her a look filled with mistrust. "You're joking, right?"

"I know, I know, but it will be different this time." Eden grabbed Lily's hands and pleaded. "Please?"

Lily shook her hands free. "Haven't we given Mrs. Roberts enough to worry about on this trip?"

"We'll leave her a note. Then she'll know we're all right."

"Why don't we just ask her to take us?"

"Mrs. Roberts? She thinks the theater is evil. I don't believe she's ever forgotten her Puritan roots. That's why my father picked her as our chaperone. He didn't want me to have any fun." Eden began to pace.

"He wouldn't have arranged invitations to tonight's party if he didn't want us to go out."

Eden flung her hands in the air. "Oh, sure. He sends us to one of his business acquaintances. I don't want to spend the evening with a bunch of stodgy old men."

Lily chewed her lip. Eden saw the indecision in her friend's expression. She stuck her hand in her pocket and rubbed the silver coin she found there. "Come on, Lily."

"I *would* like to see Mr. Kean before our friends back home do," responded Lily slowly.

"It'll be great. And nothing will happen, you'll see." Eden grinned. The coin had worked again. Her mother might not believe in its magic, but she did. Sort of. "Go get dressed and meet me back here in half an hour. Bring a wrap. We'll be outside for a while."

"Eden, I don't know—"

"Trust me." Eden ran out of the room before Lily could change her mind.

The big house was quiet. She dashed down the hall and bounded up the stairs.

"Miss Grant." The voice barked out her name in a reprimand. "Young ladies do not run up the stairs."

Eden turned around and faced Mrs. Roberts. The woman's gray dress suited her complexion. The tight chignon made her features seem even more pinched. "Yes, ma'am."

"What is the reason for your haste?"

"I need to dress for tonight's activities." Eden gave the chaperone an innocent smile.

"I'm pleased to hear you're excited about the party, but you don't need to run like a hoyden."

"Yes, ma'am."

"Go on, dear. We won't leave for an hour yet, so you have plenty of time." The older woman nodded her head in dismissal.

"Thank you, Mrs. Roberts." Eden turned back toward the stairs and remembered to climb them slowly. She lifted the lawn skirt and counted each step to herself as she ascended. . . . *thirteen, fourteen, fifteen.* At the top, she peered down the hall. Few furnishings adorned the corridor, but then again, they were just renting the house for the season. The family who owned it surely took the best pieces with them.

She pushed open the door to her room. Her footsteps crushed the thick blue carpet. The whole room was blue. Blue covered the bed, the walls, even the ceiling, although some clever artist had painted clouds on it so it looked like the sky. Ocean blue, robin's egg blue, bluebird blue, indigo blue, royal blue—they were all here in this room in one place or another. Mrs. Roberts had thought the room would suit her, since Eden's eyes were so blue. Eden hated blue. At least in such overwhelming abundance.

She pulled out a green silk dress. Now here was a color she liked. It reminded her of the forests of home. She glanced at the miniatures of her mother and father. Her European tour would be over in four months. Then she would go home to Massachusetts. And then what? Eden flopped on the bed. What would she do when she got home?

Eden stared up at the ceiling. It did no good to brood about the future. She supposed she would be getting married soon and have a family of her own. She liked the idea of children, but the idea of a husband made her cringe. All the boys she knew at home bored her. And she didn't suppose she would ever find a man who wouldn't try to control her.

Sitting up, Eden rang for the lady's maid they hired for their stay. If her future provided her no comfort, then she could at least enjoy the four months of freedom she had left.

Dressed and ready for the night's adventures, Eden made one more addition to her evening's wear. She took the coin out of the pocket of the dress she had just taken off. Silver gleamed through in the spots where the tarnish had no hold. Eden looked at Venus standing proudly on the front of the coin. On the reverse, she saw the swan that swam on its tarnished pond. The words shone into her eyes—*numquam tuas spes dedisce.*

Never forget your dreams. Ha. If I knew what my dreams were, I certainly wouldn't forget them. She placed the talisman in her reticule. Now she could leave.

Eden crept down the stairs. She inched open the door to the salon and slipped in. Lily was waiting.

"You look beautiful, Lily. That lavender gown is perfect, just as I knew it would be."

"It does look good, doesn't it?" Lily twirled around. "It's too bad we can't go dancing."

"We need more than an invitation to a dinner party for that. Unfortunately, I don't think the English are ready to invite two 'colonials' to their balls." Eden pinched her nose and altered her accent to sound more British.

"What a pity. I would so like to attend one."

"I would, too, but I don't think we're likely to receive an invitation soon. So in the meantime, let's go to the theater."

"I'm ready." Lily crossed to the door.

"Not that way." Eden strode to the window and pushed it open.

"You must be joking." Lily leaned out the window. "Why can't we just go out the front door?"

"And risk being seen? Come on, Lily. This will be easy."

"Easy for you. Your legs are long enough to reach the ground. I'm shorter than you, remember?"

"Don't worry. I'll go out first, then help you." Eden opened her reticule and pulled out the coin. "Here. Touch this for luck."

"Your coin? No, thanks. I'm beginning to think it brings bad luck, not good. Remember Florence?"

"Yes, but—"

"And Venice?"

"Yes, but—"

"And Vienna, and Paris?" Lily placed her fists on her hips. Her toes tapped her irritation on the carpet.

"Fine. I'll put it away. But don't blame me if something goes wrong tonight." Eden replaced the coin in her bag, but not before rubbing it herself. "Now come on."

Eden hoisted herself over the sill and dangled her legs above the ground. She jumped. The jump was farther than she had thought, and her teeth clicked together when she landed. But she had done it. She turned around to help Lily. Lily took the same position, but didn't move.

"It's awfully far down," whispered Lily through the darkness.

"Don't worry. I'll catch you." Eden took a place just below the window.

Lily jumped—and thudded so hard into Eden that they both sprawled onto the ground. Rolling off Eden, Lily stood first. She smoothed the front of her skirt. "I thought you were going to catch me."

"You didn't hurt yourself, did you?" Eden rose and adjusted her dress around her. She picked a twig off the cloth and twisted to view the back. Good. No damage. "Come on. We can catch a hackney at the corner."

The girls ran around the side of the house to the front.

Lights glowed in the various windows of the house. Careful not to step into the puddles of light that pooled on the ground, Eden and Lily made their way to the street without making a sound. Then Eden grabbed Lily's hand and, pulling her friend behind her, ran down the street.

"What's it to be tonight, Ryeburn? Will you attend Monkcrest's or Lockwood's soiree?"

Trevor St. John, Earl of Ryeburn, pulled the gloves higher on his hands. Night shrouded the city, but the many lights of London gave night a new color—gray, not black. He gazed out the window of his coach. "I haven't decided yet. Neither one is particularly appealing, but I should make an appearance at both of them."

"I believe I shall attend Lockwood's," said Christopher Seymour, Earl Toddington. He looked at Trevor. "Go to Monkcrest's first and meet me later."

"What shall you do after the theater, Sterling?" Trevor turned to the third man in the group.

The Honorable Martin Sterling adjusted his cravat. "I may find my own entertainment this evening. Regent Street isn't far from here. Perhaps I'll find a companion for the night."

Trevor shook his head. "I'd curb those appetites of yours, Sterling. Those women may cost you more than you can afford to lose."

"I only pick clean ones, Ryeburn. It's not as though I need fear the loss of my reputation. I'm not facing the marriage mart with a title." Sterling laughed, a coarse, mirthless sound that grated on Trevor's nerves. How had Sterling ingratiated himself upon them? Trevor didn't much like the man, but Sterling seemed to amuse Toddington.

The coach reached Drury Lane and stopped. The vehicle rocked as the driver jumped from his perch and opened the door. Trevor glanced over the crowd in front of the building.

"Good of you to let me use your box, Toddington," said Sterling.

Toddington waved his hand. "I can't use it tonight with Lockwood's soiree."

"Nevertheless—" began Sterling.

"Lily?" A shout near the carriage captured Trevor's attention. He searched the crowd for the owner of the voice. "Lily!"

A blond woman stood on tiptoe and scanned the crowd. Her hair, loosened from the knot on her head, curled around her neck and face as if flaunting its freedom. Her face was a picture of concern and worry. Trevor climbed from the coach. He ignored the startled glances of Toddington and Sterling.

"Pardon me, but are you in need of assistance?"

The girl turned to him, and he nearly backed up a step. The clear blue of her eyes stole his ability to breathe. They stared at him with a coldness he could feel. To his surprise, she was nearly as tall as Sterling. But much more pleasant to look upon.

"No, thank you." She turned her back to him. "Lily!"

"If your companion is lost in this crush, you will never find her by shouting." Trevor didn't know why he insisted on pursuing the matter. Her demeanor had made it clear that she didn't want his help.

"She isn't lost, we merely got separated." The girl didn't bother to face him as she answered.

"That doesn't sound promising," Toddington said as he joined them.

The girl turned at the new voice. "Now there are two of you?"

"Three, actually." Trevor's wave included Sterling, who gazed at the woman with keen interest. Trevor scowled at him.

"Well, thank you, gentlemen, but I don't need your assistance."

"Perhaps not, but your friend does. There are all sorts of villains in these crowds." Trevor tried not to let her gaze capture him. "What does your friend look like?"

For a moment the woman said nothing, then she gave a tiny shrug of her shoulders. "She is shorter than I and has dark hair."

"And her name is Lily," added Trevor.

The girl whirled to face him, surprise etched in her features.

"You've been calling her name," he said by way of explanation. He couldn't take his gaze from that interesting face. The fine line of her jaw seemed carved from marble, and her skin reminded him of the fresh cream that graced his table when he resided at his country home. He shook his head to clear those thoughts from his mind.

She blushed. "Yes, I forgot."

"Toddington, you and Sterling search that way. We'll try this side." Trevor took her arm and moved to the left.

The girl removed her elbow from his grasp. "You may release me." Her voice slid over him like a warm breeze, but one glance at her eyes froze him anew.

Suddenly the girl pointed toward the corner. "There. I just saw her disappear around the corner." She dashed in front of him before he could react.

Trevor followed her. She darted through the crowd, ignoring the rude glances and cries of the other theatergoers. He had some difficulty keeping pace, for as soon as she left a space, the crowd filled it. Still, his height made it easy for him to see where she went and to pick out his own trail.

She dashed around the corner just in front of him. "Lily!"

Trevor ran after her. A man dressed in dark clothing was retreating down the street. The girl held a smaller woman in her arms as that one cried.

"Shh, Lily. He's gone now. You're safe."

"I don't know what he wanted." A sob punctuated the pause between each word. The sleeve of the smaller woman's gown hung from the shoulder. Loose threads marked where the fabric should have joined.

"Most likely he thought to kidnap you and ask a ransom from your parents." Trevor pulled out a handkerchief and offered it to the sobbing girl.

The dark-haired girl looked up and gasped. Lily glanced between her friend and him and seemed to shrink in front of his eyes. Her hand flew to her mouth.

"Are you hurt?" He offered her the handkerchief again.

After a moment's hesitation, she took it. "No."

Trevor glanced around, waiting for the girls' parents or husbands to join them. No one came, yet the quality of their dress and speech indicated they weren't common women. "Where are your escorts?"

"We have none." The girl turned to her friend. "Are you sure you're not hurt?"

"I'm fine, Eden, but I want to go home."

Eden. So that was the chit's name. "You're not from around here." Trevor watched impatience flare on Eden's face. He had never seen such an expressive visage before. Her countenance revealed every emotion.

"Massachusetts."

Colonial. That explained much.

Toddington rounded the corner with Sterling in his wake. "I see you found her."

Sterling eyed the girls with interest. "Where are you going?"

"Home. Thank you for your help. Now if you will excuse us . . ." The girl called Eden pulled her friend back toward the front of the theater.

"Miss . . ." Trevor stood in front of them, blocking their path. He waited for her to tell him her name.

She shot him a testy look. "Grant. Eden Grant."

"Miss Grant, in England we do not allow our ladies to attend the theater alone."

"We don't in Massachusetts, either," the one called Lily volunteered. She cast her gaze to the ground as if she were ashamed of her behavior.

Miss Grant winced as the words spilled from her friend's lips.

Trevor glanced at Toddington, who watched the dark-haired girl with a frown on his lips. Good. Toddington was as disapproving as he. Trevor turned to the smaller woman, who clearly had more sense. "And your name is . . . ?"

"Baylor. Lily Baylor." The girl pulled her sleeve up to try to hide the tear.

"Miss Baylor," spoke Toddington. "Neither you nor your friend should be about at night. The streets of London aren't safe for young ladies without protection."

"Fiddlesticks. I can take care of myself." Miss Grant threw her shoulders back.

Trevor had to admit she made an impressive show of courage. Which only made him angrier. "Perhaps, but it is clear you cannot also take care of Miss Baylor."

That seemed to deflate her bravado.

"It wasn't Eden's fault," began Miss Baylor, her voice

steady although red still rimmed her eyes. "I let go of her hand, then suddenly there were so many people . . ."

Sterling stepped forward. "Since you gentlemen have engagements this evening, I would be more than happy to accompany these two charming ladies home." He bowed to the ladies. "Allow me to introduce myself. I am the Honorable Martin Sterling." He smirked, which caused Trevor's stomach to turn.

"The Honorable?" Miss Baylor's eyes widened.

Toddington frowned at Miss Baylor's obvious reverence. Trevor could see the muscles clenched in his friend's jaw.

Even Miss Grant seemed impressed. Trevor gritted his teeth. "No, Sterling. I will take the ladies home in my carriage."

"We can find our own hackney, thank you."

Trevor continued as if Miss Grant had not spoken. "My coach will provide the utmost discretion. Your reputations will suffer if word gets out about your behavior this evening."

"I don't give a fig for my reputation." Miss Grant scowled at him. "Besides, won't our reputations suffer if we ride with a man whose name we don't know?"

Ire rose in him. He was doing her a service, and she scorned him. "Trevor St. John, Earl of Ryeburn."

"An earl?" Miss Baylor looked as if she might faint at any moment.

"And now that we know your name, Lord St. John—"

"Ryeburn."

"Excuse me?" Miss Grant wrinkled her brow.

"Lord Ryeburn, not Lord St. John."

"I'll never learn these English conventions. Couldn't a country as old and cultured as yours come up with a simpler method of naming yourselves? I almost don't dare ask his name." She pointed at Toddington.

Toddington gave a stiff bow. "Christopher Seymour, Earl Toddington." His gaze softened as he looked at Miss Baylor. He leaned toward her and whispered, "You call me Lord Toddington."

Miss Grant sighed, a strange melodious whisper of air that sang in Trevor's ears. "I suppose I shall never get to see Edmund Kean now. Roberts is sure to double her vigilance after this."

"Roberts?" Trevor met her intense gaze with an arched brow.

"Our chaperone."

"So you do have a chaperone." Triumph rang in his voice.

"Of course. Did you really think we wouldn't?"

"I'm still willing to accompany the ladies home," interjected Sterling once again. "I've already missed the beginning of the performance at all events."

"No. My carriage is by far the better solution. Toddington, you and Sterling wait here. I won't be long. I'll come back after dropping the young ladies at home. We'll go to Lockwood's together."

"What of Monkcrest?" Toddington asked.

"I'll send my regrets." Trevor bowed to the ladies and indicated the open door of the carriage. He offered his hand to Miss Baylor.

Miss Baylor climbed in, glancing back at Toddington and chewing her lip. She settled on the seat. Trevor held out his hand to Miss Grant, who sniffed and climbed in without assistance. Trevor shook his head. A hard-headed girl was the last thing he expected to encounter this evening.

He entered the coach and paused. The girls sat opposite each other. He cleared his throat. "In England, the gentleman takes the seat facing the rear, and women do not sit beside men they have just met."

Miss Grant sniffed again and moved beside her friend. Trevor took his place. He tapped on the roof. The driver opened a small window.

"The address, Miss Grant?"

"Chipping House, Grosvenor Square."

The coach lurched into motion. Miss Baylor turned her gaze out the window, but Miss Grant met his gaze with steely blue eyes that lowered the temperature of the coach several degrees.

CHAPTER TWO

Eden stared at Lord Ryeburn. In all fairness she knew she should be angry with herself, but it was so much easier to blame him for the scare they had received this evening. Unfortunately, her conscience wouldn't let her. Guilt niggled at her until she couldn't keep silent any longer. "I apologize."

Lord Ryeburn's eyebrows shot up. "You do? How unexpected."

Heat rushed to her cheeks at the rightful reprimand. "You have disrupted your evening to see us safely home."

"Are you thanking me now?" Amusement glinted in his eyes.

"Not exactly. I did wish to see Mr. Kean perform, but I suppose I am more aware of what might have happened to us. Lily might have been hurt. We were lucky to run into you and not someone else."

"That's one of the first sensible things I've heard you say." Ryeburn crossed his arms on his chest.

"You needn't be so smug about it. I've admitted I was wrong. A gracious gentleman would let the subject drop."

"Perhaps I'm not convinced you've learned your lesson." Lord Ryeburn leaned forward. "Have you?"

Eden's breath stopped in her throat. Why hadn't she noticed the man's dark-brown eyes before? They drew her into their depths as if she were drowning. She swallowed hard, trying to restore moisture to her mouth. "Have I what?"

"Learned your lesson?"

"I doubt it," chimed in Lily.

Lord Ryeburn sat back. "Unfortunately, that's the same impression I get."

Eden frowned. "You don't even know me. I can understand Lily's attitude, but you can't possibly—"

Lord Ryeburn held up a gloved hand. "Miss Grant. You are correct. I have no right to come to such conclusions. It is my turn to apologize."

"But somehow, I don't believe you mean it," she muttered under her breath. She cast her gaze to the floor of the carriage, then sneaked a glimpse at him. His gaze was now directed out the window. Good. She took this chance to examine him.

So this was an earl. He didn't look different from any of the men at home. No, that wasn't true. He did look different, and she hadn't yet looked her fill. His hair was dark, as dark as his eyes. His jaw cut a firm line, and his face was . . . oh, so nice to look at.

His shoulders filled the confines of his jacket, which could not hide the strength evident in the man. Lord Ryeburn's legs stretched across the coach. Even so, his knees were bent as if there was inadequate room for his long limbs. She wondered why he would have such a small carriage if it didn't fit him.

In the next instant, Eden realized his attention had returned to her. He had seen her examine him. She squeezed her eyes shut in mortification. It wasn't her fault she had never seen a man like him. It wasn't her fault she wanted to see more.

"Miss Grant, are you ill?"

"No, but I wish I were." She opened her eyes to find him chuckling at her. Thank goodness they were almost home.

They pulled up in front of the house. Every window blazed with light. The door was open, and Eden could see Mrs. Roberts wringing her hands and dabbing her eyes with a handkerchief as she talked to the footman. The man seemed ready to leave the house.

"Why do you suppose Mrs. Roberts is so upset?" asked Lily.

"I don't know," replied Eden. In that moment, a coldness gripped her stomach. "Lily, did you write the note?"

"No. I thought you would."

"Oh, dear." Eden climbed from her seat and threw open the coach door. She jumped down without waiting for any assistance. Grabbing her skirts in her hands, she flew up the walk. "Mrs. Roberts. Mrs. Roberts!"

The older woman turned at the sound of her name. Tears broke out anew at the sight of her charge. "Miss Grant. Thank heavens you are safe. Is Miss Baylor with you?"

"Yes." Eden glanced back at the carriage. Lord Ryeburn was helping Lily from the vehicle.

"It seems you won't need to call the authorities after all, madam." The footman gave Eden a look that she could only construe as disapproval.

"Thank you for your assistance, Henry." Mrs. Roberts still dabbed at the corners of her eyes.

The footman bowed to Mrs. Roberts and proceeded to the kitchen.

Eden looked back at her chaperone. Mrs. Roberts had dried her tears and reinserted the steel rod that went down her back.

"Young lady, where have you been?"

"We didn't mean to frighten you, Mrs. Roberts. We meant to leave a note, but we forgot."

Mrs. Roberts turned to the door as Lord Ryeburn entered with Lily. "And who is this man?"

Lord Ryeburn stepped forward and bowed. "Trevor St. John, Earl of Ryeburn, madam. I brought the ladies home in my carriage."

Mrs. Roberts's mouth formed an O. "An earl? Miss Grant, what have you been doing?"

Eden hung her head. "We wanted to go to the theater."

"The theater? I've told you such places are immoral. Look what 'the theater' has done to you." Mrs. Roberts wagged her finger in Eden's face. "Your parents trusted me with your safety. How can I possible carry out my duties when you pay me no heed? I shall write them immediately."

"I wish you wouldn't. Daddy is sure to get angry, and I am not a child."

"Then stop behaving as one."

Eden's face flooded crimson. She could feel the heat of her blush.

Mrs. Roberts turned to Lily. "And as for you, Miss Baylor, I am shocked that you continue to allow Miss Grant to lead you astray. I had hoped you would have more sense. Just look at the tear in your new gown. How long do you think Mr. Grant will put up with squandering his money on you?"

Lily's face drained of color. "I'm sorry, Mrs. Roberts."

"It isn't every girl who is given the opportunities you have been. When I write Mr. Grant, we'll see how much more of his generosity you shall enjoy."

"Yes, ma'am." Lily cast her gaze down and twisted the handkerchief she held in her hand. Eden knew her friend was on the verge of tears. She slid beside Lily and slipped her hand into Lily's. Lily didn't look at her.

"Thank the gentleman and then take care of your appearance." Mrs. Roberts crossed her arms and frowned at Lily.

Lily bobbed a quick curtsey to Trevor. "Thank you for bringing us home, Lord Ryeburn." Her voice was so soft, he barely heard her. She turned to go, but stopped and faced him again. She extended her hand, her expression one of horror as she observed the twisted fabric of his handkerchief.

"Keep it," said Trevor. "Perhaps it will remind you of the folly of listening to your friend." From the corner of his eye, he saw Miss Grant wince.

Lily nodded and hurried up the stairs.

Mrs. Roberts beamed her approval. "Such wise words." The matron turned to Miss Grant. "We still have time to attend our engagement for the evening. I won't allow your father's business to suffer due to your foolishness. You didn't consider how your actions might harm his reputation. I don't know what you were thinking. Go upstairs and clean up."

Ryeburn watched Miss Grant straighten up and face the chaperone without fear. "Yes, Mrs. Roberts." She then turned to him. Her lovely chin inched up a notch before she spoke. "Thank you again, Lord Ryeburn, for your assistance. I'm sorry to have troubled you this evening."

He could see the pride in her eyes, the defiance etched

in the angle of her jaw. He bowed to her. "Good evening, Miss Grant."

She turned and ascended the stairs, still holding her head erect. No hint of remorse showed in her posture.

Ryeburn faced the older woman. He could see why Miss Grant would want to escape that dour mien. Still, the woman seemed concerned about her charges, as witnessed by her red-rimmed eyes.

"I must apologize for my charges, Lord Ryeburn. Miss Grant is a little high-strung."

A little? "Don't mention it, madam. I'm happy to have been of service."

"These two girls have proven difficult to control. Miss Grant's parents have spoiled her terribly, allowing her all kinds of freedoms. No discipline. They sent her on this tour with me to help curb those traits, but I'm afraid she's more than even my skills can handle. She has a sweet heart, but her actions . . ." Mrs. Roberts clicked her tongue in disapproval.

Ryeburn didn't allow himself to squirm with the discomfort he felt. This woman was telling him far more than he wanted to know about the girl. He had delivered the chit, and he would never see her again. So why did the urge to defend Miss Grant rise so strongly in him?

Mrs. Roberts continued, "What she needs is a husband, one who will not tolerate her behavior. A firm hand to guide her, one who isn't afraid—"

"Madam, I must be going. I have an engagement this evening, and I fear I shall be late if I tarry any longer." Ryeburn nodded at the woman.

"Gracious. How inconsiderate of me. I do ask your forgiveness, my lord. I shouldn't burden you with my troubles. Thank you again for bringing the girls home." Mrs. Roberts dipped into a curtsey.

"No trouble, madam. Good evening." He bowed and retreated out the door. He restrained himself from running to his coach.

Ryeburn sat back against the cushion. He hadn't felt such panic in years—not since he inherited all his father's problems. Through clenched teeth, Trevor drew in a deep breath. A brief encounter with some girl couldn't hurt him. Nothing had changed. No one need know of tonight's events, although *his* reputation wouldn't suffer even if the facts did become known.

His breathing came easier. He wasn't his father; he had proven that already. He had rebuilt his holdings, discharged his father's debts, and for the last three years, he'd had enough wealth to relax. But he wouldn't forget how hard he'd had to work to restore his reputation. The *ton* spoke his name with respect, even if those who didn't know him but knew of his father treated him with caution.

The panic slipped away; anger replaced it. That a flighty girl could elicit such turmoil in him disturbed him. Then again, look at the turmoil she caused in her own life.

He chuckled, as much at himself as at the memory of her pride and arrogance. Her name suited her. Eden. Paradise with a problem. He was glad he would never see her again.

The coach stopped in front of the theater. The crowds had dispersed, leaving only Toddington and Sterling lingering in front. Trevor climbed out and stretched his legs.

He called up to the driver, "Wait here. I won't be a moment. Then we'll go to Lockwood's."

"Very good, my lord."

Trevor's legs carried him a few steps when a glint from the walk sparkled in his eye. He looked down. A coin. Amazing that no one in the crowd had seen it before him.

He'd leave it for some unfortunate who needed it more than he.

As he stepped over it, he paused. An inexplicable urge to examine the coin overtook him. With a slight frown, he bent to retrieve it.

The coin wasn't English. Trevor turned it over in his palm. The figure of a woman graced one side, and a bird appeared on the reverse. There were words as well, but he didn't have the time to examine it further. He slipped it into his waistcoat pocket. He would look at it later.

"Back from your errand of mercy?" Toddington grinned at his friend.

"Yes, and thankfully so."

"You could have left them to me," said Sterling.

"And let them further risk their reputations?" Trevor shot back.

Sterling guffawed. "You know me too well, Ryeburn."

"Decent of you to think of them, Ryeburn." Toddington pulled his gloves on his hands.

"When have you ever known Ryeburn to think of anything but his reputation?" Sterling clapped his hand on Trevor's back.

"True," replied Toddington. "Reputation above all."

"Mock me if you will, but I find my repute comforting. In fact, I believe it's time to cement my standing in society."

"How do you propose to do that?" Toddington asked.

"Gentlemen, I plan to find a wife."

"You can't be thinking of marriage?" Toddington's eyes widened.

"Whyever not?"

Sterling eyed him with disbelief. "Taking on the shackles, when you still have so much time for freedom?"

"It is time, gentlemen. I am thirty years old, and I desire

to settle down. I have no doubt I shall find a bride this season.'' Trevor led them to his carriage.

''No doubt! With the number of mothers searching for husbands for their daughters, you'll have trouble finding just the one.'' Toddington's laugh rang out in the street.

''Knowing Ryeburn, he has the whole process mapped out,'' added Sterling. ''Step one, establish availability. Step two, determine respectability.''

''I suppose he has a working list of which ladies are eligible, which ladies have the proper qualifications.'' Toddington roared again.

''If you gentlemen are finished . . .'' Trevor waited for his friends to cease their merriment.

''He will have a problem, though. With his looks and the way the ladies swoon over him, he's bound to have a difficult choice.'' Sterling continued, ignoring Trevor's rebuke with a guffaw.

Trevor gazed at the duo with cool indifference. ''If you two idiots are through making fools of yourselves . . .''

The two men stifled their laughter, but their mirth was far from dead.

''I never realized you believed me such a cold fish.''

''None of the ladies would call you cold,'' Toddington said.

''You seem to think marriage is something more than a business arrangement,'' said Trevor.

''It would be nice to have some feelings for the girl before you wed her, something in common with the chit,'' Toddington argued.

''I'm sure she'll be pleasant enough. As for the rest, one female is much like another. With the proper organization, I shall find the proper wife, and I wager I can do it in one month.''

"A wager? I didn't think you capable of such behavior, Ryeburn," Sterling goaded.

"Then obviously you don't know me very well. One month, gentlemen, and I shall have found a wife." Trevor reached the carriage first. His driver opened the door for the men.

"What shall the wager be?" Sterling gave an eager smile.

"A token amount. One pound, say?" Trevor stood to the side to let Toddington climb in.

"No faith in your abilities, eh?" Sterling's gaze taunted him.

Trevor stepped into the vehicle rather than let loose his anger at the man.

"Sterling's right. That wager seems to lack conviction." Toddington nodded as the coach rocked with Sterling's entrance.

"I was thinking of your resources, Sterling. I didn't want you to regret the wager when it came time to settle up," said Trevor.

"Shall we say one hundred pounds then?" Toddington suggested.

"One hundred pounds," Sterling repeated.

"Agreed. One hundred pounds from each of you. I shall lose two hundred if I fail." Trevor rapped on the roof of the coach. The conveyance started.

"Finding the proper wife in one month. Not an easy task, Ryeburn." Toddington shook his head.

"Do you doubt my abilities?" Trevor raised an eyebrow at his friend.

"If you had shown some interest in a particular girl, my answer would be no. But to find a girl when you haven't begun to look . . ." Toddington shrugged his shoulders. "A pity that Miss Grant isn't available."

A rush of irritation flowed through Trevor. "I thought your tastes ran more toward her companion, Miss Baylor."

"I wasn't speaking of *my* tastes. I was thinking of yours. She's the first woman of late with whom you've spent more than a few minutes, besides your occasional mistress. You have to admit she is a beauty."

Trevor remembered the cold sparkle of her blue eyes, the soft scent of lavender, and the spirit and fire that seemed to fill her entire being. "A beauty perhaps, but entirely unsuitable as a countess. No, gentlemen. I shall find my bride in one month, and she won't be a woman as flighty and headstrong as Miss Grant."

CHAPTER THREE

Trevor sat back. Good God, what had come over him? A few minutes under the influence of that woman, and his sensibilities had flown. He was certain he could find himself the proper bride in a month, but to let his companions provoke him into a wager? Nevertheless, he wasn't worried about the outcome. After all, he knew the traits he expected in a wife. How difficult could it be to find someone who fulfilled his requirements?

The coach pulled up in front of Lockwood's house. Carriages lined the street, and drivers, wearing their different liveries, adorned each vehicle. Lights from the house spilled onto the street, splashing the ground with a harlequin mask. A footman ran up to the coach and opened the door. Trevor shook off his vexation. He wasn't going to let Miss Grant's actions spoil his evening. Lockwood was a useful ally in Parliament, as well as one of the few men who had given him a chance upon the inheritance of his title. Trevor owed the man more than he could ever repay.

Shaking off the pall of the evening's previous events, Trevor stepped from the carriage, followed by Toddington and Sterling.

The footman bowed to them. "Good evening, my lords."

Trevor nodded to the man and continued to the house, his two companions at his heels. Directing his steps to the drawing room, he saw his host circling among the guests.

Lady Lockwood greeted him at once. "Ryeburn, so good to see you again. We have missed you." His genial hostess turned to his friend. "And Lord Toddington. I see you've brought Mr. Sterling. How clever of you. One of our gentlemen has fallen ill and cannot attend. I was so afraid one of our ladies would have to go to dinner unescorted."

Trevor bowed. "Lady Lockwood, you grow more beautiful every time I see you."

"Now you know why I keep inviting you, you dear boy. You make me feel so young. Come. We are expecting a few more guests. Make yourselves comfortable until then."

The trio moved further into the room. Trevor glanced around. A good crowd, perhaps twenty people. Lady Lockwood enjoyed large dinner parties, and from her greeting he knew more were coming.

His gaze fastened upon a young lady in the corner. Trevor searched his memory for her name. Ah, yes. Lady Regina Hope. She stood with her mother, their heads bent together, probably deciding which man was the best catch in the room. He saw them glance his way, and a blush flooded Lady Regina's face. He smiled at them and nodded, then watched as they put their heads together again. Lady Regina fit his criteria, except . . .

Except she was pretty in a vapid sort of way. Her eyes lacked fire, and her skin looked more blue than pale. No roses bloomed in her cheeks. Her voice didn't caress the air, and she was short.

Trevor jerked himself upright and rubbed his forehead. He had never known himself to judge a woman in such a manner. He didn't understand his own mood tonight.

Toddington leaned over to him. "You are not going to believe who just walked in."

Trevor looked at his friend and with his gaze followed Toddington's stare to the door. Gad. It was Miss Grant. Impossible. He looked again. No mistake, it was she. Although her face revealed her anxiety, Trevor noticed that she didn't allow herself to back away from the challenge of the room. Miss Grant stood straight and tall, as if daring anyone to approach her. She must have repaired her hair, for it curled onto her head with nary a tress out of place. He found himself wishing she would pull out a few pins and let the thick lengths cascade over her shoulders. She wore the same dress of forest green he had seen her in earlier, not the usual pastel relegated to single girls. How like her to ignore the fashion dictates. Her gaze darted from one person to another.

"She looks lovely." Toddington stared at the newcomers.

Irritation flashed through Trevor, until he realized that Toddington gaped at Miss Baylor. The dark-haired girl had likewise repaired her appearance, but she seemed meek when compared to her companion.

Lady Lockwood approached the latest arrivals. She took Miss Grant's hand and pulled the girl to her. "You must be Eden. I have been eager to meet you. Your father has written us all about you. Such a dear man your father is. My husband speaks so highly of him."

Eden curtsied. "How do you do, Lady Lockwood? Please let me introduce my friend, Lily Baylor."

Lily gave a timorous smile and bobbed a quick curtsey.

"Another lovely young lady. It shouldn't surprise me that you shall attract all manner of attention while you visit us. Come. Let me introduce you to a charming young man." Lady Lockwood linked arms with Eden and Lily and crossed toward Trevor.

When Eden saw him, she stopped, jerking Lady Lockwood backward. "Oh, forgive me. My shoe slipped."

Lady Lockwood giggled like a young girl. "Think nothing of it." The older woman pulled Eden forward to Trevor. "Ryeburn, I'd like to introduce Miss Eden Grant. She's the daughter of our business acquaintance in Massachusetts."

The look on her face was worth an entire evening of boredom. She didn't know whether to admit she had met him or pretend she didn't know him. Trevor waited. He had no desire to make the decision for her.

Her face lit up. Trevor arched an eyebrow. He was curious which choice she had made.

"Lord Ryeburn. A pleasure to see you again."

Lady Lockwood looked surprised. "You know each other?"

"Only in passing. We ran into each other on the street, and Lord Ryeburn was kind enough to help us."

"I'm grateful you remember me." Trevor latched onto her meaning. Her vague words gave the impression that they might have met on Bond Street or elsewhere, when he might have given them directions. And yet she told no lie. As he bent over her hand, he smiled at her cleverness.

"This is wonderful. Will you escort Miss Grant into dinner then, Ryeburn? I'm sure you won't mind having a beautiful girl on your arm." Lady Lockwood beamed at them, then moved to Sterling, pulling Lily with her.

A servant announced dinner in the next instant. Trevor

held up his arm, and Eden placed her hand on his. The warmth and softness of her skin caught his attention. His hand burned where she touched him. He shook off that fanciful thought and took a step, but stopped when he realized she didn't follow. "Miss Grant?"

"I can't leave Lily behind."

"You needn't worry about her. Lady Lockwood will have her paired off as well."

They entered the dining room. White damask covered the table, which stretched the length of the room. Footmen stood near the high-backed chairs ready to assist the guests into their seats. Gold-edged plates adorned the table, as well as a large epergne at the center. Twelve candles glowed from the ornate silver branches, which were also heavy with fruit and flowers.

"My goodness," breathed Eden. Her gaze took it all in, from the table to the gold fabric that covered the walls.

"Impressive, isn't it?" whispered Trevor. His breath tickled her neck.

She stiffened. "I suppose, if one enjoys ostentation."

His chuckle rippled through her, like a sip of champagne. "You are determined to be contrary, aren't you?"

"Not at all." Heat pooled in her cheeks at the lie. Her conscience pricked her. "Well, maybe a little."

He laughed again, and the sound embraced her. She shot a glance at him and marveled at the way his eyes lit up in amusement. The dark depths beckoned to her. She leaned toward him. . . .

Trevor continued forward, jerking Eden from her reverie. Good heavens, what had she been thinking? This arrogant man had no hold over her. He pulled out her chair, and she took her place. To her left sat Lord Ryeburn; to her right sat an older gentleman. Eden breathed a sigh of relief. She would spend dinner in conversation with that gentleman, whoever he was. She didn't have to speak with Ryeburn again.

Eden peered down the table. Lily sat with the Honorable Martin Sterling. Lily glanced up and smiled at her. That fellow Sterling seemed to be making her comfortable, for every now and again, Lily turned to him and responded. Between Lily and herself, Eden saw Lord Toddington. He sat next to an attractive young woman Eden had not yet met, but his gaze was directed at Lily. Whenever Sterling leaned toward her friend, the earl frowned. Eden smiled. Lord Toddington seemed smitten with Lily.

"Do you find something amusing?" Ryeburn asked.

His voice startled her. "Interesting, not amusing."

The first course of soup appeared in front of her. She was happy to give her attention to the food instead of elaborating on her comment.

Course after course followed. After the soup came trout and broiled salmon. A choice of tongue in aspic or mutton chops followed as the entree, accompanied by quail or duck. She sipped her wine and enjoyed the variety of food. The older gentleman to her left talked of hunting and his collection of snuff boxes, which hardly interested her, but conversation with him was safer. The last main course finally disappeared, and the table was cleared. After champagne and dessert, the ladies retired to the drawing room.

Eden drew a deep breath. The ten or so ladies sat on the sofas and chairs around the drawing room. She had made it through without causing herself more embarrassment with Lord Ryeburn. Now she only had to wait until it was time to go home. . . .

Lady Lockwood smiled at her guests. "Octavia, would you entertain us with that lovely poem?"

An elderly woman stood, looking pleased to perform. Her voice, deep with age, began, "I shall recite a poem by Lord Byron." The woman cleared her throat. "She walks in beauty, like the night, Of cloudless climes and starry skies . . ."

Eden stopped listening. The poem was lovely, but the woman's voice was putting her to sleep. Her gaze sought Lily, who sat across the room by another matron. Eden glanced at the lady to her right. She was young and pretty.

Eden realized the ladies were applauding the performance and quickly joined in. The girl beside her stood. "If you wish, I might sing something."

"What a lovely idea, Regina." Lady Lockwood beamed at the girl.

Plastering a smile on her face, Eden hoped her discomfort didn't show. The evening was becoming frightening. Lily glanced at her, but Eden diverted her gaze. She wouldn't look at Lily. Nobody here knew. She was still safe.

The girl called Regina sat at the pianoforte and accompanied herself. Eden hoped her smile didn't fade throughout the performance. Her face hurt from the strain of holding the grin in place, but she didn't dare stop. She glanced at the clock. Only fifteen minutes had passed. Surely the men would join them soon and the performances would stop before—

From the corner, Mrs. Roberts stood. "My young ladies would love to play and sing for you."

Eden flashed a panicked plea at Lily. Lily shrugged her shoulders. There was no polite way to back out.

Inspiration hit Eden. She stood and crossed to the pianoforte. Lily took a seat on the bench.

"Eden, whatever you're thinking, don't," Lily whispered to her.

"Trust me, Lily."

"I have really come to hate those words." Lily waited for Eden to speak.

"My friend Lily has often accompanied me while I sing. That is in fact how we met. We were both taking lessons, and our teachers brought us together. Since that first day, we have become almost sisters. Her talent is quite remarkable."

"Eden, stop," whispered Lily.

"For our first song, we shall perform 'Sheep May Safely Graze,' by Johann Sebastian Bach." Eden smiled at her audience.

Lily lifted her hands, and the melody began to flow from under her fingers. Eden opened her mouth. "Sheep . . ."

The note was so far off, Eden saw the ladies wince, then stare at her in disbelief. The next note was just as far from true. She got through a whole line before the expressions of the ladies froze into smiles of pain.

Lily played the wrong note. "Eden," she hissed.

Eden ignored her friend. She sang the next three notes so off key, Lily stopped playing. She rose from the instrument.

"Forgive me, ladies. I wish to play a different song." Lily faced Eden before she sat down at the bench once again. She gave Eden a smirk so filled with mischief that Eden grew apprehensive.

Silence reigned in the room. Lily took a deep breath and began anew. The sweet notes tinkled out of the instrument, flooding the room with a new expectation. Eden groaned, or she would have if the music hadn't touched her soul. It was Mozart's "Ave Verum Corpus," one of her favorite pieces to sing. Ideally four voices sang the parts, but Lily's gifted hands would fill in for the lower voices. Eden would get even with Lily, but first she had to sing.

The first note out of her mouth met almost as big a reaction as her previous attempt. The ladies started, but this time because the note was so pure, so light, it almost was visible. Eden sang on, losing herself in the music. Her voice filled the room with beauty and joy. At the first break, Eden looked out over her audience. Rapture gripped the ladies' expressions.

She sang on, each note more beautiful than the last. She reached the climax of the music and placed each note with the delicacy of an artist until the blend of sounds was too sublime to describe. Gooseflesh rose on her arms, as it always did when she sang those notes. Her part ended, and Lily played the final three measures. For a moment, no applause greeted the end. Many of the ladies had tears in their eyes. Then the room burst out with speech and clapping and excitement.

The men were enjoying their port in the dining room. From above they heard the tinkle of music and made jokes about the ladies' entertainment. Trevor listened to the conversations without taking a real interest in any. He hated to admit it, but he was brooding. Miss Grant had avoided him for most of the meal, which shouldn't have troubled him, except it did. Now he was too busy worrying about his lack of discipline to join in the many discussions around him.

The butler brought in more port. As he opened the door, music was once again heard from above, but this time no one mocked it. The playing of the pianoforte was remarkable enough, but thereafter came an angelic voice. The men fell silent. When the song finished, excited applause drifted toward the room. Then silence, and the music started again. Most of the men put down their glasses of port and followed the sound to the drawing room. Trevor's curiosity grew. He had never known these men to join the ladies early. He trailed behind them as they ascended to the drawing room en masse.

Out in the hall, the voice was more enthralling. The exquisite tone and passion of the music captured every man's attention. As Trevor listened, his heart filled with richness of the song. One after the other, the men slipped into the drawing room.

Trevor turned through the doorway and froze. Eden. That voice belonged to Miss Grant. She continued to sing as if unaware her audience had grown. The simple ecstasy on her face stole his breath. She not only sang the music, she was the music. Her eyes glittered like diamonds, her lips caressed each word, her hands moved as softly as a butterfly, giving each note a visual accent. He had never seen anyone or, indeed, anything as beautiful in his life.

The song ended once again. This time the men joined the women with their applause. Several of the men wiped their eyes along with the women.

"Who would have thought the hoyden had such talent?"

Trevor was jerked out of the entrancement of the music. Sterling grinned at him. A strange flash of foreboding rose in him, but he dismissed it as fancy.

"Talented and rich, too. Did you know her father is one of the wealthiest men in the Colonies?" Sterling's grin held more than amusement. Trevor's unease grew.

At the request of the host, Lily began to play yet another piece, and Eden sang again. The music erased the words he was about to say to Sterling. He felt himself get lost in the music, but more than that, he felt himself get lost in her voice.

When the song ended, Trevor shook himself. He looked around the room. With the exception of Sterling, they had all fallen under her spell. She was a sorceress with her voice.

But try as he might, he couldn't keep his gaze off her. He couldn't keep his thoughts from her. He didn't want to feel any attraction for her. She was flighty, undisciplined, uncontrollable. And she was beautiful, spirited, and talented.

He cursed himself for his weakness.

CHAPTER FOUR

"Tell me it didn't happen." Eden rubbed her eyes.

"It did." Perched on the edge of Eden's bed, Lily drank from her cup of chocolate.

"I'll probably have to leave England." Eden flopped back on the bed. The contents of the tray next to her rattled.

"Careful, you'll spill."

"Careful? It's too late to be careful." Eden groaned and put her head under her pillow. "It's your fault, you know. You had to play Mozart."

"I couldn't play anything else with the way you were singing." Lily stroked her arm. "It's not so bad, Eden. There were no more than twenty people there yesterday, and this is England. They have breeding here."

Eden let out a sorrowful laugh. "I hope you're right."

An energetic knock at the door brought Eden out from under the pillow. She sat up. "Come in."

Mrs. Roberts entered. "Good morning, my dears."

Mrs. Roberts had never sounded so cheerful. Eden glanced at Lily before answering. "Good morning. I think."

"That was very wicked of you last night, pretending you couldn't sing." Mrs. Roberts laughed.

The sound surprised Eden. They had never heard Mrs. Roberts laugh.

"You can't imagine what has happened," Mrs. Roberts continued.

"Oh, no." Eden winced. "What has happened?"

"It's beyond imagining. I never hoped for such success with you two."

"Mrs. Roberts, perhaps you'd better tell us what you're talking about," Lily prompted.

"The balls, and the soirees. We've received five invitations this morning alone."

"Invitations?" Eden swallowed hard.

"Yes, my dear girl. It seems your singing so impressed Lady Lockwood last night, she has told all her friends about you." Mrs. Roberts brought forth the envelopes, each different from the other. She held up one that had a red seal, broken. "This one is for tonight. A ball. Can you imagine? It's from the Marquis and Marchioness of Heathsbury."

"A ball?" Eden closed her eyes.

"Yes. Why do you repeat everything I say?" Mrs. Roberts stared at her. "You're not feeling ill, are you?"

"No, ma'am." *I wish I were.*

"That's good to hear. You wouldn't want to miss the ball tonight." Mrs. Roberts crossed to the door, then turned back. "We have a busy day, ladies. Let's not waste it in bed." She left the room.

"I knew it. It's started." Eden tossed back the covers,

ignoring Lily's squeal as the blanket covered the food on the tray.

"You're being silly." Lily slid the tray out from under its hiding place. She crossed to the small table and placed the tray there. "At least we get to go dancing."

"How much dancing do you suppose we're going to do? They'll have us singing for most of the night." Eden opened the door to her dressing room and searched for something to wear.

"They'll already have music. You might sing one or two songs, but I doubt they'll have use of me."

"Oh, yes. You'll have a grand time, while I'm stuck entertaining." Eden tossed her nightgown onto the bed and shrugged into a simple dress.

"I was just teasing. It won't be so bad. Besides, you like to sing." Lily stepped behind her and buttoned the dress.

Eden sighed. "I know I do. It's just that people get so carried away by it. Just look at what happened last night."

"At least you haven't received any marriage proposals. Yet."

Eden glared at her friend, then burst out laughing. "You're right. It can't be as bad as it was at home."

Stepping back into the dressing room, Eden pulled out the reticule she had used the night before. "And I know just the thing to help keep me safe."

She reached into the bag and frowned. Opening the top wider, she peered inside. She thrust her hand in again. "Lily, it's gone."

"What's gone?"

"My coin. My good-luck charm." Eden turned the bag inside out. Along the bottom, the seam gaped open. "Oh, no. It must have fallen out."

"Maybe it fell out in here." Lily searched around the table.

Eden dropped to her knees. "It's got to be here." She crawled on the floor, then dove under the bed. The dust tickled her nose, and she sneezed. Retreating, she sneezed again and then once more. "Ring for the maid."

Lily pulled the cord beside the bed.

Throwing the bedclothes on the floor, Eden lifted the mattress. When she saw the maid, Eden rushed to her. "Did you find an old coin in here yesterday by chance?"

"No, miss."

"Are you sure?"

"Yes, miss."

"Where can it be?" Eden ran back to the dressing room and began to rifle through her clothes, each dress landing on the floor.

Lily dismissed the maid and followed Eden to the dressing room. "Eden, it's not here."

Eden faced Lily. Her friend shimmered and disappeared from sight as tears welled up in Eden's eyes. "I know. I could have lost it anywhere last night. We must have run over half of London." She sank down onto the floor. "It's probably in a gutter somewhere."

Kneeling, Lily hugged her. "That coin meant a lot to you."

"My mother gave it to me. It brought me luck." Eden sniffed and wiped her eyes with the back of her hand.

Lily handed her a handkerchief. "It didn't bring you luck. Remember Florence? And Vienna, and Paris?"

A smile tugged Eden's lips despite herself. "Maybe it wasn't always *good* luck, but it did bring me luck."

"I'm sorry you lost it." Lily rose. "I suppose we should straighten your room." Lily went back into the room, picking up the bedclothes as she walked.

Eden drew in a ragged breath. She picked up a dress and put it back in its place.

Numquam tuas spes dedisce.

A breeze whispered the words to her. She shook off that thought. There was no breeze in the dressing room, and no one to whisper the words in any case. She must have remembered them herself. But why? Why did she suddenly remember the words on the coin? Her dreams and hopes had no substance. Touring Europe had brought no end to the vague feeling that she was searching for something. No coin could help her find the thing even *she* couldn't name.

The coin was a lucky token, that's all. I'm just afraid of what will happen now that it's gone.

Half an hour later, her fears grew. As the two girls went downstairs, Mrs. Roberts was just closing the front door.

"Look at this, Miss Grant." The older woman held up a large basket brimming with flowers. "This is the second delivery today. And another invitation has arrived since I spoke to you."

Eden shot a glance at Lily. "Who sent the flowers?"

Mrs. Roberts placed the basket on the table in the hall and pulled out the card. She reached for her pince-nez that hung on a chain from her bodice. Clipping them to her nose, she read the card. " 'To Miss Grant. Please accept these humble posies as a token of my esteem. The Honorable Martin Sterling.' He was that nice young man Lily sat next to last night."

"I remember." Eden didn't give the flowers another glance. She stepped into the salon. Another bouquet greeted her sight. "From whom are these?"

"Lord and Lady Lockwood, thanking you for making their party a success. And they hope you will grace their house again before you return to Massachusetts."

Eden flopped onto the settee. "I'm ruined."

Mrs. Roberts sent her a puzzled look. "A young lady

doesn't flop into her seat, Miss Grant. And how are you ruined?"

"It's not important." Eden sighed.

"Not important? If you are ruined, your father will blame me for not looking after you well enough. What have you done this time?" Mrs. Roberts's voice rose a notch as her tone became shriller.

"Don't worry, Mrs. Roberts. I'm not ruined. Not in *that* way."

"Heavens, Miss Grant, don't scare me. I depend upon this position for my livelihood. My reputation can suffer because of your careless words—"

"I'm sorry, Mrs. Roberts. When our trip is finished, I shall be happy to write a testament about your conduct and the way you watched us."

"Yes, well, I didn't mean . . . never mind." Mrs. Roberts brushed an imaginary fleck off her skirt. "We'll go out this afternoon to shop for more clothes. You can't possibly have enough gowns for the upcoming events." Mrs. Roberts pivoted on her heel and left the two girls in the salon.

"It won't be so bad, Eden. Just think, the nobility vying for your attention." Lily sat beside her friend.

"Your playing is marvelous, too. Why don't they bother you?"

"Because your singing outshines anything I can do on the pianoforte."

Eden could detect no hint of rancor in Lily's voice.

Lily smiled at her. "Someday I shall make my living playing, or at least giving lessons to snotty little children. I love accompanying you, but I don't fool myself into thinking I possess a great talent." Lily lifted her hand to stave off the protest that rose to Eden's lips. "Oh, I'm good, but my talent isn't extraordinary. Yours is, and you're lucky enough not to have to worry about making a living. You can sing because you love it. And I feel lucky to play for you."

Overcome with emotion, Eden hugged Lily. "Now I know why you're my dearest friend. Well, then. Let's plan what we shall wear to the ball tonight. We'll impress the British with our style as well as our talent."

Trevor sat in his library at a small round table. This was his favorite room. Surrounded by his books, light filtering through the thick draperies, he often spent his mornings here, collecting his thoughts before the day's affairs. Here he studied Parliament's agenda, the quiet adding to his sense of ease. Steam rose from a cup of coffee in front of him. He glanced at the paper, then set it down. There was nothing interesting brewing in Parliament yet. He lifted the cup and saucer, took a sip, then replaced it so that the saucer occupied the same ring on the leather-topped table.

He reached into his pocket and pulled out the coin he had found the previous evening. He had thought to examine it during the light of day and perhaps identify it. Holding it to the lamp that stood on his desk, he turned it over in his palm.

A portrait of Venus adorned one side. On the reverse, a swan. Words encircled the fowl. *Numquam tuas spes dedisce.* His public-school Latin returned to him in a trice. *Never forget your dreams.*

An odd motto. No numbers dated the token, yet it was clearly old. Trevor turned it over in his hand again. Roman, he guessed, but he doubted it was money. Odder still was the question of how it had ended up on the streets of London.

The words echoed in his mind. He had worked hard to achieve his dreams. His father had all but destroyed the family name. Concordia, the family home, had nearly succumbed to disrepair. He had righted all that.

A knock at the door interrupted his musings. "Come."

Finch, his butler, entered. "A visitor, sir." He offered Trevor a card on a salver.

Trevor picked up the card and read it. Toddington. "Show him in, Finch. I could use the company this morning."

"Yes, sir."

Trevor placed the coin in a drawer in the table.

Toddington stepped into the room. "Good morning, Ryeburn. I hope you don't mind the early hour."

Trevor waved his hand. "Not in the least."

Toddington moved to the settee. "Still drinking that abominable stuff? Can't abide coffee myself."

"Then I shan't offer you any. Shall I get you some tea instead?"

"No, thank you." Toddington's gaze traveled to the ceiling. He cleared his throat. "Quite an unexpected evening, wouldn't you say?"

"Hmmmm." Trevor wondered what Toddington was leading to.

"That girl has an astonishing voice."

"Her voice certainly was unexpected."

"What do you think of her companion?" Toddington's face grew red.

"The dour old woman?" Trevor raised his brows.

"No, the girl who played the pianoforte, Miss Baylor." Toddington's complexion grew even ruddier.

Trevor examined his friend with wonder. Could it be that Toddington felt something for the girl? Mischief bloomed in his heart. "Ah, yes, the charming Lily."

"Charming?"

"Didn't you find her so? Miss Baylor seemed much more

refined than the incorrigible Miss Grant. I fully believe Miss Grant coerced Miss Baylor into their misadventure last evening."

"My thoughts exactly." Toddington leaned back. His face no longer held that pinch of anxiety.

"In fact," continued Trevor, "I believe Miss Baylor is quite the proper female. She speaks softly, acts demure, and is pleasant to look at. She also plays the pianoforte well, yet doesn't flaunt her talent as Miss Grant did."

"I quite agree."

"I'm glad you brought her to my attention, Toddington. I shall definitely add her to my list." Trevor waited for Toddington's reaction.

Toddington sat up. "Pardon me?"

"My list of eligible females. I have a wager to win, and Miss Baylor fits my criteria. However, she is an American, which speaks against her. Checking her family background shall prove difficult. Where do you suggest I go for the information?"

Toddington sputtered. "I? You can't mean . . . Now see here, Ryeburn—"

Trevor laughed. "It was a jest, my friend. I am not interested in Miss Baylor."

"Yes, well . . . it wasn't very funny." Toddington sat back and adjusted his waistcoat. His face wore a frown, but relief etched his features. "Not that it matters to me, but I should hate to see Miss Baylor hurt."

"She should start by avoiding Miss Grant in the future." Trevor grew annoyed with himself. That chit entered his thoughts far too often for his comfort, leaving him filled with apprehension. "Miss Baylor doesn't seem the type to befriend such a creature."

"Perhaps we misjudge Miss Grant." Toddington stroked his chin. "Perhaps Miss Baylor sees something we can't."

This topic began to irritate Trevor. "It doesn't matter. Miss Grant and Miss Baylor are leaving in a few months. Next season no one shall remember them."

A little voice in his mind laughed at him. He scowled.

"Is something wrong, Ryeburn?"

"No. What do you say to a ride in the park? There's a gelding I might purchase. Shall we put him through his paces?"

CHAPTER FIVE

Riders filled Hyde Park. Gentlemen with their long coat-tails hanging over the flanks of their horses nodded to ladies who drove their one-horse carriages or rode their ponies. The feathers and flounces outnumbered the horses. To Trevor it seemed he rode in a fashion plate rather than London. He knew these daily excursions served a multitude of purposes, social and political, but he had no desire to stop for conversation.

With a light touch, he guided his animal through the crowd. The horse beneath him responded to Trevor's every command. The roan lifted his hooves in a sprightly dance, yet never showed signs of bolting. Even so, Trevor could feel this horse had spirit. Trevor was eager to reach Rotten Row for an all out sprint.

"That's a fine-looking animal, Ryeburn." Toddington rode beside him. "I wish I had seen him first."

"I think you were too busy looking at a pretty young musician."

Toddington blushed. "Very amusing, Ryeburn."

A sense of relief stole into Trevor. This outing was just what he needed to renew his energy, revive his concentration, and remove that fog from his mind. He gazed at the bright blue sky and smiled. *There. You didn't once compare the sky to the color of Miss Grant's eyes.*

He winced.

"Are you in pain, Ryeburn?" Toddington asked.

"Muscle spasm." Trevor urged his horse forward. Perhaps a hard ride would rid him of her ghost.

Finally he reached the sandy track of the Rotten Row. "Ready to run, Toddington?"

Out of the corner of his eye, he saw a blur. Trevor looked up and blinked twice to make sure he saw clearly. Flying toward him on a horse was Miss Grant. She whooped as she passed him, sparing him not a glance. A good two lengths behind came Sterling. Even as Trevor watched, the gap between the two riders increased.

"What the devil?" Toddington clicked his tongue and galloped off in pursuit.

Trevor didn't wait any longer. He spurred his horse and entered the chase.

His judgment about the horse was correct—the roan did have spirit—but the abilities of his mount concerned him little at the moment. He sailed past Toddington and closed the distance between himself and Sterling. The roan, seeming to understand his rider desired more speed, quickened his pace. His hooves sent up little clouds of dirt. Trevor passed Sterling and neared Miss Grant.

Up ahead, a line of trees stood beside the track. Trevor's mount pulled even with Miss Grant, then shot past. A glance behind him showed she had cut her pace. He pulled back the reins, slowing his horse enough for her to reach him. By then the other two horsemen had caught them as well.

"I won," panted Eden. She turned her gaze to Trevor and flashed him a grin. "And you wouldn't have caught me either if I could have ridden astride."

"This was a race?" Trevor couldn't keep the incredulity from his voice.

"Of course. What did you think it was?" Eden turned back to Sterling. "You owe me a pound, sir."

"Indeed I do." Sterling grinned at her.

Trevor wanted to slug the man. "You urged her into this?"

"No," said Eden. "*I* challenged him to a race. Mr. Sterling was boasting about his horse, and I had to show him he was wrong. This is Hermes. I bought him in Vienna. He's one of the finest animals I've ever seen." Eden leaned forward and patted the neck of her horse. Her gaze passed over Trevor. "Although your horse looks powerful as well, Lord Ryeburn. I do so love spirit in a mount."

Desire stirred in his loins until he remembered she was talking about horses. Horses. Trevor gritted his teeth. "The race was *your* idea?"

"Yes. I haven't ridden hard since I was at home. My brother and I used to race all the time, and I would win most of the time. Well, maybe half. I can't wait to see his face when he sees Hermes."

The girl had no sense. "In England, women don't race horses, and Rotten Row is where men ride."

Eden frowned. "Are you going to lecture me again?"

"Come now, Ryeburn. It was harmless fun," Sterling interjected. "You can't expect her to know all our British customs."

"Where is your chaperone?" Trevor ignored Sterling.

"She knows I'm here if that's what you're asking." Eden lifted her chin.

"And she let you race?"

Her smug expression faded. "We ran into Mr. Sterling. Mrs. Roberts and Lily are riding a couple of slow ponies. Neither one of them is very good on a horse."

"Miss Baylor is here?" Toddington perked up at the news.

"Yes, back there somewhere."

"Do you think she would mind if I greeted them?"

Trevor's ire rose. He didn't need Toddington's infatuation to confuse the matter. "Go along, Toddington. I'll find you later." He returned his attention to Eden. "So Mrs. Roberts gave you permission to race?"

"Mr. Sterling offered to show me the best lanes to exercise Hermes." Eden didn't lift her gaze to his.

"And the race?" Trevor stifled the urge to shout the words.

"Well, he kept boasting about his horse, and I knew Hermes could beat him. What better way to prove it?"

"Do you think at all before you act, Miss Grant?"

Eden gasped. Her gaze flew to his face. No trace of the earlier joy and exuberance remained in her visage. A shimmer of tears welled up in her eyes, threatening to engulf the vivid blue.

He hated himself. He knew he was right, but he hated himself nonetheless. Trevor wanted nothing more than to restore her earlier glow and smile. Instead he clamped his mouth shut and steeled his gaze.

The struggle to win control over her emotions played out on her face. She took a deep breath, several in fact, then spoke. "Lord Ryeburn, that you disapprove of me you have made abundantly clear. It may surprise you to learn that I disapprove of you as well. Anyone who is so caught up in the rules others have placed on him cannot see the joy in living. I, sir, search for the joy. Good day." With a quick flick of the reins, she rode away from him.

He watched her until she disappeared. Had she just reprimanded him? He couldn't remember the last time someone had dressed him down. His actions always bespoke decorum, yet this high-strung female had found fault with him.

"You can be an ass, Ryeburn," Sterling muttered before he rode after her.

"So I've just been told," said Trevor to the air. *That girl flaunts her behavior in my face, then expects me to feel guilty about it. Unbelievable.* Unfortunately, guilt twisted in his gut when he recalled her expression.

He didn't know whether to laugh or get angry. Trevor kicked his heels and made ready to follow her, but thought better of it. He didn't know why he wished to aggravate himself further. Eden meant nothing to him. What did it matter if he couldn't convince her that her behavior was wrong? She would soon be gone in any case. No harm would come to him if she made a fool of herself.

Trevor turned the horse. The further he stayed from her, the safer his reputation.

He turned back.

No, he would follow her, just to make sure she got back to her chaperone. What was Mrs. Roberts thinking, allowing her charge to ride without supervision? Mrs. Roberts never should have let Sterling take Eden anywhere, and Sterling never should have offered. Unless . . .

Unless Sterling was somehow interested in Eden. What had he said last night? Something about Eden's father. The thought of Sterling's interest in Eden disturbed Trevor. Perhaps if he talked to Mrs. Roberts, he could discover what Sterling's interests were.

The roan kept pace with an easy canter. From a safe

distance, Trevor watched Eden return to her chaperone. Toddington rode beside the group, smiling like an idiot at Miss Baylor. Sterling rode alongside as well. Trevor watched as Sterling said something to Miss Grant. Even from this distance, he could see her expression brighten. Trevor knew he wasn't welcome to join them. He was the outsider here. He hadn't felt such scorn since his father was alive. But this scorn was of his own making.

He watched the group leave the park, but followed no farther.

Eden had a headache. She lay on her bed, the draperies drawn, her eyes closed, but she was far from sleeping. Thoughts whirled in her head like a hurricane. Mostly she was angry with herself for letting that pompous, arrogant, overbearing, self-righteous Lord Ryeburn rile her.

She flipped over onto her stomach and blew out a puff of air. Maybe she shouldn't have raced—she knew the behavior expected of young women—but she had enjoyed the wind streaming past her cheeks. It all seemed so unjust somehow. Her brother attended Harvard and she couldn't, simply because she was a woman—the same reason society said she couldn't race. At least society deemed her singing an appropriate pursuit, even if her talent brought its own problems. She couldn't imagine not singing. It would be like not breathing.

Tonight she would sing at the ball, she had no doubt. The Marquess and Marchioness of Heathsbury would hardly invite her for any other reason. If Ryeburn were there, he would hear her again, and—

Good heavens, what was she thinking? Never before had she thought of using her singing to impress anyone. She sang for herself. Why would she want to impress Ryeburn?

He thought her uncultured and undignified. Perhaps that was the reason. She would enjoy proving him wrong.

A smile crept onto her face. What a wonderful idea. She would be the perfect lady tonight. She would dress—and act—as society dictated, and show him how wrong he was.

She rolled off the bed, eager to start her toilette for the evening. She needed a bath after the outing in the park. On her way to the dressing room, Eden pulled the cord to summon the maid.

In the small chamber, Eden cast a discriminatory gaze over her gowns. Which dress should she wear?

A knock at her door interrupted her. "Come."

"Eden?" Lily's voice called out in the room.

"I'm here," she answered, never taking her gaze from her gowns.

Lily entered the dressing room. "Are you feeling better?"

"Definitely. Which do you think I should wear tonight?" Eden tapped her lips with her finger.

"Are you sure you're up for a night of dancing? We were worried about you—"

"My headache is gone, and I'm looking forward to this evening."

"Mrs. Roberts will be so relieved. She was afraid we would have to miss the ball because you were ill."

"You can reassure her that I am quite myself again. Now, help me decide which dress to wear."

"You have that glint in your eyes." Lily cocked her head. "What do you have planned?"

"Nothing."

"I don't believe you."

"For once, you can rely on me. I shall be on my best behavior." Eden fingered a gown of a rich topaz color. "What do you think of this one?"

"Eden, look at me." Lily stood with arms crossed. Her

gaze narrowed. "You weren't at all eager to attend this ball. What happened?"

"Trust me." Eden patted her friend's arm.

Lily frowned. "I do hate it when you say that."

"Miss?" The maid's voice called out.

Leaving Lily with her clothes, Eden returned to the room. "Will you draw a bath for me, please?"

"Yes, miss." The maid bobbed a curtsey and left.

"Will you please tell me what is going on in that devious mind of yours?"

"Devious? I am not devious." Eden grinned at Lily.

"Eden." Lily stomped her foot. "I'm getting angry."

"I promise, Lily. Tonight I shall be the perfect lady."

"I want to believe you, but—"

"Then do." Eden grabbed Lily's hands. "I know how excited you are to attend this ball. I wouldn't want to ruin that for you."

Lily blushed. "I don't know what you mean."

"You don't think I haven't noticed how you look at Lord Toddington, do you?"

Her blush deepening, Lily chewed on her bottom lip. "Do you suppose he's noticed? I would die if he thought I was chasing him."

"No, I think he's too busy looking at you to realize you're looking back."

"Stop teasing, Eden. We both know that I disappear beside you." Lily pulled her hands free.

"You can't believe that. You're everything a woman should be—petite, beautiful, and charming."

"And you are commanding, with the carriage of a queen. I'm sure he doesn't notice me when you're there. Even the Honorable Mr. Sterling seems taken with you. He talked with Mrs. Roberts today. He wants to call on you."

Eden couldn't help but grimace at that news. "And I

suppose Mrs. Roberts was so impressed with his connections, she's going to allow him."

"Don't you like him?"

"I don't dislike him, but I'm sure Mrs. Roberts would like to see me marry some member of the aristocracy. Then she could guarantee her success in the future. I can see her advertisement now. 'Chaperone. Proven ability to snare an aristocrat for your daughter'."

Lily shook her head. "He's just coming to visit."

"And you think I'm being silly." But she couldn't shake the sensation that Mr. Sterling's visits would cause trouble. Eden sighed. "Come help me decide what to wear tonight."

By the time they chose her dress, water filled the tub. Lily left Eden to her bath. Eden cleaned off the dust of the park, then leaned back in the tub. She felt guilty that she hadn't told Lily of her plan to dazzle Lord Ryeburn, but Lily would try to talk her out of it. Or make more of it than there was.

Eden shut her eyes. An image rose in her mind—Ryeburn's dark eyes shining with approval at her, his smile directed at her. She imagined him asking her to dance, how she would fit in his arms. Her heart quickened, and a flush heated her cheeks. Her eyes flew open. That wasn't supposed to happen. No. He would ask her to dance, and she would turn him down.

She splashed water on her face and stepped from the tub. Wrapped in a dressing gown, she dried her long hair with the towel, then yanked a comb through the tresses. Her anger fed her vigorous strokes, as if she were punishing herself for her stray thoughts.

Tossing her head back, she glanced in the mirror. She lifted her chin to an arrogant angle. She would show Lord Ryeburn just how perfect a lady she was.

CHAPTER SIX

The sight took her breath away.

The house twinkled with gaiety. Torches lined the path to the entrance, brightening the stones as if it were day, and the windows sparkled with lights as if stars filled the panes. Carriages lined the block as one by one they emptied their passengers in front of the great house. Eden watched as ladies in elegant attire strolled up the steps on the arms of natty gentlemen.

Remembering her pledge to herself, Eden waited until the footman reached their hired hack and helped her out, but her excitement was difficult to control. She was glad she came tonight.

Inside, the ball appeared even more magical. Chandeliers sparkled high above her head, and the many conversations made the room buzz with a convivial hum. A greenish-blue fabric covered the walls, giving the impression that the ballroom was under the sea. Indeed the sea seemed to be the theme of the decor. Scalloped shells formed the molding, with mermaids holding the corners. At the far end of the room, an orchestra tuned its instruments. The dance had not yet started, for the hostess was still greeting her guests at the door.

Jewels dripped from the ladies' necks. The gentlemen stood beside their ladies as acquaintances circled around the room greeting each other.

Eden squeezed Lily's hand. "Isn't it wonderful?"

"I can scarcely believe it's real," breathed Lily. "Do you think I look all right?"

Lily wore a pale-blue gown. Along the skirt hem ran a broad ribbon of lavender, the same color of the sash that tightened the high-waisted dress. Lace decorated the demure décolletage. She wore her hair piled atop her head in a Grecian style.

"You look lovely, just as a girl should." Eden glanced down at her own dress. It was an unusual dress of Viennese design. The light of the chandeliers burnished the topaz color until her gown seemed more copper than brown. Dark green embellished the gown in the form of a vine that seemed to grow from the hem. Burgundy roses bloomed from the vine as it climbed to her right shoulder. Eden hoped the dress gave her just the air of elegance she needed.

The music started up, and the host and hostess opened the dance.

"Do you suppose someone will ask us to dance?" Lily's gaze followed the couple on the dance floor.

"I have no doubt." Especially if Lord Toddington were here. Eden didn't voice her thought for fear of disappointing her friend if he didn't arrive.

The minuet started. Eden partnered with a young man, who was nice-looking in a nondescript way. He didn't seem much older than herself, which rather made her feel as if she danced with her brother.

The Honorable Mr. Sterling asked her for the next dance, a lengthy country-dance. As they took their places in the line, Sterling asked, "Are you enjoying yourself?"

"Yes, thank you. I've never seen anything quite like this."

As the music started, the dancers took their turns at the figures.

"I was quite surprised to find you attending tonight's affair," said Sterling as he linked arms with her and circled around.

"A pleasant surprise, I hope."

"Of course. I hadn't imagined I should be so lucky as to see you twice in one day." Sterling bowed to her and stepped forward. "So, tell me. Is America as beautiful as they say?"

"I don't know what they say, but it is pretty at home." Eden advanced, circled him, and retreated.

"May I say I doubt America has anything more beautiful than you."

Eden smiled stiffly. She didn't like the attention Mr. Sterling directed at her. Her gaze searched for Ryeburn, but she didn't see him in the throng.

"Do you plan to sing for us tonight?" Sterling continued the dance.

"If our hostess asks."

"Then I fervently hope she does so."

Would the dance never end? Keeping a courteous expression on her face was growing more difficult with each step. She didn't know why, but every word from Mr. Sterling's mouth set her nerves on edge.

"I understand your father owns an estate in Massachusetts."

"Yes, Fairlawne, my home."

"So you still consider your father's estate your home. Is there no one who has tried to tempt you away to your own home yet?"

"No, not yet."

The music ended. Sterling took her hand and bowed over it. "I shall find you later for another dance, if I may."

Sterling released her fingers with apparent reluctance. His lingering touch made her grateful they all wore gloves. She curtsied and moved to the edge of the room, careful not to give in to her desire to run.

Eden sat out the next two rounds. Lily, she noticed, had danced the first two, but was still on the floor. Since she had no desire to sit beside Mrs. Roberts, Eden found an empty seat and watched Lily.

"Miss Grant?"

Eden jumped at the unexpected voice. She turned and smiled at the gentleman. "Lord Toddington. Such a pleasure to see you again." She offered her hand.

Toddington bowed over it. "The pleasure is mine, Miss Grant." He cleared his throat and peered over the crowd. "Is Miss Baylor here as well?"

"Yes, but she's dancing at the moment. Shall I tell her you asked after her?"

"No . . . I mean, I . . . that isn't necessary." He cleared his throat again. His gaze fastened on Lily in the arms of another man, and he frowned.

Eden smiled at his discomfort.

"May I have the next dance, Miss Grant?" Toddington's gaze never left the dance floor.

If it weren't for her vow to act the perfect lady, Eden would have teased him without mercy. She hid a laugh behind her fan. "Yes, thank you."

The orchestra played a waltz. Toddington led her around the floor, never once ceasing his search for Lily.

Had he looked for anyone but Lily, Eden would have taken insult. As it was, the dance provided her with the opportunity to seek Ryeburn. She hadn't seen him this evening.

They traveled the length of the room and back, but Eden didn't spy Ryeburn. When the waltz ended, Toddington bowed to her and hurried off to claim Lily for the next dance. Eden wondered where Ryeburn could be. She decided to look in the refreshment room.

Someone pressed a drink into her hands. She thanked them absently and sipped the lemonade. The glass was still half full when she placed it on a table and left the room. Returning to the ballroom, Eden once again stood partnerless.

He wasn't here. Ryeburn wasn't coming to this ball.

Eden grew angry at herself. She had never considered that he might not attend. Such a stupid oversight.

The Marchioness of Heathsbury, a large woman with graying hair, found her at the edge of the room. Eden smiled at her hostess, but the joy had gone out of the evening.

"My dear, I was hoping to find you. Lady Lockwood tells me you have a lovely voice. Might I prevail upon you to sing something for us?"

She wanted to say no, but what purpose would that serve? She wasn't dancing much anyhow. "I would be happy to."

"Splendid. There's a pianoforte in the music room. Come this way, child."

The marchioness started to show her the way, but Eden stopped her. "Excuse me, Lady Heathsbury, but my friend, Lily, usually accompanies me on the pianoforte, and she is dancing at the moment."

"Of course. We'll wait for her as well. Which girl is she?"

"The one dancing with Lord Toddington."

When the dance ended, Lady Heathsbury marched

straight over to the pair. "Toddington, Miss Grant has kindly agreed to sing for us in the music room, but she wants to claim your partner as her accompanist."

"Of course, Lady Heathsbury." Toddington turned to Lily and offered his arm. "May I escort you to your instrument?"

Lily's face glowed. A flush colored her cheeks. Eden couldn't tell if it was from the dancing or the excitement of having Toddington's attention.

"Excellent. I'm so pleased you could attend my ball on such short notice." Lady Heathsbury linked arms with Eden and led her to the music room.

Standing at the piano, Eden looked over the full room. She sighed. At least twice as many people would hear her sing tonight, but some of those were the faces from the Lockwoods' dinner party. Without intending to, her gaze searched once again for Ryeburn.

He isn't here, you ninny. Stop looking for him.

Eden looked over to Lily and nodded. Lily bent over the keyboard and began to play. As the first notes lilted from under Lily's hands, Eden smiled. Lily had chosen a love song. They often performed this way, like a game—Lily would choose the song, and Eden would have to identify it in time for her entrance.

The song was all the more beautiful for its simplicity. Eden sang of the hope and joy of love, the richness and depth, the fears and strengths. One by one, every woman drew out a handkerchief to wipe their eyes, and many of the men did the same.

When she finished, Eden drew a deep breath, for the music had not left her unaffected. She had performed this song many times, but the words had never touched her in the past. She wanted to believe Lily's excitement was to blame, but she knew better. The song had stirred an emptiness in her soul that beckoned her as if it was trying to tell her something.

Applause engulfed her. Eden shook off the effects of the music. She curtsied to her listeners.

"Do sing another, Miss Grant," her hostess beseeched.

Lily returned to the pianoforte and began to play again. Good, thought Eden. "Psalm 26" by Haydn. Her voice rang out strong, giving the words the power and dignity they deserved.

Eden sang two more pieces after the Haydn. Then she whispered to Lily, "Play 'Jack and Joan' by Thomas Campian."

"Are you sure?" responded Lily.

"Let's see if these British have a sense of humor."

The first notes sounded in the room. Eden worked her magic with her voice. When the song ended Eden winked at Lily, then waited to hear the response.

Laughter tittered through the room, followed by loud applause. The gentlemen rose to their feet.

"Delightful," bellowed a corpulent man. "Absolutely delightful."

Eden grinned at the audience. She was glad to find that not everyone in England was as stoic as Ryeburn. She looked over the audience again and drew in a sharp breath. He was here. Ryeburn stood at the back of the room. He nodded at her, then made his way toward her.

The marchioness reached her first. "My dear, that was exquisite. Thank you so much for your lovely performance. I don't believe I shall ever be able to listen to the daughters of my friends in the future without grimacing."

Eden bowed her head. "Thank you, Lady Heathsbury."

"Come, my dear. The Duke of Welkes wishes to make your acquaintance."

Trevor watched as Eden moved away from him and

toward the duke. He had arrived late, but that didn't concern him. Most such crushes lasted until late into the night.

Eden smiled at the Duke of Welkes as he took her hand and kissed it. Trevor was too far to hear anything. The duke must have said something humorous, for Trevor heard her laugh, a joy-filled sound that washed over him, drowning him in pleasure.

Trevor shook himself. He should be analyzing his choices of girls at the ball. Realizing that Sterling's jest was indeed the most efficient way to find a bride, he had spent his afternoon drawing up lists of eligible females. And Miss Grant didn't appear on any of his lists. He spun on his heel and strode from the room.

He returned to the ballroom and glanced around. There. Three girls from his list sat together on a bench. Their mothers and chaperones hovered behind them. Here was the perfect opportunity to start his quest for a bride. So why did he feel compelled to find Mrs. Roberts? He would seek out the three ladies for a dance and check their suitability.

As he walked around the edge of the dance floor, he spotted Mrs. Roberts.

With a muffled growl of annoyance, he crossed to Miss Grant's chaperone.

Mrs. Roberts sat near a potted tree, chatting busily with another dour-faced woman. That thought gave him pause. He hadn't realized how many dour-faced women there were in the world. Habit prevented him from speaking until the lady noticed him.

After a few moments, Mrs. Roberts looked up. Her eyes widened, giving her the appearance of a startled goose. "Lord Ryeburn. Good evening."

Trevor clicked his heels together and gave a curt bow. "Mrs. Roberts."

"Allow me to introduce Mrs. Dawson. She is the Honorable Lavinia Bottomsley's chaperone."

Lavinia Bottomsley. That name was on his list. So why was he here on this fool's errand? "A pleasure, Mrs. Dawson."

The pinched face broke into a smile. At least Trevor believed it was a smile. The sight horrified him more than he cared to think.

"May I help you in some way, Lord Ryeburn?" Mrs. Roberts gazed up at him expectantly.

"I wish to discuss something of a rather delicate nature with you, Mrs. Roberts."

Mrs. Dawson stood. "Say no more, Lord Ryeburn. It is time I checked on my Lavinia. Mrs. Roberts, I am gratified to meet a lady so like myself." Mrs. Dawson strode off toward the refreshment room.

"Please sit, Lord Ryeburn." Mrs. Roberts scooted to the edge of the settee to give him more room. "You wished to speak with me?"

"It concerns your charge, Miss Grant."

A long-suffering sigh escaped the woman's lips. "What has she done this time?"

"Nothing." Trevor was taken aback.

"I'm relieved to hear that."

"I understand the Honorable Martin Sterling has expressed an interest in her."

"That sweet boy sent her flowers this morning, and he was ever so kind to her in the park. I thought perhaps at first his interest lay with Miss Baylor, but I see that I was wrong. Mr. Sterling has asked to call on her. He danced the first dance with Eden this evening."

That information sat in Trevor's stomach like bad fish.

"Can you imagine how pleased . . . but, no, I dare not think it. The son of an earl, and we shall be here for such a short while."

"Then you shall be leaving soon?" This news caused his stomach to churn further.

"Not until August, but that's hardly time for a proper courtship. Still, stranger things have happened." Mrs. Roberts smiled at him. "Think how pleased her parents would be with nobility for a son-in-law."

"He isn't nobility. He's the third son of an earl and as such is a commoner."

"Nevertheless, I'm sure they would be happy to see her settled."

Trevor rose from the seat. "I mustn't monopolize your time any longer. Good evening, Mrs. Roberts."

Trevor walked along the edge of the room trying to reach the casement doors that led out to the garden. He needed air. The thought of Eden married to Sterling made him angry. He might not like the chit, but she deserved better than Sterling. Yet Mrs. Roberts seemed certain of Sterling's interest in the girl. Trevor could warn Miss Grant. Yes, that was precisely what he would do. As a gesture of decency. The girl needed to know Sterling had no prospects or money.

"Ryeburn, I've been looking for you."

Trevor turned at the sound of his name. Toddington was bearing down on him. "We need your help."

"We?"

"Miss Baylor and I."

"You need my help with Miss Baylor?"

"Don't be an ass. We need your help with Miss Grant."

A cold chill seized Trevor. "Is she ill?" He started toward the back rooms, where he knew she must still be.

"No, but she is in a spot of trouble."

Trevor slowed his steps. "Why am I not surprised?"

"You don't understand." Toddington pulled him along. "The Duke of Welkes took her with him to play whist."

"So? She's playing whist with the duke."

"She's not playing with the duke, she's playing *against* the duke."

Trevor stopped short for an instant, then rushed forward. "Come along, man. We've had enough conflicts with the Colonies."

CHAPTER SEVEN

"Didn't anyone tell her?" Trevor quickened his steps.

"No one had a chance. The duke swept her along and then sat her down before anyone could draw her aside." Toddington's face expressed his alarm.

"Am I correct in guessing she plays well?"

"Too well. Her partner does everything she can to lose, but Miss Grant keeps winning."

Trevor rounded the corner and entered the gaming room. Their hosts had set up several card tables for those not interested in dancing. Mostly the players were the older guests, but everyone crowded around one particular table, where shouts, groans, and cheers prevailed. With a sense of impending disaster, Trevor headed straight for that table.

The duke held his cards close to his chest. His face was red, and sweat glistened on his forehead. His frown would have frightened most women. Indeed, Eden's partner couldn't sit still. Her gaze darted from her partner to the duke to the duke's partner.

But Eden played with a calm Trevor had never seen on a woman. He could detect a slight smile, but nothing else.

"Miss Grant?" Trevor stepped next to her.

"Ryeburn, do not interrupt the game," bellowed the duke.

"Forgive me, Your Grace."

"Ah-ha!" The duke slapped the ten of clubs on the table. His confident grin brought a sigh of relief from his partner.

Trevor relaxed. Maybe the game wasn't a crisis after all. The duke seemed assured of his victory. Trevor felt himself relax further when Eden's partner laid down the eight of clubs. The duke's partner played the three.

Eden returned the duke's smile. She laid down the two of hearts.

"Trump? You still had a trump card? By God, I counted wrong." The duke rose to his feet.

"Your Grace?"

Trevor didn't know who spoke, but the words had no effect. Trevor stared at the duke as the man rounded the side of the table.

The duke bent over and thrust his nose at Eden. "Do you realize what you have done, young lady?"

"No, Your Grace." The gentleness and even tone of her answer astonished Trevor.

"You have defeated a man who hasn't lost at whist in years. My girl, you are not only talented and beautiful, you are damned clever. Forgive my language." The duke grinned broadly. "By God, if I had a drink in hand, I would toast this lady."

Trevor blinked twice. Had he heard correctly? The duke

didn't mind losing to Eden? It wasn't possible. Eden had made another conquest.

"Thank you, Your Grace." Eden nodded her head.

The duke raised her hand to his lips and kissed it. "I shan't keep you from the dancing any longer. I'm sure there are many young swains who would claim your attention."

"But none as charming as you, Your Grace." Eden flashed the duke a brilliant smile.

"By God, I like this girl. If I were thirty years younger . . ." A laugh thundered from him.

"With Your Grace's permission, I should like to dance with Miss Grant." Trevor stepped forward.

"About time, Ryeburn. I wasn't so timid in my day." The duke offered Eden his hand and helped her rise. "Go on, my dear, but promise me you'll sing for me again sometime."

"Only if you promise to play whist again with me." She curtseyed.

Trevor hustled her from the room before she could say anything else. His stride carried him in front of her as he hurried toward the ballroom. Eden jerked on his arm. He turned in annoyance.

"Must we run? I didn't know you were so eager to dance." Eden slowed her steps.

Muttering a curse, Trevor matched her stride. "I can't believe it."

"What?"

"You beat the duke." He shook his head.

Eden stopped walking entirely. "Why? Don't you believe a woman can play as well as a man? Or didn't you think I was capable of anything besides trouble?"

Anger gathered in her features. Trevor watched in fascination as her expression once again revealed her every thought. He hurried to correct her impression. "It isn't that at all. The duke is notorious for his card playing."

"He isn't that good."

"That's not what I meant either. It is generally known the duke likes to play cards, but hates to lose. His reaction to a loss is frightening. Usually. For years now, whenever we have occasion to play with him, and it happens more often than you think, we let him win."

"That explains the terrible play of my partner." Eden's eyes grew wide. "Is that why she looked so frightened? Because I was winning?"

"Yes. Toddington fetched me to help stave off the scene we all believed was brewing."

"I understand now."

What did she understand? Her gaze fell to the floor, and her arrogant little smile disappeared. What had caused this sadness? He wanted to bring that smile back to her lips. "You made a conquest back there. The duke likes you."

"And I think you all underestimate him. He didn't appear so fierce to me."

What *would* seem fierce to you? he wondered. Trevor gazed into her eyes. He had never seen eyes that sparkled like the bright blue of this girl's. She wouldn't fear much. Not this one.

Eden sighed. "You've saved me from myself yet again. Your duty is done. I'll find my way back by myself."

Her attempt at sarcasm fell short. He thought he heard sadness in her voice. "What of our dance?"

"You don't have to."

"But I wish to dance with you." Trevor led her to the ballroom. The orchestra was starting a waltz. Perfect timing. He bowed to her, then held out his arms.

Eden stepped into his hold, and they twirled onto the

floor. Neither spoke. Trevor marveled at the lightness of her steps. A faint scent of lavender wafted beneath his nose. Her hair, tied up on her head with a mass of cascading curls spilling from the knot, teased his control. He wanted to remove the pins and ribbons, to bury his hands in the softness, to feel the golden lengths entwine him. He didn't dare look in her eyes. What manner of temptation would lie within those blue depths?

His hand rested against the small of her back. The thin material of her gown taunted him, denying him the feel of her skin. Images of her draped in a sheet, with her hair unbound, tantalized his imagination. He chanced a peek at her eyes.

The music ended. Trevor didn't release her. Her gaze captured him as surely as if it had chained him to her. Her mouth parted softly with her breathing, calling him, beckoning him . . .

"May I claim the next dance?"

Trevor dropped his hands and backed away. A slender youth with an eager expression bowed to Eden, who swallowed hard, then smiled. With a curt nod to her, Trevor left the floor.

He didn't know himself anymore. He had nearly risked his reputation by giving in to his urge to kiss her. In the middle of the dance floor, no less. Storming off to the refreshment room, he hoped their host had something stronger than lemonade to ease his discomfort.

The crowd at the tables jostled him, but didn't prevent him from reaching a glass. He sipped from it. Lemonade. He wondered how offended Heathsbury would be if he sought out the marquess's brandy.

A voice at his elbow caught his attention.

"Did you hear her sing?"

Trevor turned and looked for the speaker. A stout man

stood in conversation behind him. Trevor couldn't remember the man's name, but he had seen him in Parliament.

"I didn't have the pleasure, but I heard her voice is like an angel's," said a second man.

"Neither did I, but we'll have our chance. My wife plans to invite her to our next dinner party."

"An American?"

"I know, but I'm told she's quite refined."

"And beautiful." The second man laughed.

"Yes, there is that."

Trevor's grip tightened on his glass. He wanted to hear no more. He stepped away from the table.

"She raced on Rotten Row."

A new voice filled his ears.

"You don't say. Unbelievable."

"What's unbelievable is that she won."

"I don't believe it."

"Sterling told me himself. He lost a pound to her."

"She wagered on the race?"

Trevor could listen no longer. He put his glass on a convenient tray and tried to press his way out of the room.

"And she beat the duke." A woman's voice pierced his hearing next.

"My dear, you can't be serious."

"I was there. And Welkes paid homage to her. He was overjoyed to lose."

"Impossible."

Did these people have nothing else to talk about? Trevor strode back to the ballroom. Miss Grant, it seemed, had won the attention of the *ton*. They would probably embrace her as an original.

His gaze searched for her against his will. He found her at the center of a circle of ladies and gentlemen. She was holding court, beaming and chatting as if such behavior were nothing extraordinary.

The devil take it, was there no one immune to this insanity?

Trevor's ire grew. He searched for Toddington. Surely Toddington would see what a farce this situation was becoming.

Toddington danced with Miss Baylor.

He saw Sterling make his way to the center of Eden's circle and bow to her. She nodded and stood. The group around her dispersed as the couple took the floor.

Trevor watched the pair turn on the parquet. Sterling was as fair as she, but in Trevor's eyes they made a poor couple. He was too short for her. She reached the man's eyes, for goodness sake. She would look better with someone taller, a dark-haired man to provide a contrast to her blond hair.

With a snort, he realized that he described himself. He turned from the dance floor and nearly collided with the Duke of Welkes.

"Ryeburn, did you have your dance with that enchanting creature?"

"Yes." He knew his answer was curt, but he didn't trust himself to say more. Against his will, his gaze traveled back to Eden.

"Got you stirred up, did she?" The duke chuckled. "I would have thought your type to be more sedate and proper. Best be careful of her, Ryeburn. That kind of woman could slip under your guard without trying."

"I'll heed your warning well, Your Grace."

When the waltz finished, Sterling bowed to her, and Trevor saw another young man take Sterling's place. He glanced over to Toddington. The earl linked arms with

Miss Baylor and led her to the doors and out into the garden.

Hmph. Trevor wondered why he shouldn't enjoy himself as well. Plenty of eligible, proper young women waited for attention. He should get to work on finding his bride. And he would start with Lavinia Bottomsley.

He found the girl perched on a settee with her chaperone. He bowed to Mrs. Dawson. "Mrs. Dawson. May I ask you to introduce me to your charge?"

"I'd be delighted, Lord Ryeburn," cackled Mrs. Dawson. "Lavinia, dear, this is Lord Ryeburn."

The girl smiled. Trevor tried not to stare at her large front teeth. "Lord Ryeburn, thuch a pleathure to make your acquaintanth."

"The pleasure is all mine. May I have the honor of the next dance?"

"Let me check my danth card." The girl flipped the card over. "Yeth, Lord Ryeburn. My neth danth ith free."

She offered him her hand and he helped her to her feet. They took a place on the parquet as the orchestra played the first notes.

"Are you enjoying yourself, Mith, uh . . . Miss Bottomsley?"

"Immenthly. Lady Heathbury alwayth throwth thuch lovely partieth."

He nodded.

"Thtill, it'th a pity that American ith here. The'th really too vulgar for wordth."

"Miss Grant?"

"That'th the one. Thowing off her thinging like that. You wouldn't find me dithplaying mythelf in that manner."

I should hope not. Trevor wondered how much longer the waltz could last. She smiled at him, and he nearly jumped back at the renewed sight of her teeth. He would cross Miss Lavinia Bottomsley off his list as soon as he was home.

The music ended at last. With a smile pasted on his lips, he returned her to her chaperone. Mumbling an excuse, he retreated from Miss Bottomsley. He sought out the next girl.

One by one he danced or conversed with the girls on his list, and one by one he found them lacking. One was too short, the other too skinny. This one was too quiet, and that one's voice would drive a man to murder. She ate too loudly, whereas her mother wouldn't leave them alone.

By the end of the hour, Trevor was exhausted, and no female had passed his muster. Not one of these women merited a second look. Discouraged, but not disheartened, he remembered this was but the first ball he had searched, and he had two more lists at home. He would have more success next time.

Trevor slipped out the doors into the garden. He needed air. As he stood on the balcony that overlooked the garden, the night breeze soothed his nerves. He couldn't remember ever feeling so frazzled. The noise of the ball drifted out. It was too close. Trevor wandered down the steps onto the gravel path that wound through the roses.

Moonlight lit his way. The scent of the roses refreshed him, clearing his head of the dense tang of the ball. He wandered away from the house without any thought of destination. Looking over his shoulder, he thought the windows of the house watched him like giant eyes. Indeed, the whole rear facade of the house reminded him of a face, a frowning, menacing visage.

What was wrong with him? Since when did he have such fanciful thoughts? Even his nightmares held less fantastical conjecture.

He rounded a curve and found a bench half-hidden in the shadows of a tree. Taking a seat, he drew a deep breath. The air was clean, with a hint of lavender.

Lavender?

He twisted his head to see the woman hidden in the shadows at the other end of the bench.

"Good evening, Lord Ryeburn." The shadows still obscured her face, but he recognized the voice.

"Good evening, Miss Grant."

"What brings you out here? Are you hiding from your many admirers?"

"I could ask the same of you."

"Yes, but I would answer you instead of evading the question." Eden laughed. "Which we both realize I have just done."

He felt her laughter engulf him and pull a similar response from him. "So, are you hiding?"

"Yes, Lord Ryeburn, I am."

CHAPTER EIGHT

Eden couldn't turn her gaze from his face. The moonlight illuminated it, giving his skin a pale glow like one of those Greek statues she and Lily had admired. He could have stepped off the pedestal. Only he was fully clothed.

Heat rushed to her cheeks. Thankful for the darkness that hid her blush, Eden closed her eyes. It was better not to look at him than continue thinking about Greek statues.

"From whom are you hiding?" Ryeburn's voice pulled her from her imaginings.

"The crowd. Sometimes the attention overwhelms me."

"Perhaps if you controlled your impulses more often, you wouldn't be the subject of so much attention."

Anger flashed through her. "I've done nothing wrong this evening."

"No, but beating the duke at whist caused a stir."

"That wasn't my fault. Nobody told me I shouldn't play cards."

"Maybe you should have asked."

"Whom might I have asked? You?"

"That's not a bad idea. The next time you need advice, you may call on me." Ryeburn leaned back against the bench. She wanted to wipe that smug look off his face.

"Then please impart your wisdom, oh wise one."

"Sarcasm does not become a lady."

"A subject which I believe we've already discussed." Eden stood. "Very well, tell me what else I need to know."

Ryeburn examined her until she grew uncomfortable. Then he rose and circled her. "You shouldn't be out here with a man."

"I wasn't. You joined *me,* remember?"

"That is irrelevant. Your reputation will suffer if someone should happen upon us."

"Then perhaps I should leave." Eden pivoted on her heel and took a step forward. His arm reached out and jerked her back. She glared at him.

"Your dress."

"My dress? What about my dress?"

"The color. It's too bold. And the design on it—that vine—it draws the gaze upward over every . . ." He stopped, frowned, and cleared his throat. "It draws the gaze."

"I like this dress."

"It isn't suitable for a young girl."

"I'm not a young girl. I'm twenty years old."

"That old? Nevertheless, a more demure color would suit your position better. An unmarried woman doesn't wear vivid colors." His mocking tone angered her further.

"With my hair and eyes, I look ill in pastels."

"So you admit you dress to attract attention."

"I admit no such thing." Eden pulled her arm from his grasp.

"If you aren't careful, your actions will bring about consequences you don't care for."

"Such as?"

"Such as this." Ryeburn pulled her into his arms and captured her lips with his own.

Eden pulled back at the unexpected attack. His hand moved to cradle the back of her head, preventing her from breaking the contact of their lips. His other arm didn't slacken, yet she felt no pain in the confinement. Rather, she molded into his curves, fitting to him, until they stood like two pages in a book.

His lips tugged at hers, sending shivers dancing down her spine. He tasted of sunshine and ice. Eden's heart beat in her ears. The thundering roar of her blood sounded like the ocean. She was flying. Afraid of falling, she closed her eyes and clung to him.

Before she knew what happened, his tongue pried her lips open and began a gentle exploration of her mouth. Eden thought she would explode. Her mind demanded that she push him away, but her heart argued to let him stay. Her heart spoke with more force. Sense and restraint melted as Eden let her emotions consume her. She trembled inside from her toes to her fingers. She didn't understand the rollicking joy that bubbled through her; she only knew she wanted more.

Trevor pushed her away. His hands gripped her shoulders at arm's length. For an instant, Eden couldn't breath. The sudden cold startled her. She tried to return to his embrace, but his arms stayed rigid. Gazing into his face, she saw his expression of disgust. She felt the color drain from her face.

"My God, woman, in how many other ways have you been improper?" Trevor's voice filled her with dread and confusion.

Drawing in a shallow breath through her closed throat, she whispered, "What do you mean?"

"And I was worried about your reputation." He let out a caustic laugh. "You must have thought me a fool."

"I don't understand." Eden's knees felt weak, but not with the earlier ebullience.

"How many men have you been with, Miss Grant?"

Eden gasped. Anger and despair warred within her. She shoved him with all her strength. He fell back onto the bench, but his accusatory gaze never left her face. "You claim to be a gentleman, but no gentleman would ever say such things to a lady."

"And no lady would kiss like that." Trevor eyes narrowed.

"I wouldn't know. I've never been kissed before." Eden's chest heaved with every word. She knew she was close to tears, but she wouldn't give him the satisfaction of seeing them. "Between the vigilance of my father and my brother, no man has ever come close enough to me to kiss me."

She whirled on her heel and stormed farther into the garden. Her sobs broke free of their confinement, but she didn't care. She gave vent to her distress, running down the path hoping to find another secluded corner.

Trevor watched her disappear, but made no move to follow. Her sobs echoed through him, weakening his resolve to stay away from her. Could her claim be true? Had he misjudged her? The kiss had aroused him as none other in the past. Her eager reception of his tongue wasn't the action of an untried girl.

Running his hand through his hair, he pictured her face just before she left. Her eyes, beacons in the moonlight, had shimmered with the sheen of unshed tears. Her skin had lost all its color. But the look of abject betrayal haunted him. How was he to know she had never been kissed?

In the next instant, he realized he believed her. He would have to apologize to her, but not now. He couldn't trust himself around her. That kiss frightened him. It reminded him of his weakness for the wrong sort of woman. His tastes always ran to the spirited, beautiful women, the type that would never do for his countess.

It wasn't as if he were completely at fault. Her behavior brought on calamity. The few times they had met ended in disaster. She attracted trouble as a flame attracted moths. He wasn't to blame for her conduct.

But that kiss . . . If he closed his eyes, he could feel the softness of her lips, hear the little sounds she probably wasn't aware she emitted. His palm still tingled with her warmth. Blood surged in his loins as he lingered on that kiss. No, he couldn't find her now. Hell, in the state he was in, he couldn't return to the ballroom just yet either.

The wind rustled through the tree above him. The leaves whispered to him. *Numquam tuas spes dedisce.* His eyes flew open to see the moon winking through the branches. No one stood near, yet he would have sworn he had heard words. The leaves rustled above him again, but their voice remained unintelligible this time. Trevor shook his head. He was overwrought. His imagination had caused him enough trouble this evening.

How long he remained on that bench, he didn't know. Eventually the cool night air soothed him enough to risk entering the house again. The garden had lost its charm, as had the entire evening. He wouldn't find his bride here. Ignoring the ongoing festivities, he gathered his cloak, stepped into the night to his coach, and instructed his driver to take him home.

* * *

Numquam tuas spes dedisce. Eden raised her head, but she couldn't see the speaker of the words.

"Who is there?"

Silence greeted her question. She peered through the darkness, but could find no one. The breeze stirred the plants and trees around her.

Eden wiped her eyes with the back of her hands. Her imagination must have tricked her. No one stood near enough to say a word. It was just the wind through the leaves. The iron bench she had rested her head on was cold. She drew a ragged breath and rose from the garden floor. Brushing her gown off, she chastised herself for letting that man, that Lord Ryeburn, upset her so much. Just because he had ruined her first kiss didn't mean he could ruin her whole life. A kiss signified nothing. Even if she had enjoyed it more than she should.

No wonder Daddy and Nicholas had guarded her against such actions. A girl could lose her wits with such kisses.

Her breathing came more evenly, but her eyes were probably puffy and red. A few more minutes outside should cure that. Eden sat on the bench and tried to occupy her thoughts elsewhere.

She had written home about the horse she had purchased. Daddy would like Hermes, she was sure. He would outrun most every horse in their stables. Eden winced. Racing horses only reminded her of the confrontation with Ryeburn at the park.

She needed to think of something else . . . ah, yes, the gifts she had purchased for her mother and sister. Gloves of the finest kid, decorated with pearls and flowers. Just the thing to wear in Boston, where people would admire her taste, not criticize her choice of apparel. Eden frowned. She had done it again. Ryeburn was back in her thoughts.

"Go away," she said aloud. She rose from the bench.

Anger replaced self-pity. As she paced the ground, she grew more and more angry at Ryeburn. Who did he think he was? As if his title gave him leave to condemn her and accuse her of such hateful things. And he believed himself a proper gentleman. Ha.

Her fury in full reign, she started back for the ball. She would find him and tell him exactly what she thought of him. Or better yet, she would show him he didn't matter to her. She would enjoy the rest of the ball as if he had never kissed her.

The lights of the house welcomed her back. Taking one last look at her dress, Eden assured herself that she looked presentable, then swept back into the room. Her gaze sought Ryeburn as she made her way around the floor. She didn't see him anywhere. Perhaps he was in the refreshment room.

Out of the corner of her eye, she saw Mr. Sterling approach. Not wishing to insult him, she gave him a smile.

"Miss Grant, I am so glad to have found you. May I claim my third dance with you?"

Giving the room a final glance, Eden still couldn't find Ryeburn. Perhaps from the dance floor she would have a better chance. "I would love to dance, Mr. Sterling."

Sterling led her onto the parquet. As they turned, Eden kept her gaze on the periphery. Ryeburn wasn't there.

"I enjoyed your singing tonight, Miss Grant."

His words jerked Eden back to the dance. "Thank you, Mr. Sterling."

"You seemed to disappear for a while. I had hoped to escort you to dinner, but I couldn't find you."

"I was outside. The garden is quite lovely."

"Surely not by yourself? Should you feel the need to escape again, I shall be happy to accompany you."

Sterling smiled at her, but Eden thought she saw something other than friendship in his expression. An uneasiness nipped at her. She looked again, and attributed her anxiety to the events of the evening.

"Are you enjoying your visit to England?"

"Oh, yes. There's so much to see here that we don't have at home."

"If you'll allow me, I'd like to show you some of the sights of London and its surroundings. Of course, the invitation extends to your friends as well."

"I'm sure Mrs. Roberts would be happy to have you as a guide." Eden forced herself to smile. She didn't want to encourage his attention, but could think of no way to refuse his offer.

"Excellent."

The dance ended. Sterling led her back to the edge of the floor. "Alas, convention dictates I may not monopolize your attention the entire evening, so with great regret I leave you." He bowed to her.

Thank heaven for some of society's conventions, thought Eden as he left. She searched the room again and spied Lily. Threading her way through the crowd, she reached her friend.

Before Eden could speak, Lily asked, "Where have you been?"

"I? I went outside for a while."

Lily linked her arm in Eden's and pulled her to an open bench. "I've been searching for you everywhere."

"What's happened?"

"Nothing. I just wondered where you disappeared to."

Eden didn't know how to respond. Lily was her best friend, but she couldn't tell her about Ryeburn's kiss. The problem was keeping anything from her friend. Lily knew her too well.

"Are you all right?"

"Yes, just tired. Have you seen Lord Ryeburn?"

"He left about half an hour ago. Lord Toddington says he was acting strangely."

He wasn't here? Good. No sense wasting any more time over him. And that wasn't disappointment roiling in her stomach.

Eden *was* tired. She wanted to go home and crawl into her bed. "Do you think we could go home now?"

Lily searched her friend's face. "Something is wrong. I'll fetch Mrs. Roberts. We'll get you home soon."

Within a few minutes, they had said good-bye to their hostess and climbed into their hired coach. Eden sank back against the seat cushion.

"What a thrilling evening." Mrs. Roberts sat erect. Her back didn't touch the upholstery. "I shouldn't be surprised if this evening's success leads to many more invitations."

Stifling her groan, Eden shut her eyes and feigned sleep. She didn't want to encourage Mrs. Roberts.

"That nice young Mr. Sterling asked me if he might come to call tomorrow. Can you imagine? We are to entertain the son of an earl. I think I may be so bold as to say he has an interest in one of you. If he continues to show such interest, I wouldn't be surprised if an engagement might be possible before we travel home."

Oh, God. Eden didn't stir.

"Mrs. Roberts, forgive me, but I believe Eden has fallen asleep." Lily spread her coat over Eden.

"The poor girl must be exhausted. The good news about Mr. Sterling can wait until tomorrow." Mrs. Roberts sat back and soon snored in the corner.

"She's asleep, Eden. You can open your eyes now."

Eden cracked an eye open and checked for herself. Then she sat up. "You're a good friend, Lily."

"I know." Lily smiled at her. "And when you're ready, I'll listen to whatever it is that's bothering you so much."

"Aren't you tired?"

"I doubt I'll ever feel tired again." With a sigh, Lily sank against the seat cushion.

"What's made you so happy?"

"You have your secrets, and I have mine." Lily patted Eden's hand. "I'll tell you tomorrow. We're almost home." Lily turned her gaze out the window.

In a few minutes the coach pulled up in front of their house. A few minutes after that found the house quiet again, its occupants bedded down for the night.

Eden stared up at the ceiling. The blue sky looked gray in the darkness, the clouds painted on it a lighter gray. It fit her mood. She tried to sleep, but every time she closed her eyes, she was back in the garden with Ryeburn. Her lips ached for the touch of his, and her body stirred in spots she never knew she had, leaving her restless.

She tried to imagine a different kiss, someone else's kiss. She failed miserably.

CHAPTER NINE

Seated in a high-backed chair, Eden stared at the desktop. Books filled the library, but none lured her attention away from the pile of envelopes in front of her. She didn't open them; she just shook her head and stared.

She heard the door open behind her, but didn't look up.

"There you are." Lily bounded into the room. "Have you been hiding?"

"Not exactly. I don't think there is anywhere I could hide." Eden turned from the pile on the table. At the sight of Lily's cheerful face, Eden raised an eyebrow. "Why are you so happy?"

"Why are you so glum?" countered Lily with a smile.

"I'm not glum, I'm . . ." She waved her hand at the stack of envelopes on the table.

"What are those?"

"The latest set of invitations. There must be twenty here,

and Roberts keeps bringing more every hour." Eden leaned forward and cupped her chin in her hands.

"Lord Toddington told me that your name is on everyone's lips. They all want to know the American original, whatever that means."

"What *does* that mean?" Eden drew her brows together.

"It means a lot more invitations to a lot more parties. Do you really hate going out so much?" Lily's voice held a hint of disappointment.

"I don't know. If I thought these invitations were for me and not for my singing, I'd probably like it."

"Does that mean we're going to turn them down?"

Eden turned to look at her friend. Lily chewed on her bottom lip. "Is something wrong?"

"No, not wrong. I just . . ." Lily grabbed Eden's hands. "Please, let's go to as many as we can."

"We'll go to as many as you want. This is about Lord Toddington, isn't it?"

A blush crept into Lily's cheeks. As she dropped Eden's hands, Lily averted her gaze. "Promise you won't laugh or make fun of me?" She chewed her bottom lip again.

"Of course not." Eden turned her chair to face Lily.

Lily squinted at her friend as if she feared a beating. "I want to see him again."

"He does seem to have taken an interest in you."

"And I in him." Lily's blush deepened. "I know it's hopeless. He's a lord, after all, and who am I? Nobody. Just a girl from America, who can play the pianoforte a little. Besides, we're leaving in August, but I want to enjoy these next months. Do you think that's so terrible?" The words tumbled from her mouth in a rush.

"No, but—"

"Eden, I think I love him." Lily's eyes welled up.

"You've only just met him." Eden couldn't keep the disbelief from her voice.

"It's ridiculous, I know, but from the moment I saw him, I can think of little else. I'm torturing myself to spend more time with him, but I'll be miserable if I don't see him."

"He likes you, too, Lily. It's obvious from his behavior." Eden stroked Lily's dark hair, but frowned. "Are you sure you want to put yourself through this? I'll be happy to turn down every invitation."

"Oh, no. Please don't. I know I can't hope for a future with him, but let me dream."

Lily's words took Eden aback. How many times in the last few days had dreams and hopes been on her own mind? She hesitated before speaking again. "Dreams can hurt."

"Dreams are all I have. I'm not like you, Eden, I don't have a family back home who'll take care of me. If I have the opportunity to take a little happiness back with me, if only in a memory, I'll take the risk."

"You can't know what the future holds for you."

"Perhaps not, but I know what the present offers."

Eden didn't know what to say. She tried to come up with an argument against Lily's passion, but couldn't. Although Lily's eyes shimmered with tears, her demeanor was proud.

"I can't ask you to understand, I know," continued Lily. "But if he does care for me and I have the chance to respond . . ." Lily shrugged her shoulders.

"You really do love him." The realization stunned Eden. She knew her parents loved each other, but she never dreamed she'd be lucky enough to find a love like that herself. Now her dearest friend had succumbed as well. As she looked at Lily, she realized she envied her just the slightest bit.

Eden drew a deep breath. "You'll have to help me. I don't know which of these affairs your Lord Toddington is likely to attend."

Lily threw her arms around Eden's neck. "Thank you."

"Don't thank me yet. You'll have to play for me at all these functions, you know. Roberts is going to love this. She'll take all the credit for our success." Eden handed Lily a stack of the envelopes.

"Then she'll really be impossible to live with."

"Of whom are you speaking, dear?" Mrs. Roberts swished into the room. Eden always thought the woman had a second sense about such things. When Mrs. Roberts was her and Nicholas's governess, the woman always caught them in their whispers.

"Elizabeth Farley," Eden said quickly. "She'll be green when she finds out how many parties we attended." Eden didn't dare look at Lily for fear of laughing.

"A young lady doesn't boast of her accomplishments, Miss Grant."

"Yes, Mrs. Roberts."

"You have a visitor. That nice Mr. Sterling has come to see you." Mrs. Roberts beamed her approval. Then she handed Eden another batch of envelopes. "These have also arrived for you."

Eden passed them on to Lily with a wink. "You look them over. See which ones you'd like to attend." She stood and faced Mrs. Roberts. "Shall we see what Mr. Sterling wants?"

"He's in the drawing room." Mrs. Roberts waited until Eden passed her, then followed behind her charge.

Watching the street, Mr. Sterling stood by a window in the drawing room. When the ladies entered the room, he turned to them with a little bow.

"Good afternoon, Mr. Sterling." Eden offered him her hand.

Sterling bent over it. "Miss Grant. My day has grown brighter since you agreed to see me."

"Thank you. Won't you sit down?" Indicating a nearby bergère chair for him, Eden took a place on the settee. Mrs. Roberts took a seat in the corner.

"If I may say, you look lovely today."

"Thank you again, Mr. Sterling." Eden smiled, but didn't know what to say. What did he want?

"Miss Grant, I don't know if you realize just what an impression you've made on me. If your parents were here, I might speak to them, but as they are not, I have no alternative but to come directly to you."

Eden caught herself before she grimaced.

Sterling leaned toward her. "Not only are you a beautiful young woman, but you are also blessed with a talent that is unparalleled. I was hoping you would allow me to—"

The butler entered the room. "Pardon me, Miss Grant, but you have another visitor." He handed her a card.

Thank heaven. Mr. Sterling couldn't continue with his declaration if someone else were present. She read the name on the card. Her stomach dropped. Trevor St. John, Lord Ryeburn. Why did *he* have to come?

She looked back at Sterling. The man looked ready to burst, but Eden had no desire to hear the rest. Sterling or Ryeburn. What a choice. She sighed. "Show him in, please."

The butler bowed and left the room. Eden turned to Sterling and forced a smile onto her lips. "Forgive me. You were saying?"

"Yes, I wanted to tell you how much I've come to admire you in the short time I've made your acquaintance. I should like—" Sterling looked up at the doorway.

Eden followed his gaze. Ryeburn stood there scowling at them. He took two steps in the room and then noticed Mrs. Roberts in the corner. His stance relaxed.

Eden fumed. He once again had thought the worst of her until he saw her chaperone in the room.

"Good day, Miss Grant. Sterling." Ryeburn bowed to Mrs. Roberts. "Good day, madam."

"Lord Ryeburn, so good to see you again." Mrs. Roberts's face lit up.

Now she can take credit for an earl, too. Eden tried to give Trevor an icy glare, but her heart pounded and her breathing came with difficulty. She dismissed it as annoyance. "Lord Ryeburn. I certainly didn't expect to see you again."

Trevor looked at Sterling and raised an eyebrow before responding to her. "No, I can see you didn't."

"What are you doing here, Ryeburn?" Sterling clenched his fists at his side.

"Paying a visit, same as yourself."

"Well, you interrupted an important discussion." Sterling flumped back into his chair.

"I also have something to discuss with Miss Grant, but I can wait until you're finished." Trevor pointed to an armchair. "May I?"

Eden was about to say no, but Mrs. Roberts spoke first. "Of course, Lord Ryeburn. Where are our manners?" The woman glared at Eden.

"Do sit, Lord Ryeburn. I am most anxious to hear what you have to say." Although her voice was honey sweet, Eden saw Trevor's eyes narrow at the barb in her words.

Mrs. Roberts rose. "I'll see about getting us some tea." She left the room. Eden would have sworn the woman danced out, except she knew Mrs. Roberts didn't dance.

"Go ahead, Sterling. Don't mind my presence." Trevor crossed his arms on his chest and gave Sterling a nod.

Eden thought Sterling was going to growl at Trevor. Instead he faced her. "Miss Grant, I can't possibly say what I wish in front of Lord Ryeburn. Perhaps if we could withdraw elsewhere . . ."

Trevor shook his finger at Sterling. "Oh, no. That wouldn't be proper. A young lady and a gentleman alone without a chaperone? How could you even suggest such a thing, Sterling?"

If Eden hadn't thought the words directed at her, she might have laughed at Sterling's expression. But despite her desire to aggravate Trevor, she wouldn't go anywhere with Mr. Sterling. Not if he intended to finish his speech. "I'm afraid Lord Ryeburn is right. Perhaps this should wait until another day when we don't have so many interruptions."

"As you wish." Sterling bowed his head, but his fists remained clenched.

"Lord Ryeburn, what is it you wished to tell me?"

"Nothing that can't wait." Trevor sat back. He was enjoying himself. It was too easy to bait Sterling. "I missed your performance last night. I understand you sang beautifully yet again."

"She did," Sterling said. "The number of her admirers grows each day."

"Is that so? Such a pity you aren't staying longer, Miss Grant. You might find yourself a husband among the English." Trevor watched Sterling's face.

"She may succeed despite the brevity of time." Sterling tried to catch her gaze, but Eden focused on her hands.

So that was Sterling's game. He wanted to marry the chit. Trevor's mild dislike of the man bloomed into disgust. What had Sterling said? Her father was rich. Trevor now understood Sterling's urgency.

"Gentlemen, please. I didn't come to England to find

a husband. I came to enjoy the sights and learn a little of history. My father is an avid collector of Roman artifacts. He would never forgive me if I didn't explore the Roman ruins in England."

"I should love to take you on an excursion to such a site," Sterling said.

"An excellent idea. We'll make a picnic of it. Miss Baylor shall join us, and Toddington." Trevor watched as Sterling's expression hardened. "Mrs. Roberts shall accompany us as well."

"I shouldn't want to trouble you, Lord Ryeburn." Eden shot him a puzzled glance.

"Yes, Ryeburn. We needn't make an elaborate affair of a simple excursion. You needn't accompany us." Sterling's nostrils flared.

"Nonsense. It is my pleasure. Shall we set aside Tuesday for our picnic? I shall order hampers of food and pick you up in my barouche." Trevor stroked his chin. "Hmm. There shall be six of us and all that food. I'd better bring the gig along as well. Four and two . . . perfect. Room for us all. You won't mind sitting with Mrs. Roberts, will you, Sterling?"

Sterling leapt to his feet. His face turned bright red, and a white circle appeared around his mouth. After a few moments, he calmed himself. "I shall look forward to your company, Miss Grant. Until Tuesday then." He bowed to her and left the room without sparing Ryeburn another glance.

Through sheer will, Trevor kept his laughter down. Until he looked at Eden. Her cool gaze froze his humor.

"I didn't think you would have the nerve to visit me. Much less invite me on a picnic."

Trevor spread open his palms. "I came to apologize."

"Apologize? To a wanton woman?"

"Miss Grant, I erred. I misjudged you terribly."

"Did you decide this before or after you humiliated me?"

Trevor ran his hand through his hair. "Miss Grant, my behavior last night was disgraceful. I can't explain myself. I can only beg your forgiveness."

Eden fell silent. She rose and crossed to the window. "Why *did* you invite us on a picnic?"

"Are all Americans as frank as you?"

"Are all Englishmen as proper as you?" she countered.

Trevor laughed. "Hardly. If you had known my father . . ." He looked at her, then shook his head. "No, it's better you didn't know my father. He would have tried every trick to make you his paramour."

Eden gasped and whirled to face him.

"Forgive me again." What was it about this girl that caused him to forget his vow to himself? She brought out every bad trait he didn't think he possessed. She was too enticing, too bewitching. She was too dangerous. "The picnic on Tuesday was meant as a peace offering."

"And to spoil Mr. Sterling's attempt to court me." Eden smiled.

Damn, but he was beginning to like this girl. Trevor grinned. "You're not only talented, you're clever as well. Was I that obvious?"

"Yes, and I'm grateful, though I can't imagine why you did it. I know he's a friend of yours—"

"No, he's more a friend of Toddington, but I tolerate him."

Eden cocked her head. "Speaking of Lord Toddington . . ."

"And Miss Baylor?"

Her eyes widened. "You know?"

"Toddington hasn't acted this juvenile since we were boys at school together."

"So the picnic is also—"

"Another opportunity for them to meet."

"You approve?"

"It's not for me to approve or disapprove. Toddington has been rather dour lately. It's refreshing to see him changed." Trevor paused. "Am I forgiven?"

"I haven't decided yet." Eden tossed her head. "But I'll call a truce for Lily's sake."

The girl had spirit. His title didn't awe her, nor did honesty upset her. Trevor didn't know how to deal with such a woman. She wouldn't bend to the whims of society, and she wouldn't care. And yet she remained innocent. A rare combination. She would never bore him. A pity she wouldn't make a good wife.

Mrs. Roberts bustled into the room carrying a tea tray. She looked around. "Where did that nice Mr. Sterling go?"

"He couldn't stay."

Mrs. Roberts placed the tray on the table. The bang accented the frown on her face. "Miss Grant, you should have called me at once. It isn't proper for a lady to be alone with a gentleman."

"Yes, ma'am."

"I trust tales of this episode shall travel no further than this room, Lord Ryeburn?" Mrs. Roberts peered at him through her pince-nez.

"On my word as a gentleman." He gave her a bow. The last time he had heard such a reprimand was from his nanny.

"Then we are in your debt again. Tea?"

"I'm afraid I must be going as well." Trevor turned to

Eden, whose eyes shone with amusement. "Until Tuesday?"

"Tuesday? What happens on Tuesday?" asked Mrs. Roberts.

"I've invited the ladies on an excursion. You will join us as well, I hope, dear lady."

"I believe we have Tuesday free. Thank you, Lord Ryeburn."

"Then I shall bid you adieu. Good afternoon, ladies."

Trevor retreated from the room, but he heard Mrs. Roberts's voice before he left.

"Miss Grant, this is indeed a fortunate day for us. An excursion with an earl. I shall write your parents at once."

He smiled to himself. His lighter mood lasted until he realized he had just committed himself to another day with Eden. He would never find a wife if he spent all his time with her.

CHAPTER TEN

The coach pulled up in front of Trevor's townhouse. Stepping down, Trevor admired the crisp lines of his home in London, the red brick and the white columns, and the neatly trimmed hedges. Even if it lacked the majesty of Concordia, it was a fine abode nonetheless. He walked into his house. As always the clean marble floors, the white walls, the cornices cutting the space into neatly defined areas pleased his sense of dignity.

Today, however, his house also struck him as cold and lifeless.

Trevor shook off the thought. These bouts of fancy had to stop. They were disrupting his peace of mind. He handed his gloves and hat to the butler.

"Sir, the Dowager Countess of Ryeburn has arrived." The butler bowed.

Trevor ran his fingers through his hair. He had hoped the woman would spare him her company a while longer.

"I suppose she had to show up sometime. Thank you, Finch." Trevor walked up to the drawing room.

Trevor found his stepmother moving a vase of flowers from one table to another. "Hello, Vanessa."

"Trevor, my dear boy, you're always so formal." The slim brunette put the vase in the center of a side table, then crossed the room. She embraced Trevor, who stiffly received her greeting.

Vanessa looked older than the last time he saw her. She was his elder by ten years, but the years of chasing youth had taken its toll. Lines creased the corners of her eyes, and rouge put the bloom in her cheeks. Her dress would have better suited a woman half her age, but she always had tried to act like a girl out for her first season.

"Did you bring Lorane?" Trevor untangled himself from her grasp.

"Don't be silly. I came straight from Bath. Besides, Lorane is far too young to bring to London for the season. She's at home with her governess and her books."

And I'm sure she'll be happier there. Trevor didn't pretend to understand his little half-sister, but he did understand her aversion to her mother.

"How are the preparations coming?" Vanessa frowned and picked up the vase again. She moved it back to its original position.

"I'm sure the housekeeper has everything well in hand."

Vanessa widened her green eyes. "You don't know?"

"I gave Mrs. Byrd your written instructions. I have complete faith in her abilities to carry out the arrangements."

"You are such a boy in so many ways, Trevor, dear."

He didn't allow himself to react to her words.

"A masquerade takes weeks of careful planning and ceaseless preparation." Vanessa took a seat, spreading her skirt out beside her as if she sat on a throne. "You can't depend on the lower classes to carry out the instructions properly. They need supervision, someone to command them."

"Then it's a good thing you came to town when you did." Trevor didn't bother to hide the sarcasm in his voice. Sarcasm was beyond Vanessa. Just as he never thought to remind his stepmother that Mrs. Byrd ran his household without interference from anyone. Nor would he tell Vanessa how he had to plead with his housekeeper to stay on after Vanessa's last visit. He would pay Mrs. Byrd a healthy bonus for putting up with Vanessa this time.

"You need a wife, Trevor." Vanessa poured herself a cup of tea.

Trevor smiled. He knew full well Vanessa didn't expect him to marry for years. She expected her position as countess to remain secure. "I've been thinking the same thing lately."

The cup wobbled on the saucer as Vanessa nearly dropped her tea. "Excuse me?"

"I've decided it's time I married. It's my intention to find a bride before the season is out."

The color drained from his stepmother's face. She gulped so hard, he almost heard it. "And have you found anyone suitable yet?"

"No, but I have made a list of eligible girls, any one of whom I believe will make me an admirable countess."

"Well, now, this is exciting news." Her face still lacked color and her tone enthusiasm. "And when you marry, shall you bring her to Concordia?"

"Of course. She will be the countess, after all." Trevor wished he were cruel enough to continue his torture. "But there will always be room for you and Lorane there. It is her home and yours for as long as you wish."

"That's very generous of you, Trevor." The cup finally reached Vanessa's lips.

"I wouldn't let my sister live without a home."

Vanessa's eyes narrowed. Of all her faults, he couldn't say she wasn't shrewd when it came to her security. She had just been told that her position remained hers only because of her daughter. Vanessa placed the cup back on the table. "But we needn't worry about such things yet. You haven't made a choice. Who knows how long it will take you to find a bride?"

She smoothed her hair with her hand. "Until then, I shall help you with the annual masquerade. We have but a week. Let's hope your Mrs. Byrd isn't too far behind in the preparations. I shall need an allowance."

"You shall have it." Trevor almost wished his father hadn't started the tradition of throwing a masquerade every year, but the *ton* expected it, and in truth it was the one legacy of his father's he didn't mind. But Vanessa knew too well how to spend an exorbitant amount of money.

"Have you thought of a costume yet?"

"No."

"Leave it in my hands." Vanessa clapped her hands together. "I shall find the perfect guise for you."

Trevor hesitated. He didn't want anything outlandish, but he would be happy not to worry about it. And choosing his costume would please Vanessa. He could offer her this small boon. "Thank you, Vanessa."

"Now you must do me a favor."

"Yes?"

"I have heard of a girl who is visiting London. They are calling her the American Nightingale."

Trevor raised his eyebrows.

"Don't look so surprised. We get the news even in Bath. Everyone is talking about her."

"You're speaking of Miss Eden Grant."

Vanessa waved her hand. "I don't know the girl's name,

just that her voice is angelic. All the *ton* is clamoring to have her at their soirees. I want you to invite her to the masquerade."

"You can't be sure she'll come."

"Of course she'll attend. You've never had a problem attracting women before when you've had the desire. I want you to meet her and make her come to our fete."

Disgust for his stepmother had never hit him as deeply before. "I won't seduce the girl to make your party a success."

Vanessa looked taken aback. "Good heavens, I didn't mean that. She is an American, after all. But I would like to hear her sing. I just want you to invite her."

"She isn't here for your amusement or anyone else's." He didn't know why he jumped to Miss Grant's defense with such vehemence. He enjoyed hearing her sing as much as anyone. "She's on a tour of Europe. This is her last stop before she returns to Massachusetts."

"You've already met her? Why didn't you tell me you've made her acquaintance instead of protesting so? You had me worried." Vanessa sipped her tea. "The masquerade will be the event of the season."

"I'll invite her, but I can't guarantee she'll come."

"Nonsense. Why would she turn down an invitation from an earl? She's an American."

Trevor refused to argue any further. "I said I would invite her. Now if you will excuse me, I have work." Leaving Vanessa to herself, Trevor went to his study.

Invite Eden to Concordia? She would be under his roof, under his care. A weekend with her would test his resolve to the limits, and he feared he wasn't strong enough to resist the temptation.

Trevor sat at his desk and pulled out a sheet of his stationery. Pen poised in hand, he couldn't bring himself to dip the point in the inkwell.

Coward.

Dipping the quill in ink, he wrote the invitation. When he finished, he blotted the paper, folded it, and sealed it in an envelope. He left it on a salver in the hall for Finch.

Before he returned to his desk, he poured himself a brandy. Trevor swallowed the amber liquor, letting the mellow burn smooth its way down his throat. He had nothing to fear. She wouldn't be alone with him. Mrs. Roberts would see that Miss Grant behaved herself. Miss Baylor would be there as well. Of course, that young lady would be too busy with Toddington to notice her friend. On the other hand, there would be a house full of people. He never had to be alone with her.

So why did the thought still terrify him?

Trevor frowned. Eden Grant had no hold over him. Shuffling through a drawer in his desk he brought forth the list. Several of these young ladies would also attend the masquerade. He would focus his attention on them. It didn't matter that none of them sparkled the way Eden did, or spoke the way she did, or fit in his arms the way she did. Their bloodlines were pure, their behavior refined, their training complete.

Was he looking for a wife or buying a hound?

Trevor rubbed his forehead. These rebel thoughts had to stop. His plans had not changed. He would find a wife this season, a woman who would behave and not bring any scandal to his name. And if she didn't sing like an angel, it mattered not.

He leaned back in his chair and closed his eyes. Startling blue eyes filled his memory. With little effort, he brought forth the memory of the peach-soft taste of Eden's lips. His blood surged. He would have a hard time finding a proper countess if he couldn't banish Eden from his mind.

He couldn't invite her. It was that simple. Despite his

stepmother's plea, he wouldn't invite her to the masquerade. She would only distract him from his goal. Taking another swallow of the brandy, he rose. With purpose-filled strides, he stepped into the hall.

The salver was empty.

Eden opened the most recent envelope. It had arrived much later than the rest. She removed the sheet and scanned the contents. It was from Ryeburn. Her heart started to pound. He was inviting her to the masquerade at his home.

She clutched the letter to her chest. She twirled, letting her arms fly out, giddy with joy.

She stopped so suddenly she almost fell.

He wasn't inviting her because he cared for her, he was inviting her because Lord Toddington would be there, and she would bring Lily.

The joy drained from her as if her body had become a sieve. Why should it matter to her how Ryeburn felt toward her? She read the letter again. Coached in formal terms, it held nothing she could remotely consider a sign of friendship. He would probably expect her to sing as well.

They would attend for Lily's sake, but Eden didn't have to spend more time with him than was necessary. Surely there would be many other guests as well. She would ignore him.

The trouble was she couldn't forget him. Their kiss in the garden haunted her. It sneaked into her thoughts by day and crept into her dreams at night. Even now she felt the heat rush to her cheeks at the remembrance of his lips against hers. The hateful exchange that had followed did little to diminish the effect of that kiss. Her first.

Pressing her fingers against her mouth, Eden tried to

imagine a different kiss, one that might take her mind from Ryeburn. Fingers were a poor substitute for a man.

"Miss Grant, what are you doing?" asked Mrs. Roberts.

Eden whirled around. Her cheeks flamed, and no answer came to her. "I . . . I . . ." She thrust the letter toward the chaperone. "Another invitation."

"From whom?" Mrs. Roberts placed her pince-nez on the bridge of her nose.

"The Earl of Ryeburn. He wants us to attend a masquerade he's giving at his country house next weekend."

"What a delightful idea. We have nothing planned, unless you would rather attend a different event."

"No. I would like to attend a masquerade."

"Very well. We shall accept the invitation. Perhaps that nice Mr. Sterling will be there." Mrs. Roberts smiled at her charge.

Eden could see the woman's hopes as if she had written them on her forehead. "Most likely."

"He is the son of an earl, and quite distinguished looking, if I may add."

Sterling? Distinguished looking? Eden thought he looked like a washed-out ferret compared with Ryeburn. She sighed. What use was it to compare the two men? One didn't care for her, and she didn't care for the other. "I'll tell Lily about it. She'll be excited to hear of our plans."

"Perhaps the two of you should discuss possible costumes. It might be amusing for you to dress as a famous pair."

"Yes, Mrs. Roberts." Eden fled the room. She couldn't pretend enthusiasm any longer. Maybe she could change her mind. Maybe she could turn down the invitation. . . .

No, Lily wouldn't forgive her, and Eden couldn't be that cruel to her friend in any case.

Resigned to her fate, Eden went in search of Lily.

CHAPTER ELEVEN

The item in the newspaper was small, but enough to annoy Eden.

Those privileged to hear the American Nightingale sing at the ball of the Marquess and Marchioness of Heathsbury two evenings past will surely never forget the experience. The ton *is buzzing with guesses of where she will appear next. The hostess lucky enough to have her is assured of success.*

A nickname. The English had given her a nickname. At least her actual name hadn't appeared in the newspaper. Not that she hoped to remain anonymous now.

Eden put the paper aside. With luck only a few people would read the spot. She reached for the coin in her pocket, remembering too late that she no longer had it. That explained 'the American Nightingale.' Bad luck courted her now that she no longer had her talisman to guard her.

Thank goodness one couldn't carry a pianoforte, else she'd probably have to sing on today's picnic.

Eden looked over the pile of invitations. The article in the newspaper would only make the stack grow. She didn't remember meeting most of these people. She wondered how many invited her without ever seeing her. One particular ornate envelope made her smile. That party she would attend and enjoy. The Duke of Welkes had taken a fancy to her, and she liked the eccentric man in return.

But the rest . . . Eden pulled out a sheet of paper. She had already accepted Lord Ryeburn's weekend party, so she had an excuse for many of these galas. She wrote her regrets without feeling a twinge of the real thing. That took care of five envelopes.

She couldn't possibly attend all the rest without suffering exhaustion. She sorted the invitations by date and laid them out in order on the desk. The first ones she eliminated were balls that fell on nights immediately following other balls. No one could dance that much. That still left too many envelopes.

Between now and the weekend they could attend two different events. Eden looked at four cards. Another ball and a tea. That would suit her. And with any luck, Lily would see her Lord Toddington again. Eden penned the two regrets and two acceptances.

Finishing her responses would take more time than she had. She glanced at the mantle clock. Ryeburn was due to arrive in about fifteen minutes. Lily was still busy dressing, trying on one outfit after the other. Eden had lost patience with her half an hour ago.

Eden's own dress was yellow, bright and sunny. Part of her wanted to irk Ryeburn with the color, but the dress was also well suited for a picnic. Truth was, she regretted agreeing to the excursion. Lily thought of nothing else but Toddington, and Mrs. Roberts hadn't stopped talking about the desirable match Eden might make if she charmed Mr. Sterling enough. Eden snorted in disgust.

Mrs. Roberts entered the room in time to hear. "I hope you won't make a sound like that on the picnic."

"No, ma'am."

"Have you finished the correspondence?"

"Not entirely."

Mrs. Roberts clicked her tongue. "You cannot let these people wait for your reply."

"I realize that, but there are so many to answer." Eden handed her the nine she had finished.

"I'll leave these for the butler to send. These arrived for you as well." Mrs. Roberts handed her three more envelopes.

Eden sighed. "More?"

"Honestly, Miss Grant. Most girls would be thrilled to receive such attention." Mrs. Roberts shook her head.

Most girls didn't have to perform in exchange for the attention. "Yes, Mrs. Roberts."

The invitations didn't bother her as much as the thought that she only received them because she could sing. How much attention would she attract if she were plain Eden Grant? How many balls would she attend if she had no talent?

None at all.

That answer soured her mood further. She wanted someone to notice her for herself.

The butler entered the room. "Lord Ryeburn, Lord Toddington, and the Honorable Martin Sterling have arrived."

"Thank you. Show them in." Mrs. Roberts straightened her skirt.

Ryeburn bowed in greeting. "My carriages await, ladies. Are we ready to depart?"

Eden rose. "I'll fetch Lily." She fled the room before her expression could reveal the distress of her thoughts.

Rushing up the stairs, Eden headed to Lily's room. She found Lily dressed only in her shift. "Lily, the gentlemen are here. They're waiting for us."

"I can't go. I have nothing to wear." Lily stood in a colorful pile of discarded dresses.

"Don't be a donkey." Eden bent down and lifted one from the ground. "What's wrong with this one?"

"It's too blue."

Too blue? Eden could agree with that sentiment. She lifted another. "Wear this."

"No. It's too breezy."

Eden crossed her arms. "If you don't put something on right this minute, I'll drag you downstairs just as you are. I swear I will."

"I don't doubt it," Lily murmured with a frown. She picked up a soft green dress. "This will have to do." She pulled the dress over her head and let it flow over her.

"That's the first one we tried on. You could have saved us a lot of time."

"But do you think—"

"I do. Now, come on." Eden did up the back of the dress. "Shoes."

Lily stepped into her shoes.

"Good. Let's go." Eden grabbed Lily's hand.

"My hair."

"Your hair looks fine. It's still up . . . mostly."

"E-den!"

"Trust me. You look charming." Eden dragged her out the door.

"I do hate it when you say that."

The gentlemen all stood as they entered the room. Toddington's cheeks grew red as he smiled at Lily. "Good morning, Miss Baylor."

Lily blushed as well. "Good morning, Lord Toddington."

Eden sent her gaze heavenward. "Where are we going?"

Ryeburn gave her a crooked grin. "We'll drive along the London Wall and stop at the Tower of London. Those are probably the best views of Roman ruins in London."

"The best ruins lie outside London." Sterling stepped forward. "If you wish, Miss Grant, I should be happy to take you to see them."

"That's a kind offer, but this is my father's passion, not mine. I only promised him I would try to see why he thinks the Romans were so great by looking at the ruins in every city I visited," said Eden.

"The morning flies. Shall we depart?" Ryeburn offered his arm to Eden.

The party made its way to the carriages standing outside. Ryeburn helped Eden into the barouche, then climbed in himself. Toddington assisted Lily. But for the slight flare to his nostrils, Sterling's face betrayed no anger as he helped Mrs. Roberts into the gig. Sterling didn't spare the barouche a glance, but kept his gaze focused on the road ahead.

Eden sat back in open coach. The warm spring air had a distinct odor. It must be London, she thought, but Eden enjoyed the breeze on her face anyway.

As they passed the London Wall, Ryeburn pointed out the remains of the original Roman fortress. It looked like a bunch of rocks stuck together, and rather sloppily at that. Eden supposed it was impressive that such a thing still stood after fifteen-hundred years, but it didn't move her.

The things she did for her father.

At least the Tower of London was interesting. After showing her the Roman parts of the fortress, Ryeburn took her and the others to see the crown jewels. The regalia glowed even in the dim indoor lights. Eden looked at the treasures with awe, but decided she would probably get a headache if she had to wear one of the crowns.

They traveled outside the city for their picnic. Finding a shaded spot by a brook, Ryeburn's footmen spread out a large ground cloth and brought forth the hampers. The meal was a sumptuous feast—patés and meat pies, cold roasts and game birds, preserved cherries, raspberry tarts, and to wash it all down, champagne. By the end of the meal, Mrs. Roberts was suppressing yawns. It wasn't long before the woman leaned against a tree, and her snores grated upon the ears of the picnickers.

Trevor found his gaze drawn to Eden time and again. Her natural grace blended with the wild beauty of the woods. At any moment, he expected her to dance in the water and reveal herself as a water sprite, then disappear in a magical mist.

He nearly snorted with disgust.

She had done it again. She had led his thoughts down a path of fancy he never knew he was capable of. He didn't like it. If she could conjure such behavior in him, he could imagine the havoc she could wreak on a weaker person. No wonder Mrs. Roberts had difficulty controlling her charge.

Ryeburn cast his gaze at the sleeping chaperone. "Does she always watch you with such vigilance?"

"Only when her belly is full of fine food," answered Eden.

"I'll take that to understand you enjoyed the repast." Ryeburn lifted another bottle of champagne and filled Eden's glass again.

"No more. Too much, and I won't be able to sing tonight."

"Where are you performing tonight?"

Eden hesitated a moment. "The Countess of . . . What was her name again?"

"Thornley?" offered Trevor.

"No, that wasn't it. The Countess of . . . Featherstone. She's having a ball tonight and invited us to attend."

Trevor found that information interesting. Perhaps he would rethink his plans for tonight. If she were going to the Featherstone ball, he could attend as well, and see her again. . . .

Gad, what was he thinking? He didn't want to see her again. No, that wasn't entirely true. He wanted to see her again, but he shouldn't. Toddington would likely attend Featherstone's ball, but Trevor would attend Thornley's affair instead.

As Trevor pondered his evening plans, he saw Sterling slide closer to Eden. Trevor held down the rush of irritation that seized him.

"Then I shall have pleasure of hearing you sing again, for I shall attend the Featherstone ball tonight as well." Sterling preened his cravat.

Trevor's hands itched to tighten the damn cloth around Sterling's neck. The smug cur. He used every opportunity to wheedle his way into her graces. Trevor turned to Eden. "What makes you think you will perform?"

Eden gazed at him. "For what other reason do you think she invited me?"

Her words took Trevor aback. She didn't sound bitter, but a sadness lurked in her eyes. A wave of guilt washed over him. Hadn't he invited her to the masquerade because his stepmother wanted her to sing?

"You can rest assured that when I invite you, it shan't be for your talent." Sterling bowed his head to her.

"And just where will you invite her, Sterling?" Trevor couldn't prevent the words.

Sterling reddened like a glowing ember. "I, that is, we were just speaking . . ."

"Gentlemen, if you wouldn't mind, I don't wish to speak of invitations or parties. I have enough of that at the house. I wish to enjoy the day."

"Perhaps we could take a stroll?" suggested Sterling.

"An excellent idea. Miss Baylor, will you walk?" Toddington stood and reached his hand to Lily.

"And how do you propose we do that without compromising the ladies? Their chaperone is asleep." Trevor waved his hand at the snoring woman.

"Wake her up, Ryeburn. She can walk with you." Sterling offered his arm to Eden. "Miss Grant?"

Trevor watched as Eden stood and took Sterling's arm. If Sterling thought he wouldn't wake the woman, Sterling was wrong. Grumbling to himself, he crossed to Mrs. Roberts. "Madam?"

Mrs. Roberts didn't stir.

Raising his voice, Trevor bent down and shook her shoulder. "Madam."

"Wha—excuse me?" Mrs. Roberts blinked several times and sat up.

Trevor jumped back as Mrs. Roberts glared into his face. "Madam, I was wondering if you would accompany us on a stroll through the woods. The ladies don't wish to go without you."

"As is well and proper." Mrs. Roberts stood and brushed off her skirt. "You mustn't think I would allow my girls to do anything questionable."

"I wouldn't dream of it." Trevor offered his arm. "Shall we?"

Mrs. Roberts giggled like a schoolgirl, a frightening sound indeed. "Thank you, Lord Ryeburn." She took his arm. "Where are they?"

Trevor bit back a curse. Sterling and Toddington had already disappeared down the path. "I'm afraid they've started without us. We must make haste if we are to catch them."

"By all means." Mrs. Roberts pulled on his arm. "I cannot allow them to go off alone. It isn't proper."

Trevor spied the two couples as soon as they rounded the curve in the path. Mrs. Roberts slowed her pace. Apparently this distance satisfied her sense of duty. Trevor matched her pace with impatience. He was too far behind the others for his peace of mind.

As the three pairs walked through the cool woods, Trevor paid little heed to the woman on his arm. His attention never wavered from the two heads in front of him. Sterling would lean over and whisper something to Eden, and often she would laugh in return, the mellifluous sound washing over him like cold water. The irony of his anger irritated him all the more. She wasn't the right woman for him, but, by God, he didn't want Sterling to win her either.

"Your generosity overwhelms me." Mrs. Roberts patted his arm.

Too late he realized the woman had been prattling their entire walk. "It was my pleasure, Madam."

"I shall write Miss Grant's parents."

Panic gripped him. His heart raced. What had he just agreed to?

"They shall be quite happy to hear how kind you have been to their daughter. I'm sure they shall wish to thank you personally."

His panic subsided. "That isn't necessary. I'm enjoying myself just as much as the young ladies."

"The Grants are an unusual family. Quite close to one another."

Quite different from his own. "Is Miss Grant eager to return home?"

"I'm sure she misses her parents, but I cannot tell." Mrs. Roberts lowered her voice as if taking him into her confidence. "She's unlike most young ladies. She has had several offers for her hand and refused every one."

Trevor mulled that information over in his mind. From the way she had kissed him, he knew it wasn't because she lacked passion. But she had also claimed she had never been kissed. How did those two facts reconcile themselves? Several marriage proposals, yet never been kissed? With each day, with each fact, Eden became more intriguing, much to his dismay.

Her laughter floated back to him yet again. He clenched his teeth. If he didn't know better, he would swear jealousy raged within him, but jealousy would require a degree of entanglement, and while he liked the girl, he would not have her in his life.

He quickened his pace, ignoring the startled glance Mrs. Roberts sent him. Soon he could hear the conversation between Sterling and Eden without straining.

"Remember, you've promised me your first dance."

"I shan't forget, Mr. Sterling." Eden smiled at him.

Trevor fumed.

"Perhaps tonight I shall have the opportunity to speak with you when there are fewer ears." Sterling all but drooled on her shoulder.

"Fewer ears? At a ball? I don't believe that possible, Mr. Sterling." Eden's attempt at lightness seemed strained. Or was that a wish on Trevor's part?

"Perhaps. But a man can only hope."

Trevor snarled at Sterling's obsequious tone.

"Lord Ryeburn, are you ill?" Mrs. Roberts searched his face.

"I fear something has indeed upset my stomach."

"Oh, dear." Mrs. Roberts waved her hands and shouted to the others, "We must return. Lord Ryeburn is ill."

Trevor bit back his denial. This was the best and fastest way to keep Sterling from Eden.

The group hurried back to the carriages. While the women expressed their concern for his health, Trevor celebrated the success of his ploy. Sterling had to ride in the gig, while Eden rode with Trevor. He felt a little guilt at the deception, but one look at Sterling's icy expression as he rode beside Mrs. Roberts erased that.

His joy at interrupting Sterling's awkward attempt at courtship was short-lived. The man would be at the Featherstone ball tonight. Trevor winced. And he himself had invited Sterling to his masquerade. Two days with Eden. Sterling would have ample opportunity to court Eden at Concordia, away from the stifling conventions of London society. The last thing Trevor wanted to do was give Sterling another opportunity to win her.

The nagging feeling that perhaps Miss Grant might change her mind about Sterling and welcome his suit bothered Trevor. What right had he to deny her possible happiness?

With Sterling? Never.

His conscience soothed, he enjoyed the ride to Grosvenor Square. Tonight at the ball, he would make sure Sterling would have no chance to corner Eden and press his suit.

Trevor's serenity fled as he realized he had just decided to attend Featherstone's ball after all.

CHAPTER TWELVE

Since the night of the Featherstones' ball, a restlessness he had never experienced before filled Trevor. Although he had prevented Sterling from monopolizing Miss Grant's time at the ball, he couldn't prevent other swains from vying for her attention. Their simpering ploys irritated him nearly as much as Sterling's. He had left the next day for Concordia, where he hoped his sanity would return to him.

Concordia stood ready for the masquerade. Ryeburn paused in front of the looking glass and adjusted his costume. As he tugged at the toga, his wreath fell off. With a soft grunt of disgust, he bent and retrieved the offensive article. Why had he agreed to let Vanessa pick his costume? He hated the toga, the laurel wreath he wore in his hair, the bow upon his back, and the lyre on his arm. The sun mask he wore obscured his features, but gave the final clue to his personage. Only the truly obtuse would fail to recognize him as Apollo.

The arrival of the guests had caused little stir. The household staff had prepared well for the days of revelry. Each room now housed one or two guests. After a light supper on the day of their arrival, the travelers retired to their rooms. Today they breakfasted at their leisure, then spent the day reading or strolling through the gardens. For those interested, Trevor had arranged an excursion to the local abbey ruins.

Nothing marred the festive atmosphere and air of anticipation. Trevor's sister, Lorane, had withdrawn to the nursery and hadn't reappeared. Trevor often wondered why she was so reclusive, but at least he needn't worry about her as he worried about her mother.

Vanessa had found fault with almost every aspect of the event. Trevor followed her for two days to soothe his put-upon servants. Vanessa's behavior had cemented his resolve to find a wife. He couldn't continue to subject the help to Vanessa's tirades. He needed a countess.

His thoughts strayed to Eden. He was growing accustomed to having her intrude upon his thoughts and interrupt his search for a countess. He hadn't spoken to her since the night of the Featherstones' ball. Although aware of her arrival at Concordia, he had managed to avoid her. But he hadn't failed to notice how his guests flocked around her when she appeared. Sterling seemed glued to her side.

Trevor adjusted his wreath and took a final glance in the viewing glass. Shaking his head, he turned from his image. Only Vanessa would deem it appropriate to give a dark-haired man the costume of the sun god.

The music of the orchestra sounded in his ears. He had to hurry. As host, he should be downstairs already. He flicked the end of the toga over his shoulder and left the room.

The many guests appeared in groups, but soon the ballroom teemed with brightly colored creatures and characters. Trevor gazed over the room. The masquerade promised to be a success again this year.

Gold fabric draped the walls, and gold chains hung from the chandeliers. Trevor didn't know what effect Vanessa wanted to achieve with this decoration, except a show of opulence. Small potted orange trees stood in the corners, their fruit fragrant and ripe among the green leaves. Silver candelabra stood on pedestals every few feet. The orchestra played behind a screen of palm fronds, leaving Trevor to suppose that the orangery stood empty of plants at the moment. But the effect was magical. It was as if the music rose from a secret source. As much as he hated to, he had to admit Vanessa had succeeded in creating a mood that pleased.

Trevor moved among his guests. Only a few faces were uncovered, but he didn't find it difficult to recognize the people behind the masks. He noticed peacocks and swans, kings and queens, fairies and elves. The gaiety of his guests seemed elevated because of their anonymity. He wondered how many of them would be quite so bold if they realized their identities weren't as hidden as they believed.

He spotted Vanessa. Her costume was outrageous as usual. She wore a long blond wig that fell over a flesh-colored sheath. Flowers adorned the hair, and she was barefoot. As Lady Godiva, she would attract a great deal of attention, which was exactly her idea of success. Trevor laughed to himself. She wouldn't be happy after Eden sang. Few would pay attention to an older widow after a beautiful young girl had enchanted them.

He furrowed his brow. He hadn't seen Eden yet. What was her costume? Casting his gaze over the room, he searched for her blond head. Instead he found Toddington. Toddington's garb was that of a Viking. Beside him stood a shepherdess. Miss Baylor, of course. She looked charming in the full peasant's skirt, blouse, and bonnet. She held a crook in her hand. The only thing missing was a lamb to follow her around.

If Miss Baylor was the shepherdess, Eden must be the sheep. He searched the room once again. No sheep. He spotted a horse and an elephant, but no lamb.

A vision glided across the floor. Her dress was green at the top, but blended into brown at the bottom. The texture and pattern gave the impression of leaves on a tree. Long brown gloves covered her arms. Tiny leaflets covered the gloves. Leafy twigs crowned her head. She wore a simple green domino on her face. Stunning blue eyes gazed out from the holes in the mask.

Eden.

He stared at her. It wasn't possible. They would certainly provide fodder for the gossips after this evening. His Apollo to her Daphne—the forest nymph who spurned Apollo's advances by turning herself into a tree. What chance did he have to convince anyone he wasn't interested in her after tonight?

Eden turned. When her gaze fell on him, she stopped short. Her expressive face told him the same thoughts were running through her mind. She grimaced, tried to ignore him, then turned and came directly toward him.

"Why didn't you warn me?" Her voice held an accusation.

"This costume was Vanessa's idea. I had no knowledge of it until this evening. Why aren't you Miss Baylor's sheep?"

"Can you picture me as a meek lamb?" She crossed her arms.

He chuckled. "No. The wolf in sheep's clothing perhaps, but the lamb, never."

She looked disgruntled. "Thank you for that amusing analogy."

"I meant no insult."

"Yes, you did, but that seems to be your standard behavior when you're talking to me."

He had the grace to feel guilty. "Yet you're still talking to me. You don't seem very offended."

"If it wasn't so true, I would be." She laughed softly, a mix of humor and sadness. All the more striking for beaming from a field of green, her blue gaze latched onto his.

Trevor couldn't avert his stare. She held him spellbound. Her honesty captivated him. He might not approve of her, but she didn't shy away from the truth. He shook his head. "So why did you choose Daphne?"

"Need you ask?"

"I think I can guess. You would prefer your freedom than tie yourself down."

"No one ever said you weren't perceptive. So what are we going to do about this?" She waved her hand over her costume.

"Nothing. You look charming. But perhaps it's best we aren't seen together much this evening."

Her eyes changed somehow. Was that hurt that sparkled in those blue depths?

"You are right, of course." Eden tossed her head back. "It shouldn't be difficult to avoid you. There are plenty of others who might welcome my company." Eden turned and started to walk away.

"Miss Grant . . ." Trevor stopped. Without turning back, she stopped for a moment. He didn't continue. She moved on.

Damn. His gut felt empty, devoid of feelings and life. His every nerve screamed to follow her, but he pushed those urges down. He had done the right thing. He was protecting himself and his name. Hadn't she just admitted as much to him?

So why couldn't he stop thinking about her?

He needed a distraction. No, he needed a countess. Angelica Breensbury, the next name on his list, was here. She should provide ample diversion. Trevor had seen her earlier dressed as a faerie. Spotting her across the room, he set off to determine whether the faerie would make a suitable countess.

Eden watched him talk to that pretty girl dressed as a faerie. She tried to concentrate on the conversation with Mr. Sterling, but her attention wandered. Who was she? Probably some proper English girl with a title. Did he find her attractive?

The music started, and Ryeburn took the floor with the faerie. They glided across the polished wood. She was petite—her head scarcely reached his chest. Her dark hair complemented his, and she seemed to anticipate his every move, as if she were born to take that position. Breeding, Lily called it. "Annoying" would be Eden's choice. She frowned.

"I didn't mean to offend you." Sterling's quick apology cut through her musings.

Eden tried to think back to what Sterling had said. "Pardon me?"

"I said I didn't mean to offend you. You couldn't have chosen your costume to coincide with his, not knowing how he feels about you." Sterling smiled at her. "I fear my jealous nature appears when I'm with you."

Eden didn't know which statement panicked her more—the bald truth about Ryeburn's opinion of her or Sterling's declaration of affection for her.

"I've startled you. Surely you must have guessed how fond I've become of you."

She was glad a mask hid most of her face. "I think I see Lily over there. I must speak with her."

Sterling grabbed her hand before she could rush away. He bent over it and kissed it. "Promise me a dance, and I shall let you go."

Her glove did little to protect her from the feel of his lips. Suppressing the urge to wrench her hand free, she nodded. "A dance. Later."

"Until then, my dear, I shall count the seconds." Sterling kissed her hand again, then released it.

She scurried away like a mouse unwillingly freed by the cat. Eden entered the ladies' salon and crossed straight to the washbasin, peeling her gloves from her as she walked. She scrubbed her hands until she could no longer feel Sterling's lips on her skin. A shudder ran through her. Mrs. Roberts found the man pleasant enough. Why couldn't she?

Because Sterling wasn't Ryeburn.

Her face grew cold as the color drained away. Eden stared at herself in the mirror. Ryeburn meant nothing to her. Why would he? Just because he was the first man to kiss her. . . .

And she had enjoyed it. . . .

Eden shook her head. Nonsense. She found Ryeburn interesting because he disapproved of her. She enjoyed goading him, even if he made an easy target.

She just wished she had someone to talk to. Lily was less than useless at the moment. Her friend was too busy worrying about Lord Toddington to help with Eden's turmoil. Mrs. Roberts would probably have an apoplectic fit if Eden tried to take the woman into her confidence. Her mother was far away. Even her lucky coin was gone.

Eden felt alone for the first time in her life, an unfamiliar experience, especially for a twin.

She heard the music start again in the ballroom. If she returned now, Sterling would no doubt seek her out for that dance. She couldn't interrupt Lily, she didn't want to spend more time with Mrs. Roberts, and she was avoiding Ryeburn. That exhausted the list of people she knew.

The refreshment table would offer some sanctuary. Just before she reached it, she heard a voice speak her name. Turning her head, she saw her hostess, Lady Godiva, in conversation with an older woman.

"This Miss Grant has a remarkable voice, I've heard. I had Trevor invite her so that we may decide for ourselves."

Disappointment crashed through her. Ryeburn had invited her for her singing. She had hoped he wouldn't be like the others. She had thought he invited her to bring Lily and Lord Toddington together.

"It's hard to believe an American could possess such talent." said the older woman.

"I have my doubts, but her performance tonight shall prove whether she truly can sing or if the stories exaggerate her talent."

Lady Godiva's smile reminded Eden of a cat's. If Ryeburn's betrayal didn't hurt so much, Eden would have liked to scratch the smile from the woman's face.

Ducking back through the corridor, she made her way to the garden. She remembered the twists of the hedges that lined a maze and the round gazebo at the center. The perfect refuge.

In the cool of the evening, far from the cheerful lights of the ball, Eden tried to compose herself. She didn't understand the emptiness that plagued her. She didn't understand the yearnings that echoed within her. She didn't understand herself.

Numquam tuas spes dedisce. The words of that stupid motto whirled in her head. Her dreams had never included a pompous earl with no sense of humor. Sitting on the iron bench, Eden let her emotions wash over her. Anger mixed with sorrow, fear blended with hope, until confusion reigned. She wasn't one to weep, but tonight the tears fell unchecked.

Sterling tapped Trevor on the shoulder. "Have you seen Miss Grant?"

At Sterling's words, Trevor's gaze scanned the room. "Not since the beginning of the masquerade."

"I've been looking for her for the past fifteen minutes and can't seem to find her anywhere."

"Perhaps you should ask Miss Baylor."

"I have. She hasn't seen her either. If you spy her, tell her I'm waiting for the dance she promised me." Sterling ambled away, craning his neck over the crowd as he searched for Eden.

An uncharitable sense of satisfaction ran through Trevor at the thought that Eden wasn't there to dance with Sterling, but part of him wondered where she had gone. If she were in the ballroom, he would see her. Hell, every time he blinked he saw her in his mind's eye. She shouldn't be hard to spot in her costume. Even among all the glittering attire, she stood out.

Trevor saw the faerie. She waved to him, and he gave a halfhearted wave back. The girl hadn't met his expectations, but he had yet to seek out the other two women on his list. He chided himself. Instead of worrying about Eden, he should be striking up an acquaintance with the other candidates.

But first he would check by the refreshment table just to be sure.

As Trevor circled the dance floor, he found his way barred by Vanessa. "There you are, my dear boy."

"Hello, Vanessa."

"The evening is progressing wonderfully, wouldn't you agree?" Vanessa preened her hair, adjusting it over the crucial body parts.

The movement drew his attention and, before he could prevent it, he glanced down.

"You naughty boy. You mustn't look at me in that way."

He met her gaze with disinterest. "I wouldn't dream of it."

He saw her lips harden. Her eyes narrowed a fraction. Then she forced a smile to her lips. "Lord Buckley hasn't kept his gaze from me the entire evening."

Lord Buckley was an ass. "Can I assume you hope to remarry then?"

"I couldn't marry beneath me. If I wed Buckley, I'd only be a viscountess. Besides, how would you manage without my guidance?"

Trevor drew in a deep breath to still his annoyance with her. "What do you want, Vanessa?"

"It's time for that girl to sing. I want to see if it was worth inviting an American." Vanessa's voice crackled with superiority.

"I haven't seen her for a while."

"Go find her. She can't expect our hospitality without doing her part."

Anger chilled his blood. "She is my *guest,* and I won't have you or anyone bully her into performing like a trained animal."

Vanessa widened her eyes. "Good heavens, Trevor. I didn't realize she meant so much to you."

Through clenched teeth, Trevor said, "She doesn't

mean anything to me. She is my guest and a visitor to our land."

"Of course. I didn't mean anything else." Vanessa patted his arm. "But do go find her and ask her. Perhaps she will indulge you."

Trevor shook his arm free. Without another word to his stepmother, he walked from the ballroom. He would find Eden, and would try to convince her to sing as a favor to him. Nothing would please him more at the moment than to see his stepmother's face fall in disbelief at the beauty of Eden's voice.

CHAPTER THIRTEEN

Trevor didn't know where to search next. She was nowhere in the house. Miss Baylor hadn't seen her, and Mrs. Roberts was too busy exchanging stories with the other chaperones. Sterling still waited for his dance. Trevor had sent a maid to see if Eden was in her room, but the servant reported that the room was empty.

If Eden wasn't in the house, she must be out. By now urgency filled his steps. He needed to find her and make sure she was safe. His mask long since discarded, Trevor dashed through the conservatory and stepped out into the garden.

Although a few indiscreet couples occupied the near benches and corners, Eden wasn't among them. His search led him farther from the house. He stopped at the edge of the maze. Nothing lay beyond these hedges except the expanse of lawn and forest that encircled Concordia. If she had fled there, he'd never find her. The only haven left to explore was the gazebo at the center of the maze.

He raced onto the winding paths and reached the center in little time. "Eden . . . Miss Grant?"

"Is it time for me to perform?"

The bitterness in her voice startled him. He stepped into the small shelter. She sat on the bench, her domino on the seat beside her. Her hair loose, she exhibited a wild beauty. Then he noticed the tears. "Is something amiss?"

Eden wiped her eyes. "No. I'm a bit disappointed, that's all."

"Can I somehow help?"

"I doubt it." She flicked another drop off her cheek.

"You're crying."

"Obviously."

"I'd offer you a handkerchief, but I'm afraid Apollo doesn't have a place to carry them."

An impatient glare was the only response to his levity.

"Miss Grant, I was worried about you. Nobody knew where you were."

"And heaven forbid that something should happen to the entertainment."

Her words confused him. "You're angry."

"Yes, I am."

"Why?"

Arms akimbo, she stood and faced him. "Because I had hoped you'd be different from the others."

"You're angry at *me?*"

"I realize you invited me at the last moment, but you didn't have to let me think it was because you wanted to give Lord Toddington and Lily another chance to see each other."

He raked his hand through his hair. "I admit my stepmother wanted me to invite you to sing, but you are here as my guest. You don't need to do anything you don't wish."

"That's not what Lady Godiva said."

"What did Vanessa say to you?" Anger stirred within him, but not at Eden.

"She didn't say it to me. I heard her speaking to someone else." Eden glanced away.

"If I know Vanessa, it was something rude and showed her ignorance."

The hint of a smile appeared on her lips. "Well, it wasn't complimentary."

"Vanessa can't abide anyone outshining her. People talk about you. She probably hates you for that."

"I'm almost tempted to sing just to spite her."

"You'd spite her either way. She's told everyone you'd sing tonight. If you don't, she'll come off as a liar, and if you do, the attention you'll receive won't sit well with her." Trevor paused. "Do you hate to sing that much?"

"Oh no, I love to sing. It's the fuss I hate."

"The fuss?"

Eden raised her eyebrows. "Would I be here now if it weren't for my singing?"

Trevor chuckled. "Probably not."

"At least you're honest about it. Since that night at Lord Lockwood's, I've received at least thirty invitations. And I read about myself in the newspaper."

"Ah, yes, the article on the American Nightingale."

"You saw it? I still can't believe they gave me a nickname."

"I've heard Vanessa call you that more than once."

Eden flounced onto the bench. "That's the fuss. And it's worse at home."

Trevor took a seat beside her. "Worse?"

She sent him a look of disgust. "Did you know I've received seven proposals of marriage?"

A jolt of surprise slammed through him. "Seven?"

She nodded. "All from boys who thought they were in love with me after hearing me sing. Their declarations annoyed Daddy, but you should have seen Nicholas when they followed me around."

"Nicholas?"

"My twin." She looked at Trevor out of the corner of her eye. "He always tries to correct my behavior as well."

"He hasn't succeeded much." Ryeburn rubbed his forehead. The thought of her suitors disturbed him. "What did Nicholas think of your suitors?"

"He was livid. They were his friends until they met me."

Seven suitors and never been kissed? It was hard to believe. "Your brother protects you with diligence, I'd say."

"Too much diligence, I'm afraid."

He could understand her need to rebel a little better. Trevor examined her face. The tears had disappeared, leaving the reddened rim of her eyes as the only evidence she had cried. He wanted to hold her against him until her eyes recovered as well.

Errant thoughts again. He cleared his throat. "Will the seven be waiting for you when you return?"

"I hope not. They are part of the reason my parents agreed to this trip. By now they should have regained their sanity and found themselves a new hobby." She fell silent, but then laughed.

"Pardon me?"

"I was just remembering something. One of the boys fancied himself a composer. After hearing me sing, he wrote me a song."

"How charming."

"You haven't heard the song." Eden thought for a moment, then began.

A tree covered a lazy brook
Its leaves were green and cool,
And in the pool beneath the limb
There swam a trout in its school.
My love is like that trout
Gasping for air in the water.
Hoping your hook will pull him out
Sooner, not at all later.

At the first notes, the magic of her voice almost claimed him, but through sheer effort of will he concentrated on the words. His mouth dropped open.

"Wait, I'm not finished yet." Eden smiled and drew another breath.

Oh pull me out, dear one,
Let my fish nourish you.
For you alone I am meant
Or I will drown in that cold brook.

"Gad, that's terrible."

Eden laughed. "There can't be a more atrocious piece of music in existence. And it continues for another three verses."

"Please spare me." He grinned at her.

"I sang it once, because I didn't want to hurt his feelings. No one noticed how dreadful it was except my family. Everyone else seemed entranced." She shrugged her shoulders.

Thinking of how her voice had nearly mesmerized him, he shook his head. "Your voice is capable of such power.

But it is difficult to imagine no one noticed the song." He thought of the first night he heard her sing. The only one who escaped her spell had been Sterling. Trevor frowned. What could that mean?

"Perhaps I should sing it for Lady Ryeburn."

"You wouldn't dare." He paused. A slow grin spread over his lips. "On the other hand, it might be rather amusing."

"Why, Lord Ryeburn, I never knew you had a streak of devilishness in you."

"If you tell anyone, I shall deny it."

Her laugh washed over him like a warm bath, soothing and all too comfortable. He wearied of fighting his attraction to her. His every muscle strained to pull her near. He wanted to smell her lavender scent, touch her velvety skin, taste her delectable essence. "I am going to kiss you, Miss Grant."

Eden eyes widened for an instant. Then she leaned into him and lifted her face to his.

He touched his lips to hers with a gentleness that tantalized rather than satisfied. He savored the moment, the prolonged agony, before he gave into his craving to crush her to him. The malleable softness of her lips molded to his, urging, sending innocent promises of the treasure within. Kissing her was a mistake, he knew, but what a glorious error.

Eden closed her eyes. Her face appeared all the more delicate for the absence of the intense blue gaze. He kissed her as if he might break her. Tiny fires danced in his blood.

Trevor pulled her closer. His lips demanded more from her. She gave to him willingly, fanning the tiny fires into a conflagration. His tongue asked admittance, and she welcomed it with her own. He explored her mouth with a hunger he couldn't control.

He withdrew from the kiss, but didn't break contact. Brushing little kisses along her jaw, he moved lower, over her neck, stopping at the indentation at the base of her throat. As he tasted the spot, she let out a faint moan. She trembled in his arms.

His head moved lower still, his lips gliding over the creaminess of her skin. Her heart pounded below his mouth; her breathing grew uneven. His hand strayed to her décolletage, stroking the hint of a satin swell. Her sharp intake of breath cut through the haze of passion to remind him of her innocence.

"God help me," muttered Trevor. He lifted his head and stared into her eyes. "You must stop me."

"But I don't want you to stop." Her voice was feeble.

Trevor sat up. "We can't do this."

"What are we doing?" The invitation in her eyes called him like a siren.

"You are such an innocent." He pushed away from her. His breath came in deep bursts. "If we don't stop, I will ruin you."

Eden slid closer. "Once again you talk of my reputation."

"The smile in your eyes tempts me, woman, but this isn't right. You deserve someone who can offer you more than a moment."

Eden stopped. "I see."

"No, I don't believe you do." Trevor took her hands in his. "You are a beautiful and talented woman. Someday you will find someone who can give you what you seek."

His words sobered her. Withdrawing her hands from his, she scrunched her mouth to the side. "You sound like my father."

"Not that old, I hope."

"Nearly."

He chuckled. "We've already established how dissimilar we are. But perhaps we can agree to be friends."

Disappointment settled in his stomach like a rock. Why did this particular woman have to be so reckless and headstrong? Why did this particular woman have the power to make his emotions reel?

She extended her hand. "Friends."

"Friends." He grasped her fingers. He knew he was right. They weren't suited to each other. So why wouldn't the disappointment vanish?

"Well, friend, would you like me to perform for your guests this evening?"

"Only if you wish. You are my guest, too." He grinned at her. "But I would love hearing you sing again."

Eden lifted her mask from the bench. "I would enjoy singing for your guests. And Lady Ryeburn."

The wicked glint in her eyes nearly undid him. He had just regained control of the passion that had raged through him during the kiss, and now it threatened to overpower him anew.

"We'd best return separately. Miss Baylor is probably worried about you."

"I'll go then." Eden rose, then turned to face him. "Are my eyes red from crying?"

He almost groaned. The moon lit her hair and costume so that she did indeed look like the nymph Daphne. His body hardened. "You look lovely," he managed to say.

"Don't be too long. You won't want to miss your stepmother's expression." At the first twist of the path, she vanished from his view, disappearing into the night like the goddess of nature she portrayed.

Trevor closed his eyes. If he weren't still seated, his knees would have buckled beneath him. How could a woman have such power over him? He prided himself on his strength, yet now he felt weaker than a babe—except in his manhood. It was harder than a rock.

He did groan now. Friends, indeed. He dropped his forehead into his hands. He wanted to take her to his bed and spend the night entwined in her legs, discovering how deep her passion ran. And such thoughts wouldn't help him regain control any time soon.

Trevor clenched his teeth. His guests awaited him. He couldn't spend the night in the maze because he had no more control over himself than a schoolboy. Drawing a deep breath, he concentrated on the conjugation of Latin irregular verbs. That seemed to help. Next he recited the fifth declension of masculine nouns. Just for fun he also recited the first through fourth. By the end of his Latin review, he had regained full control of his body.

The words of the coin sprang unbidden to his mind. *Numquam tuas spes dedisce.* Ha. If his dream was an American Nightingale, he was better off forgetting his sleep entirely.

CHAPTER FOURTEEN

Eden followed the path through the maze, but her thoughts remained in the gazebo with Trevor. Her lips still pulsed from their unaccustomed activity. She pressed her fingers to her lips. If she didn't push too hard, she could pretend she was still kissing him.

Her hand dropped to her side. Silly, childish games wouldn't soothe her. Trevor disturbed her. He had revealed a sense of humor and a spirit she guessed he kept hidden because he was ashamed of it. His touch wakened her in places she didn't know she had. When he kissed the skin of her chest, she had felt the stirrings deep within, leaving her longing for more. But more of what?

She rounded the corner and stopped. A hedge greeted her sight and cut off her progress. She had gone the wrong way. Returning along the same route, she plunged down a different trail. A few yards later, this path, too, ended in a hedge.

Eden wrinkled her brow. She backed up and tried a third path. Two new trails branched from this one. She didn't know which one to try. With a puff of exasperation, she admitted she was lost.

"Lord Ryeburn," she shouted. No response greeted her call.

Once again she shouted, "Lord Ryeburn!"

She waited a moment. From somewhere to the left, she heard something. "Lord Ryeburn, is that you?"

"Miss Grant? I thought you went back to the house."

"I got lost."

His chuckle rumbled through her like a wave of heat. "I thought you knew the way."

"So did I."

"Stay where you are. I'll come get you."

"How will you find me?"

She jumped as his voice came from beside her. "I grew up playing in this maze. Do you really think I don't know every corner?"

Eden looked up at him. "You realize we have to go back together now. Either that or I spend the night here."

Trevor smiled. "I'll lead you out." He offered her his arm.

Placing her hand on his forearm, Eden followed. His arm was warm under her touch, and his confident strides comforted her. They walked in silence until they reached the edge of the maze. There she withdrew her hand. At his questioning glance, she nodded at the people taking the air in the garden. "Perhaps it *is* better if they don't see us together."

Knowing that the sight of two people emerging from the maze would start tales, Eden realized she wanted to spare him any further embarrassment. For the first time in her life, she wished she were a proper lady, one Trevor could hold on his arm without explanation and be proud to do so. Her sudden concern for reputation confused her.

Troubled by the turn of her thoughts, Eden picked up her skirt and dashed into the house. She heard Trevor call after her, but she didn't pause. Stopping only long enough in her room to fix her appearance, Eden returned to the ballroom. As she expected, Mr. Sterling spotted her at once and crossed to her. She inhaled deeply, resigned to her fate.

"Miss Grant, you promised me a dance."

"I did, Mr. Sterling." Eden forced a smile to her lips.

The orchestra struck up a waltz. Sterling led her to the floor and took her in his arms. She suppressed the urge to squirm. His hold didn't envelop her with the same sense of well-being and security as Trevor's had.

Thank heavens the waltz didn't last long. Sterling released her. "May I have the next dance, as well?"

"Forgive me, Mr. Sterling, but I promised our host that I would sing tonight."

"For your singing, I shall gladly relinquish you from my arms." Sterling bowed to her.

Eden couldn't find the words to respond. She bobbed a quick curtsey and left the floor.

Since she had given voice to her decision, she searched for Lady Godiva. Eden laughed to herself. She would have to remember not to use that name any longer. If she wasn't careful, she would address Lady Ryeburn incorrectly.

In a secluded corner of the house, she found the woman encircled by three gentlemen. From their laughter and hushed tones, Eden guessed they shared gossip and secrets. Although they seemed in good spirits, their laughter sounded hollow. Their convivial mood rang false, as if it served some other purpose. Loathe to interrupt, Eden waited to the side.

"Rufus, you scoundrel. You cannot think I would enjoy such a thing." Lady Ryeburn stroked the man's arm, corrupting the meaning of her words.

"My wife couldn't attend your masquerade this year. Who knows when I shall have the chance to be your favorite again?" Laughter surrounded the man as he placed his hand on Lady Ryeburn's breast. Looking up, he noticed Eden. He dropped his hand to his side and nudged the fellow beside him. One by one the men's attention drifted from Lady Ryeburn and focused on Eden.

When Lady Ryeburn noticed the straying regard of her admirers, she looked for the source of the disruption. Her gaze latched on to Eden. She frowned. "What do you want?" As if she remembered too late how impolite her words sounded, Lady Ryeburn smiled and crossed to Eden. "How can I help you, my dear?"

The woman's behavior confused Eden. "I'm sorry. I fear I'm interrupting. Perhaps I should return some other time." Eden turned to leave.

"Nonsense. You have my attention now." Lady Ryeburn cocked her head. "Ah, yes, you are the American girl. I almost didn't recognize you in that costume. I sent Ryeburn to fetch you. Are you ready to sing?"

"If you wish." Eden moistened her lips. She didn't like this woman or the distasteful men who surrounded her.

"Of course, my dear. That is why I invited you to my party." Lady Ryeburn pushed through the circle and took Eden's arm. "Gentlemen, you are in for a treat tonight. The American Nightingale shall sing for us."

Irritation whirled in Eden. Despite Lady Ryeburn's breeding, she was as crass as a washerwoman. Eden bristled at the use of the nickname. But she refrained from pulling her arm away. Trevor had warned her about his stepmother. Eden would enjoy singing for this woman.

Within a few minutes, Lily sat at a pianoforte in the music room, and Eden stood beside the instrument. Lady Ryeburn had given the orchestra a well-deserved break and invited everyone to listen to the American Nightingale.

Eden looked over the crowd. Lady Ryeburn sat in the front row beside that odious man Eden had seen her with earlier. Lord Toddington sat at the end of the row, but his gaze never strayed from Lily. A few rows back sat Mr. Sterling. She averted her gaze so she didn't have to acknowledge him. Her gaze scanned the room once more. There. Trevor sat at the very back of the room. He gave her a wink. An impish glint gleamed in his eyes. It robbed her of the ability to think clearly.

The first notes floated from the pianoforte and beckoned her attention. Eden glanced at Lily. The bright aria was the perfect antidote to the chaos of her thoughts. Closing her eyes, she let the music touch her, and she sang.

From the back of the room, Trevor felt the enchantment begin. He no longer cared how Vanessa reacted to Eden's singing; he was grateful he could hear Eden again. When the first piece ended, the brevity left him dissatisfied, until she began anew. Her sorcery grew stronger with each song, filling the room with her spell. The listeners could no more stir from their chairs than prevent the tears that flowed during a poignant song. When she finished a rollicking melody, his guests stood and thundered their applause.

Eden curtseyed to them, then whispered something to Lily. Lily glanced up at her, then shrugged. Eden turned to the audience. "This next song I would like to dedicate to a new friend." Her eyes glittered with mischief.

Trevor wrinkled his brow. What was Eden planning?

Lily played a few chords, then began to embellish upon the simple melody. Eden's gaze landed directly on him, and then he heard her sing.

> A tree covered a lazy brook
> Its leaves were green and cool,
> And in the pool beneath the limb
> There swam a trout in its school.

Trevor started. It was the atrocious song from the maze. She couldn't be serious. He glanced around the room. No one seemed to notice. The music was innocuous enough, and under Lily's skilled fingers, it sounded gay, but the words . . . He waited for the audience to fidget under the strain of listening to it.

And he waited. No one stirred. To his amazement, the enraptured look never left the faces of his guests. He glanced at Eden, who sang the song in the most dulcet tones she could achieve. He started to laugh.

A woman near him shot him a look of reproof. Trevor hastened to muffle the sound, but his shoulders shook. Another woman near him clicked her tongue, and a third hissed at him to be quiet. He tried, but the song was so bad and the audience so oblivious, he couldn't stop.

At last the song ended, and once again the listeners burst into applause. He let loose the roar he had suppressed. The people around him shot him looks of concern, but it didn't matter. If she hadn't warned him, he never would have believed it.

Her program at an end, Eden acknowledged the delight of the audience with a thank-you. Lily and Toddington stood to one side as the guests dispersed. Many stopped to speak with her, often to get her promise of sometime performing for them again. Trevor listened in disbelief. Now he understood what she meant by "fuss."

Lady Ryeburn remained behind the others. She stepped forward, dragging Lord Buckley with her. That man's gaze never left Eden, which Trevor imagined irked Vanessa to no end. Trevor stayed to see what his stepmother had to say.

"Well, my dear, you do have a gift." Her eyes were cold and held little warmth. "A pity you are an American. Your talent shall be wasted in the Colonies."

"She could tour Europe," said Buckley. "I'm sure I could convince several of us to sponsor her. With her abilities and looks, she'll make a fortune."

"Shut up, Rufus," said Vanessa.

"Thank you very much, but I have no need of a fortune, nor am I interested in performing for the public." Eden's response eased the hard lines around Vanessa's mouth.

"Of course not. Thank you for performing for us this evening." Vanessa smiled at her as if she had just bestowed a blessing on her. As Vanessa left, dragging the unwilling lord behind her, Trevor heard his stepmother say, "Ignorant chit. Turning down a fortune. Doesn't she know what you are worth?"

"How do you think she would respond if I told her my family already has a fortune?" Eden stood beside him and grinned.

"That was extremely ill-mannered of you to sing that song."

"I know."

"And I enjoyed it tremendously."

"I saw."

Lily crossed to Eden. "What was that thing you sang?"

"You've never heard it? Yet you played so well." Trevor looked at Lily.

Lily shrugged. "Eden explained the chord order and tempo. It wasn't a difficult piece. Rather insipid, really, so I embellished." She turned to Eden. "What was it?"

"A song written by Neville."

"You needn't say more."

Toddington frowned. "I don't understand. What was wrong with that song?"

"You fell under the enchantment," said Trevor. "I'll explain later."

For a moment Toddington looked confused. "As you wish. Miss Baylor, may I escort you back to the dancing? It is nearly midnight. Almost time for the unmasking."

A blush pinkened Lily's cheeks. "Thank you, Lord Toddington." The pair left.

"It's hard to believe no one heard the words to that song."

Eden lifted her hands. "I did tell you."

For a moment neither spoke. He was loathe to leave her, but Trevor remembered his duty as host. "Thank you for the unforgettable performance." He lifted her hand and kissed it, cherishing the contact for an instant longer than propriety allowed. Releasing her, he ignored his desire to stay with her and returned to the ballroom without much enthusiasm.

He surveyed the dancing, once again in full swing. He understood the politics of hosting this masquerade, and he understood that the affair would garner him more influence. So why did he feel as if he were perpetrating a sham?

"She must be his mistress," a woman's voice near him spoke. "Did they really think they could hide it? He's dressed as Apollo, and she's Daphne."

Dear God. They were speaking of Eden and him.

"She has a great talent, but you know how performers are. No morals whatsoever."

"I understand they were out in the garden together tonight. I saw her as they came in. Thoroughly disheveled," a second woman said.

"In the garden? How primitive. But what can you expect from an American."

"I have heard she is a wild thing. She races horses."

"All the men are falling at her feet. She could choose any one of them. Not that I blame her for choosing Ryeburn. That dark coloring of his fascinates most women."

"Who can say how soon he'll tire of her? He's never been known to fancy any woman for long."

"But to invite her to the masquerade? Scandalous."

"Blood will tell. He is his father's son, after all."

Trevor's face showed none of the fury that roiled within him. He stepped into the ballroom and stared at the two women talking near him. They reddened, but didn't hide their laughter. They moved away, heads bent together.

He viewed his guests in a different manner now. No longer were they his friends and acquaintances. They were the enemy. How dare they compare him to his father? His father hadn't a moral bone in his body. Any money his father made was soon gambled away. His second wife had cuckolded him with his knowledge, almost as often as he had cheated on her. Trevor couldn't even be sure his sister really was his sister. Only his father's fortuitous death had saved the family.

Seven years Trevor had spent rebuilding his fortunes, seven years of denying himself any pleasure in order to achieve the stature he desired. And in little more than two weeks, a woman had caused the gossips to bandy his name on their tongues.

Eden returned to the ballroom at that moment. He

saw her look about the room. He turned away. The best recourse was to ignore her. Here, tomorrow, anywhere. Let the *ton* think he tired of her. She would be gone in three months. He need never see her again.

The events of the evening unsettled him. Once again he had given in to his weakness for the wrong woman. He had worked far too long and hard to restore dignity to his family. He couldn't risk further harm to his name. It was enough he had to worry about Vanessa's indiscretions.

The guilt that troubled him about the damage to Eden's reputation he dismissed as irrelevant. In three months, she would return to Massachusetts, where no one would hear of her escapades in London. In three months, the *ton* would remember her fondly for her singing, then forget about her.

In three months, she would be out of his life forever.

CHAPTER FIFTEEN

Across the ballroom, Eden caught Trevor's gaze for an instant. He frowned and turned away. Eden wrinkled her brow. She hadn't expected that reaction.

Sterling appeared at her elbow. "Is something troubling you?"

"No, nothing." She cast one last glance at Trevor and saw only his back.

"You were magnificent this evening."

"Thank you."

"The man who marries you is fortunate indeed."

Eden gave him a quizzical look. "Why do you say that?"

Sterling gave a flip of his hand. "Not only are you beautiful, but talented as well. With the proper husband, your talent could amass a fortune."

"I have no need of a fortune."

"Ah, yes, your father." Sterling took her by the arm and led her toward the refreshment room. "Did you know, in

England only the eldest son inherits? Any other progeny must fend for themselves."

"I wasn't aware." Eden glanced around. Short of yanking her arm from his grip, she had no choice but to follow him.

Sterling paused at the table. "A lemonade, my dear?"

She wasn't particularly thirsty, but after singing, she would welcome a lemonade. "Yes, please."

He reached for a glass and passed it to her. Without pausing to let her drink, Sterling continued to pull her along. Eden held the glass in her free hand, struggling to keep the beverage from sloshing over the side.

" 'Tis a terribly unfair thing, this primogeniture," continued Sterling. "Many younger sons are much more competent than their older brothers. Unfortunately, that is never taken into account. I hear it is different in America."

Disquiet alighted on Eden. "Where are you taking me?"

Sterling gazed down at her. "Good heavens, I haven't given you a chance to drink your lemonade." He pulled her into the study. "Here you are, my dear. A nice quiet corner where you can enjoy your drink, and we can talk."

He led her to a leather armchair and waited until she sat. Eden stared up at him.

"Drink. It will refresh you." Sterling crossed to the casement doors that led out to the front of the house. "Where was I? Ah, yes. Primogeniture. Drink."

Eden took a gulp. What did Sterling want? His behavior alarmed her. She glanced at the door. It wasn't too far. She could dash out before Sterling caught her. Placing her glass on a nearby table, Eden waited for her chance to leave.

"Do you have it in America? How much do you inherit upon your father's death?"

"I don't know that I inherit anything."

"Well, you are a woman, after all. One would hardly expect one's parents to discuss such things with you." Clasping his hands behind his back, Sterling stared out the window.

"I think we should return to the party. It's almost time to unmask." Eden rose from the chair.

"Sit. I haven't finished speaking with you yet."

Eden remained standing. "I wish to return to the ball."

With a quickness she had never seen in him before, Sterling crossed the room and blocked her way. "Sit. We have not finished our conversation."

Her alarm grew as she took in the lines of anger on his face. She sat again. Eden eyed the man with fear and loathing. "What do you want?"

Sterling knelt in front of her. "Miss Grant, I am sure you have noticed how fond I have become of you. Although we have only known each other for a short time, it is time enough to know I wish to spend the rest of my life with you. Since your parents are absent, I cannot do the proper thing and ask for your hand from your father, so I shall ask you. Will you marry me?" He took her hand.

She snatched it back. "No."

"Are you sure?"

"Definitely."

"I'm sorry to hear you say that."

Eden rose. "I'm returning to the ballroom now."

"No, you are not." He stood and pushed her back into the chair. Sterling leaned over her. "I'm waiting for my coach. Until it arrives, I have time to explain why you are here." He returned to the window.

Inching up, Eden attempted to stand.

"Sit. Don't even think of leaving. We'll go when I'm ready. Finish your lemonade."

"You're mad."

"You don't care for me any more? You might later." Sterling returned to her. "When my coach arrives, we shall leave and head for Scotland."

"What?"

"My dear Miss Grant, I am the third son of an earl. My elder brother is the Viscount of Harbroke, whereas I am simply the Honorable Martin Sterling. I receive nothing upon my father's death. Oh, a small stipend to be sure, but not nearly enough to set me up in the lifestyle I wish to pursue. With no title to attract an heiress and no money of my own, I have had to survive by other means. My circle of friends who will support me has diminished. In simple terms, I need a new source of revenue.

"When I met you, I realized you were the perfect answer to my problems. Your father is rich. He will support us. And if he chooses not to, I can always put you on stage to perform for our living."

"I'm not leaving with you."

"You don't have the choice. 'Tis a shame you turned down my proposal. It would have made things easier."

"For whom?"

"Such a pity your mouth is worth so much to me. I would enjoy stitching it shut." Sterling reached into his pocket. He pulled out a small brown bottle and a handkerchief stuffed thick with cotton. Unstopping the vial, he poured the liquid onto the pad.

Eden leapt out of the chair. She dodged his reach, but couldn't outrun him. He grabbed her arm and yanked her back. "I told you to sit." He threw her into the chair, then bent to retrieve the cloth, which had fallen to the floor.

Pinning her head with his hand, Sterling pressed the damp material onto her nose.

Eden thrashed her head from side to side, or tried to, but Sterling's grip was firm. She held her breath until she felt her lungs would burst, but in the end she exhaled and drew in air. Her vision began to swim. She no longer struggled to control her breathing, until the world slipped away from her sight and blackness claimed her.

The bouncing of her seat jarred her awake. She couldn't understand why her chair undulated beneath her. Blinking didn't clear her vision. Darkness held her sight captive. Trying to discern where she was, Eden sat up.

"I see you've awakened." Sterling's voice came out of the darkness.

Eden blinked some more. With the aid of moonlight, she finally determined that she rode in a coach. "Where are you taking me?"

"To Gretna Green. We'll be married as soon as we cross the border."

"I won't say the words."

"That doesn't matter. The joy of being married among the Scottish is that one can always find a barbarian willing to ignore convention." Sterling leaned forward. "By the time we get to Scotland, you'll have to marry me. No one will believe you haven't been ruined."

"If you touch me, I'll kill you," she hissed.

"No need for dramatics. Whether I have you now or wait for our wedding night makes no difference to me. To all eyes, you are already bedded."

Fury raged in Eden. She wanted to scream, but to what purpose? No one would hear her, except the coachman, but he was most likely in Sterling's control. Frustration agitated her further. She balled her fist and let it fly.

Sterling screamed as her fist hit his eye. He flew back against the seat, and his hand covered the offended area.

"You miserable bitch." He raised his free arm to strike her.

Eden waited for his blow, but it never came. Lowering his arm, Sterling snarled at her. "I will repay you for this, but I prefer a bride without damage. I have plenty of time to teach you obedience after we are wed." He lowered his hand from his eye. Even in the dim light, Eden saw the redness from her punch. "Go to sleep. We have a long journey ahead of us."

Folding his arms across his chest, Sterling leaned his head back. Within minutes, he slept.

Eden glanced out the window. The ground sped underneath the wheels. If she were to jump, she would most likely break an arm or leg. Or both. Perhaps if the coach slowed . . .

A tear trickled from her eye. What hope did she have to escape? No one at the masquerade would miss her. Except Lily. Eden straightened. Yes, Lily. Lily would raise the alarm that she was missing. Surely someone would come after her. If only Nicholas traveled with her. Her brother wouldn't let Sterling succeed.

She needed a champion. She needed a hero.

Lily tapped on Trevor's arm. "Lord Ryeburn, I need to speak with you."

"Yes, Miss Baylor?" Trevor noticed Toddington standing beside the girl. The two hadn't been apart for longer than a few minutes all evening.

"I can't find Eden anywhere."

Trevor looked among the unmasked faces in the ballroom. He saw no sight of Eden. "I shouldn't worry about her. She tends to disappear at parties."

Lily furrowed her brow. "She wouldn't have missed the unmasking."

"This is a large house. There are many places she could be."

"She isn't in her room, or anywhere else I've looked."

"Check the garden." The bitterness in his tone surprised himself.

"She isn't in the garden." A blush crept onto Lily's cheeks. "We . . . that is, I . . . She isn't there."

Trevor shot Toddington a glance. His friend's color was high as well. He smiled knowingly. "I'm sure she'll turn up soon."

Lily frowned. "Lord Ryeburn, no one has seen her since she sang."

That was over two hours ago. A hint of unease stole over him. His gaze searched the room. He spied his butler, Finch. "Let me make inquiries, Miss Baylor."

Trevor crossed to Finch. "Have you seen Miss Grant lately, Finch?"

"No, my lord. Not since she sang."

"Would you ask the others if they have seen her?"

"Yes, sir." Finch moved away. Trevor scanned the room. He saw nothing out of the ordinary, and he didn't see Eden. Where was she?

This was ridiculous. Miss Baylor's imaginings were unfounded. Eden had to be somewhere in the house. But he couldn't turn his gaze from the crowd.

From the corner of his eye, he saw Finch return.

"My lord?"

"Yes, Finch?"

"Miss Grant was seen in the refreshment room with Mr. Sterling."

"And now?"

"I do not know, my lord."

Trevor searched the room for Sterling. His disquiet grew. Sterling wasn't here either. "Ask if anyone knows where Sterling is."

"Yes, my lord."

He didn't trust Sterling with Eden. Sterling had made his attraction for Eden plain. Now they were both missing. Trevor's stomach churned. She wouldn't have gone with Sterling, would she?

"My lord?"

Finch's voice broke Trevor from his rumination. He turned toward the butler.

"One of the footmen remembers Mr. Sterling ordering his coach about two hours ago. He left with a guest shortly afterward."

Sterling didn't have a coach. "Which guest went with him?"

"I shall ask, sir."

"I'll come with you."

Trevor followed Finch into the back rooms of the house. The footman in question was flirting with a housemaid in the kitchen. The man straightened as soon as he saw Trevor. "My lord."

"Did you see who Mr. Sterling took with him in the coach?"

"Yes, my lord. It was the American girl, the one who sang."

Trevor's heart stopped for an instant. A coldness spread through his limbs at the news. "I understand. Did she go willingly?"

"I couldn't see, it being dark and all, but I don't think she complained, for Mr. Sterling carried her, and she didn't raise her voice none."

"Thank you."

The man nodded his head. "My lord."

Trevor returned to the ballroom. The music of the ball sounded discordant to his ears. His gut twisted in anger and disgust. He knew he had no right to feel betrayed, yet betrayal was the exact word he'd use to describe the taste that soured his mouth. How could she go with Sterling? She had led him to believe she didn't care for the man. Then why would she leave with him?

He found Lily waiting for him. "Did you discover anything?"

"Yes. She left with Sterling two hours ago."

Lily drew her brows together. "That isn't possible."

"I assure you it's true. One of my servants saw her in Sterling's arms. He carried her to a coach."

"Sterling doesn't have a coach. He drove here with me," said Toddington.

"He got use of one somewhere. And he left with Eden—I mean, Miss Grant."

"She wouldn't do such a thing." Lily's voice grew louder.

"She did."

"Then something is wrong."

Lily's statement drew worried glances from the guests standing close enough to hear. The last thing he wanted was more gossip this evening involving himself and Miss Grant. Trevor took her by the arm. "Let's continue this discussion in my study. You come, too, Toddington."

He led them down the hall to his study. Pushing open the door, he noticed a strange, slightly sweet smell. The casement doors were cracked open. Trevor frowned. On the floor was a handkerchief and a small brown bottle.

Lily wiped away a tear. "Something is wrong. Lord Ryeburn, Eden wouldn't leave with Mr. Sterling. You may think her improper, but she isn't. I know her. You have to believe me."

Trevor half listened. Kneeling, he picked up the bottle

and cloth from the floor. The cloth was dry, but the bottle still had a drop or two inside. He sniffed the contents, then shoved the vial from his face. He blinked a few times to clear his vision.

"I believe you," replied Toddington. "I'll send for my coach at once and give chase."

"Thank you." Lily's mouth quivered when she smiled at Toddington. She cast a contempt-filled glance at Ryeburn. "It's nice to know someone cares about Eden."

"Toddington, what do you make of this?" Trevor handed him the bottle.

Toddington turned the small object in his hands. He, too, smelled the contents, blinking furiously afterward. "I remember it too well from my time in the army. It's something you never forget. It smells like ether."

"That's what I thought as well." Trevor glanced to the window, then crossed to Lily. "Forgive me for doubting you, Miss Baylor. Miss Grant is indeed in trouble."

CHAPTER SIXTEEN

Trevor rang the bell cord. "Toddington, will you go with me?"

"Of course—if only to keep you from killing Sterling."

"Thank you." Trevor clapped his friend on the shoulder.

Within minutes, Trevor transformed himself from host to the efficient man who had rebuilt his fortune. He sent Finch to inquire of the remaining coachmen whom Sterling had hired and whether any of them knew the destination. Trevor told Toddington to change his clothing and sent another servant to prepare their horses. Trevor himself dashed up the stairs to disrobe and put on practical clothes.

By the time he donned dark trousers, boots, shirt, and coat, Finch had returned. Toddington and Miss Baylor waited in the study.

Trevor tied a cravat around his neck as he returned to the quiet room. "What did you find, Finch?"

"Two of the grooms and one of the coachmen agree that Mr. Sterling intended to take Miss Grant to Gretna Green."

Trevor and Toddington exchanged a look.

"What does that mean?" asked Lily.

"Sterling intends to marry her."

"Eden wouldn't agree to that. She doesn't like Mr. Sterling, at least not enough to marry."

"That won't matter." A fresh wave of anger rolled over Trevor.

"Why is he doing this?" asked Lily.

Trevor shook his head. "I can't say for certain, but I think he has found a way to support himself without working."

"Eden?" Lily sent Toddington a puzzled look.

Toddington took Lily's hands. "Sterling is almost a pauper. He's relied on the largesse of the *ton* for his existence. With a rich wife, or in your friend's case, a wife with a rich father, his income would no longer depend on others. "I've always found him despicable."

"You have? I tolerated him because I thought he amused you." Trevor rubbed his forehead.

"He told me you were going to sponsor him for the House of Commons, so I never said anything," responded Toddington.

"Insufferable bastard." Trevor bowed to Lily. "Excuse me, Miss Baylor."

"No need. You've expressed my sentiments exactly. Poor Eden must be out of her head with fright. Do you think you'll find her?" Lily bit her bottom lip.

"You may count on it, Miss Baylor." Trevor didn't have the heart to tell the girl Eden would be ruined, even if they brought her home by morning.

Lily turned to Toddington. "Please find her."

"We shall, my dear." Toddington lifted her hand and kissed it.

"And be careful," she whispered.

Finch stepped forward. "If I may be of aid, my lord . . ."

"Thank you, Finch, but I need you here. Make sure Lady Ryeburn doesn't get carried away in my absence."

"Very good, my lord."

The servant returned with the news that the horses were ready. The two men ran out into the night without a thought to the gaiety they left behind.

The sun's rays touched the sky with their first color. Eden's eyes burned. She wanted to close them, to find refuge in slumber, but she was afraid to sleep. Across from her, Sterling drowsed. His mouth hung open, and a trickle of spit ran down his chin. If she wasn't so tired, she would laugh at his appearance.

She closed her eyes for a moment, giving in to the temptation of sleep. When she next opened her eyes, the sun was high, and Sterling gave her an indifferent glance. The coach had stopped at an old inn.

"You may as well sleep some more. We won't reach Scotland until after midnight."

"Where are we?"

"We're just changing horses. We'll be on our way in a moment."

Eden straightened her skirts. She eyed him with loathing. "I don't wish to sleep anymore."

"You've nothing to fear from me. I'm as tired and cranky as you. I won't touch you. Consider it an early wedding present." His cackle disgusted Eden.

"I'm hungry."

Sterling glanced out the window. "I suppose a short stop

won't hurt. I need to relieve myself, and I could use a bit of food."

He climbed from the coach and turned to help her down. His grip encircled her arm, and he showed no signs of releasing her. He dragged her inside.

Sterling pointed at a plump woman wearing an apron. "You there. Pack us some food."

"Where's yer blunt?"

Sterling reached in his pocket and pulled out a coin. He tossed it to the woman. "Here. If you keep an eye on her," he pulled Eden forward, "I'll give you another beside."

"Anything for you, dearie."

Sterling left her in search of a privy. Eden waited until she couldn't see him, then turned to the woman. "If you help me escape, I'll give you one hundred pounds."

The woman roared. "Now where would you be carrying one hundred pounds? In that tree you're wearing?"

The few others in the room laughed with the woman. Eden reddened, but continued. "I can't give it to you now, but I promise I shall send it to you."

"Why should I be trusting you? The gentleman has cash I seen."

"Please. He's kidnapped me."

"Sorry, miss. I don't know nothing about a kidnapping, but that's betwixt you and the gentleman. But just in case you get any ideas of making me lose me money . . ." The woman waved to a huge man. The man lumbered to them. "This is me son. Luther, go block the door. Don't let the lady out."

"Yes, Ma." The hulk took a place by the door.

Eden swallowed her scream of frustration. "Can I at least find a place to relieve myself? I've been in that coach for hours."

"Sure, dearie. Don't let it be said that Old Maggie were a cruel one. But you won't mind if I accompany you."

Gritting her teeth, Eden shook her head.

A half an hour later, she sat across from Sterling as they again traveled north. A cold meat pie sat uneaten beside her.

"I thought you said you were hungry." Sterling spewed crumbs as he talked.

"Watching you eat has made me lose my appetite."

"A pity. Then you won't mind if I eat yours. These pasties are remarkably delicious for peasant food. We shall have to stop for more on our way home. Where shall we make our home? I've always wanted to live on the park."

Eden ignored his question and stared out the window. The afternoon shadows had started to stretch, but the idea of time passing brought her no comfort. Every minute seemed to bring her closer to her fate, one she seemed destined to share with Sterling. A burning lump formed in her throat. She wouldn't cry again. She wouldn't.

She wiped a tear away.

The horses wouldn't last much longer. Trevor sat in the saddle, weary, angry, and frustrated. They had seen no sign of Sterling since they left Concordia. Toddington looked spent, and Trevor had to admit he would soon topple from the saddle himself. An inn appeared in his sight. They would change horses here and perhaps get some food as well.

Trevor rode into the courtyard. A huge monster of a man swept the stones in front of the door.

"Ma, more visitors," bellowed the giant.

A plump woman ambled out the door and wiped her hands on her apron. "Well, if this ain't me lucky day. The second set of gentry to appear on my doorstep. Come in, gentlemen. What can I get for ye?"

Trevor dismounted and tied the horse to the railing. "We need fresh horses."

"Of course. Yer fortunate that coach didn't take all of 'em."

"Coach?"

"Aye. The one what came through here not half an hour ago. Brought another gentleman to my inn. Only he had a lady with him. Not that she was too happy about it." She winked at the large man at her side.

Trevor's blood quickened. "Was the woman tall and blonde?"

"Indeed she was, sir."

"And you say she was unhappy to be in the man's company?"

"Aye. She even tried to bribe me to help her escape. Offered me a hundred pound to help her. 'He's kidnapping me,' says she, but I didn't believe her."

"Which way did they drive?"

"North. He was very generous, he was."

"If you can get those horses here in five minutes, you'll see how generous I can be."

The woman knocked the man on the head. "Don't just stand there, Luther. Go get the man his horses."

"Yes, Ma."

Trevor pulled out two gold coins. "For your help, madam."

"Anytime, dearie. I don't rightly know how I helped, but you just tell me, and I'll be happy to do it again."

Her son led two horses to them. With ease, he unsaddled the spent mounts and readied the two fresh horses.

"It's not much farther now, Toddington," said Trevor. "We can rest after we save her."

"You mean she weren't lying?" The woman's eyes widened in horror.

"No, she wasn't."

"I thought they were husband and wife having a little tiff." The woman extended her hand with the two coins. "I'm not deserving of these."

Trevor smiled at the innkeeper. "Madam, you're an honest woman, and for that alone you deserve them." He mounted the horse. "Let's go, Toddington. We almost have them."

His exhaustion forgotten, Trevor drove the horse at a furious pace. Toddington followed behind. An hour later the coach came in view. Trevor eyed the thing with relief and hatred. If this wasn't the right coach, he knew he would have to admit failure. Neither he nor Toddington could continue much longer.

His face set with determination, Trevor rode up beside the driver. "Stop this vehicle."

The coachman looked down, but didn't slow. "If yer're robbers, I carry no money, only passengers."

"I know that, man. Now stop this coach. We are not highwaymen."

The driver pulled back on the reins, and the conveyance eased into a stop. Trevor jumped from his horse.

"What's going on?" Sterling leaned out the window. He saw Trevor and screamed to the driver, "Get going, you fool. You won't get paid if he stops us."

Toddington grabbed the reins of the animals. "I'll pay him for his trouble."

The coachman didn't stir. He looked too interested in the action to want to move.

Trevor yanked open the door of the coach. Sterling cowered in the corner. Across from him sat Eden, looking tired and a bit disheveled, but smiling with a joy that brought gladness to his heart. "Eden."

Eden flung her arms around his neck. She kissed him on the lips, heedless of the gasp that came from Sterling. Trevor lifted her from the carriage and placed her on the ground. She still embraced him.

"You came for me." Her voice held more amazement than relief.

Trevor clamped down the giddy satisfaction he felt as he held her. He cleared his throat. "It was the proper thing to do. You were under my roof. I had a responsibility to keep you safe."

The joy disappeared from her face. Her arms dropped to her sides. "Yes, well, thank you." She lifted her chin. "And thank you, Lord Toddington."

Toddington nodded.

Sterling climbed out of the vehicle. "Do you know what you are doing to me? I'll be ruined."

"Yet you had no qualms that you ruined Miss Grant." Trevor's cheek twitched in anger.

"I was going to marry her," whined Sterling "She wouldn't have been ruined."

"Did you ask her if she wanted to marry you?"

"Of course."

Surprised, Trevor turned to Eden. His gaze narrowed. "He did?"

"Yes," she answered. Her arms akimbo, she pursed her lips.

"Then why the joy at your rescue? Did you change your mind?"

"No."

Trevor stepped back. "My apologies. Forgive the interruption. Let us help you return to your coach."

"I don't wish to return to the coach."

Toddington stepped between them. "Ryeburn, you're being an ass. Why don't you ask if she accepted his proposal?"

Trevor refused to acknowledge the chagrin that sped through him. He turned to Eden. "Did you?"

"No. I refused him, so he kidnapped me."

Something akin to relief spread through Trevor. Then he grew angry again. "Why would you let me think you accepted?"

"Because you are so quick to judge me and find fault with everything I do. He says he proposed, so you automatically assumed I went with him willingly. You knew how I felt about him." She stomped to the side of the road and sat beneath a tree.

Toddington's shoulders shook, and he sucked in his upper lip. Trevor glared at his friend. Only Toddington would dare laugh at him. In a few moments Toddington regained control. "What are we going to do with him?" He pointed to Sterling.

Trevor tore his gaze from Eden. Her behavior still infuriated him. He drew a few deep breaths. Finally he turned his attention to Sterling. A circle of purple and blue surrounded Sterling's left eye. "What happened to your eye?"

Sterling covered it with his hand. "I knocked it against something."

"Yes, my fist," shouted Eden from the side of the road.

"She punched you?" Trevor faced Eden.

"Jolly good blow, Miss Grant," said Toddington.

"Thank you."

"I think, for your own safety, we should return Miss Grant to her chaperone." Trevor chuckled.

"You can't do this. Once word of this gets out, no one will take me in. How am I supposed to live?"

"Get a job." Trevor turned from Sterling.

Sterling grabbed Trevor's sleeve. "She can't mean anything to you. I'll still marry her. I'll be good to her."

Without warning, Trevor whirled and punched the man in his right eye.

Reeling back, Sterling covered his right eye and screamed. "Why did you do that?"

Trevor grabbed the man's collar and pulled him so that Sterling's nose was just inches from his. "Just be glad I didn't decide to castrate you."

The color blanched from Sterling's face. Trevor shoved him. Sterling landed in the dust.

Toddington spoke to the coachman. "I am the Earl of Toddington. We wish to hire you. Will this cover your expenses?" He handed the man a five-pound note.

The man looked at the fiver. "This will more than cover my expenses. But I feel a bit guilty taking it, seeing as how I enjoyed the show so much."

Toddington smiled. "That's fine. We'll take care of the young lady, then tell you where we wish to go."

"What of him?" The coachman pointed to Sterling.

"He has chosen to walk." Trevor yanked Sterling to his feet and pushed him down the road a few steps.

Sterling's jaw dropped. "You can't leave me here."

Trevor grinned. "We can, and we will. I suggest you start if you wish to reach shelter before dark."

"All this because of that bitch?" Sterling waved his hand toward Eden.

Before Trevor could react, Toddington stopped him. "He isn't worth it, Ryeburn."

Trevor glared at Sterling, then smiled. "If I can still see you in five minutes, I will give you a lot more than another black eye."

Sterling stumbled as he took a step backward. He whirled on his heel and started down the road, tiny clouds of dust chasing his feet as he walked.

CHAPTER SEVENTEEN

Eden's gaze never drifted from Sterling until he disappeared. She gave a sniff of indignation. That serpent deserved his comeuppance.

Ryeburn and Toddington joined her at the side of the road. "Miss Grant, we need to speak," said Ryeburn.

Eden looked at him. A shadow of dark growth colored his chin, and his hair looked unkempt. His eyes were red, and he blinked too often. Toddington didn't fare any better. "Couldn't it wait until we've all slept a little in the coach?"

"I'm afraid not." Ryeburn ran his fingers through his hair. "Miss Grant, Sterling has caused more trouble than you are aware."

"I know. He kidnapped me. Mrs. Roberts must be frantic with worry. I can't imagine what Lily thinks."

"It's more than that. Sterling's actions have ruined you."

"He didn't touch me."

"Be that as it may, no one will believe you."

"But it's the truth." A tremor of disquiet wriggled in Eden's stomach.

"You spent the night with him alone in a coach headed for Gretna Green. The truth matters little to the *ton.* If you return now, your reputation will not survive the scandal."

Her anxiety grew. "Then I'll return home."

"What would happen if your father heard of the scandal?"

Eden grimaced. "You don't want to know."

"He would be angry." Trevor sounded like a tutor giving a lesson.

"Yes, but he'd believe me." Eden felt as if the air closed around her.

"Perhaps, but could he make others believe as well? He has business connections in London. Don't you think someone will confront him with his daughter's disgrace?"

Oh, God. If Daddy found out, he would kill Sterling. If not Daddy, then Nicholas. Eden closed her eyes in dismay.

Toddington took her hand. "I'm afraid there's very little we can do to prevent the rumors from spreading. If I could, I would take it all upon myself."

"There's no need, Toddington. I've considered our every option, and I have found a solution." Trevor turned to Eden. "You will marry me."

"What?" Eden jerked her head back.

"Ryeburn, are you sure?"

Trevor ignored Toddington. "We're near Gretna Green. We can be wed on the morrow."

Eden stared at him. "But I—"

"As my countess, no one would dare accuse you of impropriety. The story will still circulate, but the *ton* will assign it some romantic significance."

Eden didn't understand the flurry of activity in her stomach. Her insides tingled, and her blood roared in her ears. She was too tired for such teasing. "Why would you do this?"

"As I said earlier, your safety was my responsibility. I failed. The fault is mine that your reputation is in shreds."

"Such an admirable reason for marriage," remarked Eden. She couldn't lift her gaze to meet his. Disappointment tasted bitter on her tongue. "And if I refuse?"

Trevor gave her a look of patience. "You don't seem to understand the severity of your situation."

"I most certainly do." Eden stood. "My reputation is worth nothing here, and soon will be worth the same at home. My choice is either to live fighting off the consequences of my lost reputation, even if Sterling didn't touch me, or to remain in England married to a man who's only offered because it is the right thing to do."

"I had planned on taking a countess soon at all events."

This news bothered Eden more than she cared to admit. "So now I'm taking a position meant for someone else. Will she forgive you?"

"I had no one specific in mind."

"So I'll do." Eden tossed her hands in the air. She began to pace, knowing that if she stopped, she would cry.

"Miss Grant," said Lord Toddington, "would it really be so bad to be a countess?"

Eden stopped, and as she had expected, tears welled up in her eyes. She drew in a ragged breath. "How would you react if the only way you could return to some semblance of a normal life was never to return home?" She closed her eyes. "I'll do it. I'll marry Lord Ryeburn."

The only sound that greeted her announcement was the song of the birds twittering in the trees. When she felt someone touch her arm, Eden opened her eyes.

Lord Toddington stood beside her. "You won't regret this."

"I hope not," she whispered.

Trevor rose from the ground. "Let's get going. We can sleep a little in the coach before we reach Gretna Green."

Eden stared down at the simple skirt and blouse. With the encouragement of Trevor's money, the innkeeper's wife had provided the coarse brown wool and white linen garments. Eden's tree dress would not stand another day of wearing, and in all honesty, the simple garb proved comfortable. Yet Eden frowned. This was not how she had pictured her wedding attire.

She ran a brush, another of Trevor's purchases, through her hair, then tied it back with a ribbon. She had no other adornment. How could she? Her belongings were in London. With a sigh, she acknowledged that she had nothing left to do—except step out of the room and get married.

Trevor waited downstairs. He didn't look much better than she. His trousers were of the same brown wool as her skirt, although his boots shone. He hadn't had to replace those. His shirt was gray. No one would mistake them for the Earl and soon-to-be-Countess of Ryeburn.

Toddington stood next to Trevor. His clothes had likewise transformed him from earl to peasant. Eden had to chuckle. What a trio they made. They seemed better dressed for the masquerade than a wedding.

"Are you hungry? We could eat first." Toddington waved his hand toward a table.

"No, thank you. I'd rather get this over with." Eden noticed that Trevor didn't protest. His face showed nothing of his thoughts. She wondered if he was angry or happy or indifferent. Indifferent, she decided.

"Right. Let's go." Trevor's voice held all the enthusiasm of a block of ice.

Toddington led the way out of the inn. Eden followed. A few steps later, she jumped as Trevor took her arm. Shooting him a glance, she saw that his expression was unchanged. So much for being the happy couple.

The morning had dawned gray, and the advance of the early hours had done little to change it. The sky was perhaps a lighter gray now, but still unfriendly.

"I don't see a church. Where are we going?"

"To the blacksmith's." Trevor didn't look at her.

"The blacksmith's? We're to be married in a smithy?"

"Yes." Trevor's terse reply gave her no comfort.

"This keeps getting better and better," she mumbled. From the corner of her eye, she saw Trevor glance at her. She didn't care. This was her wedding day. If she wanted to grumble, she would.

A few minutes later found them in the smithy. A large, red-haired man boomed out a welcome. "Good morrrning to ye. Bonny day for a wedding. I'll need yer names."

Trevor released his hold on her. "Trevor St. John, Earl of Ryeburn, and Miss Eden Grant."

"Earl, is it? I havena married many o' those." The smith peered at Eden. "Such a bonny bride. I ken your hurry now. Won't be more than a few more minutes." His laughter irritated Eden. The smith wiped his hands on his leather apron. He moved the pig iron away from the flames of his furnace and closed the door. "Pardon the mess, but I have horseshoes to make."

Hysterical laughter threatened to spill from Eden at the absurdity of the situation. She bit her lip.

"I see ye brought a witness. Excellent. We'll need another. Mother!" he called.

A round woman, well suited to the large man, entered the smithy. "Ye wanted me?"

"Aye. I need you for a witness."

The woman clapped her hands together. "I love weddings, and ye perform them so glaidsome, Father."

"Thank ye, Mother. We can begin."

The smith raised his voice and began the ceremony. Eden didn't think the man could get any louder. She was wrong. The smith thundered out each word. Eden winced several times at the volume.

All too soon the smith asked for their vows. Trevor spoke without hesitation, his voice clear and strong, although Eden had to admit, when compared with the smith, Trevor sounded quiet. Her turn came next. A movement caught her attention. Eden saw the woman dab a tear away from her cheek. The sight surprised Eden so, she almost forgot to repeat her vows, but repeat them she did.

At the end of her turn, the blacksmith's wife sobbed loudly. "I do so love weddings."

"We're almost done, Mother." The smith turned to Eden and Trevor. "Having made your vows in front of these witnesses, I now pronounce you husband and wife."

Trevor turned to Eden. "I believe it is customary for the husband to kiss his bride."

Eden didn't trust her voice. She nodded.

Trevor bent his head to hers and gave her a chaste kiss, then broke away. Disappointment flared up in Eden.

"Youth is wasted on the young," muttered the woman.

"That's no kiss, mon!" roared the blacksmith. "I thought ye was eager to wed."

Toddington stepped forward. "I'm sure his lordship is

waiting for a more private moment." He turned to Trevor and extended his hand. "Congratulations, Ryeburn."

Trevor shook the proffered hand. "Thank you."

Toddington faced Eden. "Congratulations to you as well, Countess." He placed a kiss on her cheek.

Countess? Good heavens, she was a countess now, wasn't she? What would her parents say? Eden froze. Her parents. She hadn't considered her parents' reaction to her nuptials. "I need to write my parents."

"You can do that at Concordia. We'll be leaving shortly." Trevor pulled out a twenty-pound note, which he handed to the blacksmith. "I trust this will cover your services."

"More than enough, my lord. Happy to oblige ye."

"Good-bye, my lord and lady," said the blacksmith's wife, still sniffing. "Much happiness to the both of ye."

Trevor led Eden back to the inn where the coach waited for them. He handed her into the coach, then turned to the driver. "We'll return along the same route. I will ride beside for a while."

Eden sat back in a huff. Her new husband was leaving her to sit alone.

"Very good, sir." The driver took his place.

"Toddington?" Trevor mounted his horse.

Lord Toddington flashed Trevor a disapproving glance. He climbed into the saddle of the other horse. "Don't you think it might be better form to join your wife in the coach?"

Curious to hear his answer, Eden leaned toward the window of the coach. His gaze caught hers. Without turning away, Trevor shook his head. "I've already performed with all the honor expected of me."

His words hit her like a blow, and her breath whooshed out of her like a freakish wind. The wedding was his idea. He had insisted upon marrying her. How dare he now imply that she had somehow tricked him? She sat back. The thump rocked the entire coach.

A few minutes later, the coach lurched into motion. As much as she tried to repress her thoughts, Trevor's words echoed though her mind. His abhorrence of the marriage didn't surprise her, but her own reaction did. She waited for the cold in the pit of her stomach to grow into anger, but in its place an anticipation grew, spreading its warmth through her. No dire impression of doom invaded her. Images of Trevor holding her, kissing her as he had in the garden, filled her. Why did she feel no anger, no bitterness at her fate?

She looked out the window. The stiff back of her husband greeted her sight. Maybe because he felt all of that anger for her. Leaning against the upholstery, Eden sighed. If she had to remain alone for the entire trip back, the miles would pass very slowly indeed.

Late that evening they reached Old Maggie's inn. The coach jerked to a stop, wakening Eden from her dreamless sleep.

Trevor pulled the door open. "We've stopped to change horses. I thought you might like a bite to eat."

Eden hadn't thought of her stomach all day, but the mention of food brought a loud growl from the neglected area. "So kind of you to think of me." She stepped from the coach. The lights of the inn flickered in welcome. Her stomach growled again.

"Let's get you some food before you frighten the horses." Trevor led her inside. Toddington followed.

Old Maggie spotted them at once. "You found her then. I've been wondering what happened. Where's the other gent?"

"I have no idea." Trevor pulled a chair from a table and waited to seat Eden.

"Is the young miss safe?" Old Maggie hurried to the table with three pints of ale.

"The young miss is now the Countess of Ryeburn."

Old Maggie eyed Eden, then bobbed a curtsey. "My lady. I wish to ask yer forgiveness. I didn't know—"

Eden waved her hand. She smiled at the woman. "It's all forgotten, if you bring me some food. I am so hungry."

Old Maggie grinned back at her. "Coming right away, my lady." The woman retreated to the rear of the room. "Luther, make sure their mugs is never empty."

"Yes, Ma." Luther lumbered over to the table and peered into each cup.

"Not yet, Luther," said Toddington.

Luther nodded and backed away, but not too far.

Aware that everyone stared at her, Eden smoothed her hair. "Did you have to pick the most central table?" she whispered to Trevor.

"We won't be here long. You may as well get accustomed to the stares. When we return to London, we shall be the focus of all the gossip. You didn't think our marriage would escape notice?"

Eden glared at him. "I don't see why you have to be so hateful. It wasn't as if I asked to wed you." She crossed her arms and turned away from him.

Trevor gazed at her profile. Even in anger she was beautiful. And now she was his wife. The events of the day had left his emotions in confusion. His hands itched to touch her, to stroke her skin, to kiss and explore her. Gad, his body grew hard just thinking of it. So why did he feel such anger toward her as well?

The truth slapped him. He wasn't angry with her, he was angry with himself. If he hadn't been so blind, if he had only recognized Sterling as the threat he was, he wouldn't have a countess who didn't know the first thing about propriety. Perhaps he could teach her to behave. Had she not promised to obey?

Now there was a promise he never expected her to keep.

The notion of Eden as an obedient wife brought a frown to his face. Why did the thought displease him? He imagined her as one of the bland young women he had considered so perfect. He pictured her without the fire, the sparkle in her blue eyes, the laugh that was closer to a caress than a sound.

Maggie's return interrupted his musings. She laid down three steaming bowls of stew served with a chunk of bread. "It's not the food ye might be accustomed to, but it'll give you strength for the rest of your journey."

"Thank you, Maggie." Eden sniffed the steam "It smells delicious. The cook at home couldn't do better."

Trevor watched the older woman redden with pleasure. Eden's words rang with sincerity. He was suddenly proud of his wife. Mayhap she wouldn't make such a bad countess after all.

CHAPTER EIGHTEEN

She fell asleep in the coach. After a filling meal and the long day, sleep came without a struggle, even though she had never expected to spend her wedding night tossed about in the belly of a vehicle. She stirred twice during the long night: once when her husband and Toddington joined her in the coach to sleep, and once more when they changed horses sometime during night's darkest hours.

They reached Concordia late the following afternoon. Eden was once again alone in the coach. Ryeburn and Toddington had retrieved their horses and ridden back to the estate. As the coach wheels crunched over the gravel of the drive, Eden leaned out the window. This was her home now. Somehow it seemed more imposing than it had when she arrived for the masquerade five days earlier. Had it only been five days? Her entire life had changed since then.

The expanse of green lawn stretched from the gates to

the house. House? Eden wouldn't have used that term to describe such a building back home. No house was this big in Massachusetts. Even Fairlawne, although large, seemed dwarfish in comparison. The edifice rose four stories above the ground, its gray stone tinged with the green moss of centuries' growth. In among the spires and towers, chimneys jutted from the roof at almost every junction. Parts of it looked distinctly like a castle. She would have to remember to ask about that later. Toward the end of the drive, the road circled around a grand fountain. Flowers filled neatly outlined beds.

When Eden looked up at the front steps, she noticed the servants pouring out of the house to line up in two neat rows along the entrance, men on one side, women on the other. Then she saw Ryeburn make his way to the coach. He had arrived sooner than she. The coach stopped at the apex of the drive. Two footmen hurried to the vehicle, one to open the door and the other to help her disembark. Ryeburn stood a few feet away. He offered her his arm. She stepped to him and took his arm, but said nothing.

"The servants are waiting to greet their new mistress," he whispered in her ear.

Oh, heavens. Did these people expect her to give the orders now? Eden knew how to run a household, but one the size of a house, not a government.

"Don't look so frightened. They're harmless."

Eden shot Ryeburn an impatient glance. "How would you know?" she whispered back.

"They've had to deal with Vanessa for years. They've got to be happy to see you take her place."

His answer stunned her for an instant; then she laughed. His responding smile lifted her spirits, and by the time she reached the lines, she was able to greet each servant with grace and, she hoped, charm.

Just inside the door waited Lily and Mrs. Roberts. Eden forgot decorum and rushed to hug Lily. Lily, in turn, burst into tears.

"I can't believe all this," sniffed Lily. "Were you hurt? I was so worried."

"I'm fine, Lily. I can't believe all this yet either."

Mrs. Roberts wiped away her own tears. "To think I considered that man an admirable suitor for you. If I had known what he planned, I never would have let him past the door."

"It doesn't matter now, Mrs. Roberts." Eden patted the woman's arm.

"It most certainly doesn't. You are a countess now, even if those clothes don't suit your new position. Where did you get them?"

Eden had forgotten about her lack of appropriate clothing. The simple skirt and blouse showed the days' travel. "It will be nice to change into my own things."

"Under the circumstances, I suppose those were the best you could find." Mrs. Roberts refolded her handkerchief and tucked it up her sleeve. "No use fretting over what can't be changed. It all turned out for the best in the end. My own little charge a countess. Miss Baylor shall be lonely without you in the house."

Eden froze. She had forgotten that Lily would no longer be with her. "She can stay with me until you have to return home."

"Nonsense," snapped Mrs. Roberts. "We wouldn't dream of intruding upon you at this time. We'll return to the London house and wait out the end of our journey there."

Ryeburn stepped up to his wife. "We need to return to

London as well. You'll have plenty of opportunity to see Miss Baylor before she leaves."

"We're going to London?"

"Yes. Parliament is in session, and I can't afford to miss the season. Not if I want to maintain the influence I've achieved," said Ryeburn. "As it is too late to start for London tonight, we shall travel together in the morning. Ladies, if you will excuse me, I have neglected some business that I must have finished before I return to London. I shall see you at dinner." Ryeburn bowed and left the group.

Mrs. Roberts nodded her head. "You have a fine husband, Lady Ryeburn. He knows his responsibilities and duties. A woman cannot ask for more."

Yes, she can. Eden glanced after him. The hallway had swallowed every trace of his presence. Is this what her married life would be like? Loneliness settled upon her like a damp blanket.

"I will take it upon myself to write to your parents, Lady Ryeburn." Mrs. Roberts pressed her hand to her breast. "You cannot imagine the joy I feel when I call you by your new name. Lady Ryeburn. Knowing I have done my job so well brings me great comfort. I believe I shall rest before dinner. The adventures of the past days have exhausted me. You ladies will excuse me."

Eden peered after Mrs. Roberts. The hallway swallowed her as well.

"Are you happy, Eden?" Lily's voice startled Eden.

Eden couldn't control the emotional whirlwind within. Tears filled her eyes and dripped out before she could even consider her answer. "I don't know."

"Let's find a quiet corner." Lily linked her arm in her friend's.

"I don't know where to go. Some countess I shall make. I don't even know my way around my home."

"You will in time." Lily handed Eden a handkerchief and led her to the study. "Here. This is where Lord Ryeburn planned your rescue."

Dabbing her eyes with the handkerchief, Eden said, "I wasn't sure anyone was going to come after me."

Lily planted her fists on her hips. "What kind of friend do you think I am? I wouldn't let that monster take you and do nothing about it."

"Yes, I knew you would want to rescue me. I just wasn't sure anyone would help you."

"Eden Grant, you stop feeling sorry for yourself."

"I'm not Eden Grant anymore. I'm Lady Ryeburn." A fresh round of sobs burst from her throat.

Lily put her arm around her friend. "You poor thing. You've been through too much in the past few days. When Christopher told me you married—"

"Christopher?"

"Lord Toddington." A blush crept into Lily's face.

"I don't even know what to call my husband." Eden gave Lily a sad smile. "Sounds like you and Lord Toddington are getting along well."

Lily's blush grew deeper. She nodded.

"Good. One of us deserves to have her dreams come true." Eden stilled. Her words too closely echoed the motto on the coin. She wasn't sure she believed in it, but bad luck had plagued her life since she lost the coin. Her sadness melted away. Resignation washed over her. *Numquam tuas spes dedisce.* Ha.

"Eden?"

"I'm fine, just tired. I think I'll follow Roberts's example and rest before dinner."

"Are you sure?"

"Yes. Go find Toddington. Enjoy yourself." Eden gave a reassuring squeeze to Lily's hand and left.

She wandered to the room she had occupied when she arrived. It was empty. All her belongings were gone. She opened every drawer, the armoire, looked under the bed. Nothing remained of her presence. Gritting her teeth, she exited. What was the name of the housekeeper? Eden went through the receiving line in her mind. Some animal. Sparrow, Hawk, Chicken? Byrd. That was it.

Eden returned to the study. Lily was no longer there. She rang the bell. Mrs. Byrd appeared in a few moments. "Yes, my lady?"

"My things have been moved from my room."

"Yes, my lady. When his lordship arrived home, he gave orders to put you in your new chambers."

"I don't know where they are."

Mrs. Byrd eyes widened. "I beg your pardon, your ladyship. I should have shown you at once. Please follow me."

Mrs. Byrd led her down the hallway and up the grand staircase. Turning left down a corridor, the housekeeper opened the third set of double doors. "Your chambers, Countess Ryeburn."

Eden stepped in and almost let her jaw drop. Gold accented the ivory-colored walls. The scrollwork in the corners resembled vines growing over columns. "There's no blue."

"I'm sure you can change whatever you wish, my lady."

"No, I don't like . . . Never mind." As she circled to view it all, the fireplace caught her attention. Above the mantle on a green heraldic crest posed a swan. "What's that?"

"That's the family coat of arms, my lady."

Of course. She had seen it on the side of Ryeburn's

barouche and coach. "I have a lot to learn." At Mrs. Byrd's surprised glance, Eden realized she had spoken aloud.

"Will you be needing anything else, my lady?"

"A bath, perhaps, and then a little sleep."

"Very good, my lady."

When Mrs. Byrd left, Eden continued her perusal of her room. The forechamber contained a desk and settee and several armchairs. A second door led to the bedroom proper. An enormous bed covered one wall. Deep greens, golds, and russets warmed the room, inviting her to touch the bedclothes and draperies. The elegance astounded her.

"Do you like it?"

She whirled around at the voice. Her heart pounded in her chest. Trevor leaned against a doorway she had not explored yet. "Where did you come from?"

"My room. They attach through here, although I have my own entrance from the hall, just as you do."

She peered behind him. His room was the mirror image of hers, only done in browns and greens. Ryeburn stepped aside. "You may come in if you wish."

Eden stepped back. "No, thank you. Perhaps later."

Trevor lifted an eyebrow.

Heat rushed into Eden's cheeks. "I mean . . . I don't . . . Oh, dear."

Trevor laughed. "No, I don't expect you did." He stepped closer to her and raised his hand. With a feathery caress, he stroked her cheek, gliding his fingers down the line of her jaw. Eden shivered from the deliciousness of his touch.

A maidservant appeared with a bucket of water on each arm. "Excuse me, milady. You wanted a bath?"

"Yes, thank you." Eden stepped away from Trevor.

The maid carried the buckets into the bathing chamber.

Eden heard the water splash against the side of the tub. The maid returned through the room. She bobbed a quick curtsey. "Just a few more should fill it, milady." The maid left.

Trevor crossed back to his room. "You must be tired. Why don't you rest after your bath. I'll have Mrs. Byrd wake you in plenty of time to dress."

"I think that might be best."

"Until later then. Sleep well, Eden."

"What do I call you?"

He paused. A moment later, an enigmatic smile curved his lips. "Whatever you wish." He withdrew from her room through the connecting door.

Eden stood in the same spot a few hours later. A sheer white nightgown veiled her, but she couldn't sleep. The night beckoned her to the window. Crossing to the glass, she pressed her face against the pane. Her stomach churned with anxiety. He would come to her tonight. She knew they had to consummate the marriage sometime. Although he had said nothing to her, she had seen it in his eyes. She couldn't help her nerves.

But a part of her tingled at the thought of his touch.

After dinner, after they had exhausted all conversation, their guests had retired to their chambers. Trevor escorted her to her room and left her in the care of her new lady's maid. Before helping to brush the tangles from Eden's blond lengths, the girl laid out the white nightgown on the bed and placed a flagon of wine with two glasses on the bedside table. Eden soon realized the girl's intentions—to make Eden beautiful for her husband. When Eden slipped the nightgown over her head, the scent of lavender assailed her. The maid must have found her bottle of fragrance and sprinkled it on the material. After stoking the fire, the girl left. The quiet of the room deafened Eden. Only the occasional cracking of a log on the fire reassured her that the world had not stopped.

At the sound of the door opening, Eden turned, but didn't move from the window. The fire cast an uneven glow over him, giving him a sheen of gold, burnishing his dark hair. Her breath caught in her throat. She was his wife. She belonged to him.

Trevor held out his hand. "Come here, Eden."

She willed her feet to move. With each step she grew more tense. When she slipped her palm into his, the warmth of his skin surprised her. She had not realized how cold she had become.

"You are chilled." He took her other hand and gently rubbed them between his own.

She was surprised to see that sparks did not fly out at his touch. She trembled. He gathered her in his arms.

"You shouldn't stand by the window if you are cold."

His heat drew her in, covered her, threatened to block all reasonable thought. She couldn't lift her gaze to his for fear of losing herself in the dark depths of his eyes. "Why did you marry me?" she whispered.

"Knowing how Toddington feels about Miss Baylor, I couldn't let him marry you." He chuckled.

She didn't join in his mirth. "Why?"

"Does it really matter?" he whispered against her hair.

"I suppose not. 'Tis done. But it would be nice to know you cared for me just a little."

Trevor sighed. "I thought we had established that in the garden."

"We also agreed that I had no place in your life." Eden lifted her gaze to him.

"That has changed." He outlined her lips with his finger. "I do care for you."

"A little," she added.

He smiled. "A little."

His lips replaced his finger against her lips. At the first touch of his kiss, his warmth spread through her, lighting every corner of her soul. His fire skipped along her nerves. Her heart sang, and for once it was someone else's song she heard.

The kiss ended when Trevor lifted her in his arms. He looked down into her eyes. "You are my wife."

She laid her head against his chest. The soft scent of sandalwood mixed with her lavender in a gentle combination. She inhaled deeply.

"You do know . . ."

When he didn't continue, Eden lifted her gaze. His expression was so full of concern, she reached up her hand and cupped his cheek. "I know. My mother explained."

With swift, fluid steps, he crossed the room to her bed. Placing her in the middle as if she were an invaluable treasure, Trevor let his hand run from her shoulder to her waist to her hip, but he himself came no closer. Only the thin lawn of her gown separated his palm from her skin.

Eden's heart raced. She wanted more of his touch, and she wanted to touch him in return. Her heart pounding, she moistened her lips and drew an uneven breath. "You are my husband."

CHAPTER NINETEEN

Trevor's legs nearly buckled at her words. He gazed upon the vision in the bed. She couldn't hide her apprehension of the unknown, nor could she hide the eagerness that glowed in her eyes. That gleam nearly undid him.

"You are so beautiful." He knelt beside her. With gentle fingers he inched the first button out of its fastener. She never removed her gaze from him even as color darkened her cheeks. Her mouth parted, and her breathing became a soft whisper in the night air. As his fingers brushed against a round breast, she sucked in her breath with a tiny gasp, but didn't move. When all the buttons were unfastened, he brushed the bodice of her gown open. In the golden light of the room, the pale creaminess of her skin beckoned him. He traced the round aureole with his finger and saw it pucker. Her nipple thrust forward as if demanding its due attention.

Eden's flush covered her whole body now. With a

crooked grin, he bent his head and took the nipple in his mouth. With a quiet scream, Eden arched her back, offering herself to his taste. His hand moved to her other breast, teasing it to attention.

"Are you supposed to do that?" she asked, her voice wispy and airy.

"Do you like it?" he countered, never lifting his head from the round softness.

"Very much."

"Then I am supposed to do it." Trevor flicked his tongue over the peak. Eden moaned.

His hands pushed her gown further down to her waist, further still past her hips. She lay fully exposed to his gaze. Eden fought the urge to cover herself. He opened his dressing gown and discarded it. He wore no shirt underneath, only a pair of trousers. Eden lifted her hand to touch his chest. She felt the solid strength of the lightly haired expanse, yet his heartbeat penetrated through the muscled wall to her palm.

Running his palm down her stomach, Trevor reached the apex of her legs. Eden cried out in surprise. He lifted his gaze to hers. "Trust me."

Eden nodded.

He kissed her then, his tongue leading hers in a lustful dance. Her head spun with a delicious vertigo. Her blood sang as it raced through her. From deep within, her body ached for him. As if in answer to her need, Trevor moved his hand. His fingers delved into her feminine valley, rubbing the sensitive bud he found there.

Eden writhed at the sensation. Her skin tingled as if each spot clamored for attention. Sparks scattered inside her, burning her without harm. And yet the ache for him grew stronger, more unbearable.

"Trevor, please." Though what she asked for she didn't know.

"Not yet, sweet."

He lowered his head to her breasts and feasted upon their bounty once again. Easing his hand between her legs, he slipped a finger into her innermost haven. Eden bucked against him. Trevor chuckled and slid his finger out, then back in again.

"You're almost ready for me." His voice was deeper, husky. His thumb still rubbing her bud, he slipped another finger inside.

A wordless entreaty glided from her lips. The noise sounded foreign to her, as if her voice were not under her control. She realized she wasn't under her own control. Another wave of emotion washed over her, obliterating any further thoughts.

Trevor withdrew from her. For an instant she felt bereft of his warmth until she saw that he had removed his trousers. Her eyes widened as she took in the sight of his magnificence. His dark hair curled over his shoulders. The broad chest led to a well muscled abdomen, tapering to his slender hips and his . . .

"Oh. . . ."

Trevor eyes gleamed with amusement . . . and something else. Eden caught her breath. The ache for him grew sharper yet.

"Spread your legs for me."

She did so. Trevor climbed between her limbs. He leaned over her, supporting himself on his hands. Her tongue darted out to moisten her lips, tempting him to kiss her once more. He smiled at her. "You're ready. Wrap your legs around my waist."

Straightening, Trevor lifted her hips. Mustering as much control and patience as he could, Trevor eased his manhood into the opening meant just for him. She was slick and wet and hot. He fought the urge to bury himself within her, reminding himself that she was an innocent. He pressed forward, each inch an exquisite torture. At her maidenhead he stopped. Finding the sensitive nub, he rolled it gently between his fingers. Eden writhed beneath him. Her breath came in little gasps, her back arched, and her mouth parted in a sound of pure enjoyment. At this same moment, he broke through her maidenhead, masking the pain in her pleasure.

Eden's senses returned to her for an instant only, for in the next moment, Trevor moved above her, thrusting himself in and out of her. Eden wrapped her legs more tightly around him. The delicious ache grew until it threatened to explode. She held her breath, for that was easier than breathing. She never knew such sensation existed. And still it continued, intensified, blossomed until she thought it might consume her.

Above her Trevor's eyes grew darker, if that was at all possible. His features sharpened, the intensity evident on his face. Eden rolled her head back, not trying to understand any of the feelings, just letting the waves take her further and further from herself. Something elusive lingered just out of her reach, tantalizing her, teasing her, frustrating her. She rocked her hips to meet his thrusts.

And then she reached the elusive shore and shattered. Her cry disappeared in the frenzy of sensation roaring through her. Stars shot through her, leaving sparkling trails in their wake. Her entire body quivered with the explosion.

And as her senses slowly returned to her, Eden realized that Trevor, too, had shared the experience. He withdrew from her and lay beside her, gathering her in his arms, heart to heart. Her cheek rested against his, their breath mingled, their heartbeats still strong and powerful.

Trevor held her without saying a word. In truth, he wasn't sure he could speak. And if he did, he was sure he would say the wrong thing. Eden's passion had shaken him to his very core. Never had he experienced such an extraordinary coupling, and it filled him with fear. She matched him in passion; gad, she fit in mood, in wit, in pride better than any woman in the past. All the more reason to believe her an unsuitable countess. She didn't know how he struggled to maintain his correctness, how he had suffered through his father's debauchery.

But Eden *was* his countess.

He rolled away from her. She let out a moan in protest.

"I'll be back shortly." He crossed the room, oblivious to his nakedness, but not to her gaze, which followed him. Already he felt the stirrings of renewed passion, another sign that she could wield great power over him if he let her. He returned with a basin and towel. "Let me clean you."

She flushed. "Oh, no. I couldn't."

"After your first time, you should be treated with respect and tenderness. As your husband, I am the logical choice." He dipped the cloth into the warm water. With gentle strokes, he washed the blood from her legs. His thoughts strayed from his task all too easily, drifting to the memory of her entwined with him in passion. His loins hardened. At last he finished. Turning from her, Trevor hid his arousal from her. He reached for his trousers and pulled them on.

Eden lay in her bed uncovered save for the blush that colored her skin. His control could not bear her charm any longer. He drew the sheet over her. "Good night, Eden."

Clutching the sheet to her breast, she sat up. "You're leaving?"

"I am returning to my room." He stood and walked toward the connecting door.

"Won't you stay?"

He turned back and saw the plea in her eyes. He almost took a step back to her, but stopped himself in time. "You need your rest."

"And if I don't want to rest?" She sent him a smile filled with promise.

Trevor swallowed hard. "You need to rest." Without waiting for her reaction, he turned and left the room, shutting the door with more force than he intended.

The chambermaid had turned down his bed, but the mattress was far from inviting. He paced the floor. In this state of arousal, sleep would be impossible at all events. He ran his hand through his hair. Proper women weren't supposed to have such deep passion. Proper women didn't tempt their husbands with their bodies. Proper women never interfered with their husband's thoughts.

He had expected some fondness for his wife, a quiet coexistence, filled with mutual respect and admiration. Enough to provide incentive to produce an heir or two. He hadn't expected to react like a rutting stag when he saw his wife, to be so caught up in her as to forget he was a gentleman and she a lady.

Perhaps it wouldn't last. Yes, of course. This feeling would diminish over time. This was the first time he had made love to Eden. In London, when he returned to his duties, his desire for her would settle down. He should have expected such a reaction. He had thought of little else since he met her.

He ignored the little voice that told him he erred.

Eden watched the door close. Was he really leaving her alone after they had shared such intimacy? Several minutes passed before she believed he wasn't coming back. She wrapped the sheet around her and strode to the door. If he wouldn't come to her, she would go to him. Her hand stayed on the latch without turning it. She couldn't go to him. His expression had been so cold when he left her.

She returned to the bed, only to stare at the spot where they had shared such passion. She turned on her heel and crossed to the window. Why had he withdrawn so abruptly? Didn't he want to be with her?

The answer hit her with the force of a blow. Air rushed out of her, and she found it difficult to breathe. He had done his duty. The marriage was now consummated. It didn't matter that she had just experienced the most glorious night of her life—his job was over.

Her chest constricted as she tried to breathe. Tears formed in her eyes and spilled onto her cheeks. With an angry swipe, she wiped them away. How could she forget that she wasn't meant to be his countess? That he married her because he felt obligated?

Just her luck to marry the one man who really didn't care for her.

She stared out the window toward the west. *Mother, why can't you be here? I need to talk to you. I miss you.*

Oh, sure. That would solve nothing. Her mother told

everything to her father, and her father would, well, he would probably kill Trevor. Daddy was very protective of her. Her marriage would be shock enough for them. She didn't need to tell them Trevor felt obligated to marry her.

This is quite a mess you've created for yourself, Eden. Only this time, you married it.

Trevor stood by the desk in his study. The sky was still the blue-gray of early morning when night still fought to keep its hold on the heavens. The sun would rise soon, thank goodness. They could be off then.

He knew he must look a fright. He hadn't slept the entire night. When he realized slumber was a futile effort, he had risen, dressed, and gone down to his study. Two hours later, his thoughts plagued him with as much energy as they had in his bedroom.

Reaching into his waistcoat pocket, he pulled out the coin. He had taken to carrying the thing with him. Flipping it in his hand, he read the inscription on the back. *Numquam tuas spes dedisce.* His dreams didn't include a headstrong countess or losing his wits when she was about. The words encircled the swan. Funny. He had never given the swan much thought. Perhaps because the bird was part of his coat of arms, and he was used to seeing it around him.

He flipped it over again. Venus seemed happier than the last time he looked at her. Gad, he must be tired. Imagining a figure on a coin expressing emotion. Indeed.

The coin hadn't proven itself much of a talisman. It certainly didn't ward off bad luck. Actually his turn of luck had started when he met Eden. He could believe *her* the bearer of ill fortune more easily than the coin.

He dropped the coin to his desk and turned to leave the room. He stopped at the doorway. Retracing his steps, he retrieved the coin and placed it in his pocket again with a smile. He'd gotten used to its weight there.

He turned again and froze. Eden stood in the door. Red rimmed her eyes, and her skin lacked its usual luster. "You're up early."

"So are you. I couldn't sleep. I was hoping to find something to read until breakfast."

"Why didn't you wake your maid? She would have fetched some food."

"Just because I couldn't sleep doesn't mean that poor girl has to stay awake as well."

"That's her job."

"Perhaps, but I'm not an evil taskmistress."

"Suit yourself. You are the countess."

"And you are the earl." She moved down the hall toward the library.

What had she meant by that? Trevor shook his head. Of course he was the earl. Perhaps if he were more alert he might understand her. No, probably not.

A few hours later, the household, guests and all, had breakfasted and packed their belongings for the return to London. Two coaches stood ready—one to return Mrs. Roberts, Lily, and Toddington to their London addresses, and the other to speed the Earl and Countess of Ryeburn to their London townhouse. After seeing their guests settled and on their way, Trevor handed Eden into the coach and climbed in after her. She sat in the far corner, her face turned out the window. He took his place and told the driver to start. The coach lurched into motion. Eden said nothing, and Trevor didn't trust himself to speak to her.

He stretched out his legs as best he could and leaned his head back. With any luck, he could catch up on his sleep during the journey.

CHAPTER TWENTY

"The Earl and Countess of Ryeburn."

Eden held her breath as she walked beside Trevor. Every gaze turned to view the couple as they entered the room. Trevor had warned her. This was only the second night back from Concordia, their first appearance since they wed.

After arriving in London two days ago, Trevor had her things sent to his house. She settled into her rooms, separate from his, in little time. She had, after all, only a portion of her wardrobe with her. The rest hung in an armoire in Massachusetts.

Hermes stood in a stall maintained by Ryeburn. The gelding seemed little put out by the move. With Hermes and the purchase of the roan, Ryeburn had added to his formidable stable. Eden wondered if he were as proud of his addition of her to his collection.

The myriad chandeliers lit the massive ballroom almost

as if it were day. As they made their entrance, the murmur rose like a roar. Heads bent together whispering behind fans and gloves.

"Courage, Eden," said Trevor out of the corner of his mouth. "You are now a countess."

"You forget I am the American Nightingale. Crowds don't frighten me," Eden shot back.

Trevor chuckled. "Perhaps I should warn the crowd instead."

As they pushed their way through the throng in the ballroom, a booming voice greeted them. "Excellent move, Ryeburn."

Eden turned to see the Duke of Welkes bearing down upon them. The duke grinned at the pair.

"My dear." The duke took her hand and kissed it. "I am so happy to hear you won't be leaving us after all. I was afraid I should have to travel to the Colonies to get a decent game of whist."

"I'm sure my father would have loved to meet you, Your Grace." Eden beamed at the man. He, she was sure, was genuinely happy to see her. "You should plan a trip anyway."

"I just might, Countess. Perhaps we can play a little whist tonight?"

"Only if you'll be my partner."

"I do like you forward American women." The duke bellowed with laughter. He clapped Ryeburn on the back. "I knew she had gotten to you. Don't deny it, Ryeburn. Eloping to Gretna Green. If I were thirty years younger, I'd have done the same."

"Yes, Your Grace."

"Frankly, I never would have thought you had the gumption to marry the girl. You're usually so proper." The duke fell silent for a moment, then grinned again. "Doesn't matter. You showed your stuff when called upon. Ha."

The duke bellowed again. Eden laughed with him, but also at the pained look on her husband's face. He didn't seem to enjoy the attention they garnered.

"Courage, Ryeburn," she whispered.

"Very funny," he muttered.

When the duke left them, Trevor led her to the dance floor. For a few minutes Eden forgot her cares and enjoyed his embrace. The waltz was all too short. The music ended, and Trevor escorted her from the floor. She wanted to dance again with him, to feel his arms around her, but his stiff demeanor let her know he didn't feel the same.

Trevor took her to the edge of the dance floor and leaned toward her ear. "I believe Miss Baylor has arrived." He nodded toward the entrance.

Lily appeared at the top of the stairs. Her gaze searched for a familiar face. Mrs. Roberts stood at her side.

"May I go to her?"

Trevor gave her a puzzled look. "Of course you may. She is your friend."

Eden picked up her skirts and hurried to the staircase. "Lily."

Lily turned her head. Her eyes lit up when she saw Eden. Lily rushed down the stairs and clasped Eden's hands in hers. "I'm so glad you're here. I was so hoping for a chance to talk to you."

"It seems odd that we don't see each other every day."

Mrs. Roberts embraced her. "Lady Ryeburn. You're looking well. I have written your parents with the news."

"Thank you, Mrs. Roberts. I've only had time enough to send a short note."

"I'm sure you ladies would like to catch up. I'll leave you." Mrs. Roberts nodded at them and moved off.

Eden shook her head. "You'd think she arranged the marriage."

Lily leaned back and examined her. "You look like you haven't slept."

"I haven't much."

"Oh, Eden."

"It's nothing, truly. I'm fine. Is Mrs. Roberts treating you well?"

"She has, since Lord Toddington visits us every day."

"Nothing like another earl to mollify Mrs. Roberts."

Lily paused. "Mrs. Roberts thinks we should go home as soon as possible."

"Why?"

"She doesn't believe it right that we stay on at your father's expense."

"Nonsense. Daddy expects us to stay until August. You know he thinks of you as one of the family. If he balks at paying the rent, I'll pay it. Lily, you can't leave me yet."

"Thank you."

"There's no thanks involved. I'm being completely selfish in keeping you here. Besides, if you leave now, how can we get Toddington to propose to you?"

"E-den." But Lily giggled. "He promised he would come tonight. Have you seen him?"

"Not yet, but in this crush, the king could be here, and I wouldn't know."

"Are you singing tonight?"

"No one has asked. But if they do, you will accompany me, won't you?"

"As if I ever let you down before."

The friends linked arms and disappeared into the crush.

* * *

Trevor watched from the edge of the floor as one swain after another danced with his wife. In one hand he held a drink, stronger than the usual lemonade. His other hand he clenched in a fist. Downing a swallow, he felt it burn the entire length to his stomach. *I really should eat something.* He saw his wife smile at her next partner as the two whirled away on the parquet. He took another swig.

"You look angry." Toddington appeared by his side.

"Don't those men know she's married?"

"Some do, some don't."

Trevor glared at his friend.

Toddington shrugged. "They're only dancing with her."

"Hmph."

"If it troubles you that much, dance with her yourself."

"I think I will."

Trevor shoved his drink into Toddington's hand and stormed to the dance floor. He tapped the offending swain on the shoulder. "Excuse me, but I wish to dance with *my wife.*"

The gentleman looked surprised, then stepped aside. Eden gave the man an apologetic smile, which irritated Trevor further. He held his arms ready, waited until she stepped into them, and led her away in the three-count dance.

As they turned on the floor, Eden said nothing, but her gaze lifted to his, questioning his actions. He didn't answer. She sighed, then focused on the dance. Trevor knew he should say something, but he couldn't explain himself. Instead he enjoyed the feel of her fluid grace and the fit of his arms around her.

The dance ended. Trevor gazed into her eyes. Gad, that blue was distracting. So distracting, in fact, that he failed to notice the hostess approach until she stood beside them. He recovered and bowed to the woman.

"Would it be too much of an imposition to ask your wife to sing for us this evening?"

Yes, damn it, when all he wanted to do was take her home to his bed and—

"I would love to, your ladyship."

The woman took Eden by the arm. "I'm so pleased you were able to make it after your little adventure."

They moved too far away for him to hear any more of the conversation. Trevor wanted his drink back.

Trevor's head ached. He had imbibed far too much the previous evening. And why? He laughed at himself. Because he worried that his wife might embarrass him. Eden had displayed regal manners and charmed all who met her for the first time. She couldn't help that she attracted so much attention. She must be used to it, because she handled it with so much aplomb.

He would get used to it in time, too.

Stretching in his bed, Trevor winced. He hadn't indulged so much in years. The ache in his head reminded him why. How could his father have done it night after night? With ever so much care, he placed his feet on the floor. Good. It remained still. He stood. His heart immediately moved from his chest to his head. Closing his eyes until the pain subsided, Trevor grasped the bedpost for strength. When the pounding stopped, or rather slowed, he moved to his dressing area. Splashing water on his face helped, but not much. Perhaps he should call for help in dressing.

Pride forbade it.

With deliberate motions, he dressed himself, but forwent

his usual cravat. The skill of tying a knot around his neck escaped him at the moment.

A knock at the door brought the pounding back to his head. "Come."

Finch opened the door. "Excuse me, my lord. You have a visitor."

"At this hour?" He winced at the sound of his voice.

"The dowager countess."

Gad. "Tell her I'll be down shortly."

Finch nodded and retreated from the room.

He knew why Vanessa had come. Her timing was terrible. He pulled on his Hessians and went to greet his stepmother.

Vanessa was in the library. She had pulled a book off the shelf, but Trevor knew it was for show. He had never seen her actually read a book.

"Good morning, Vanessa."

She stuffed the book back on the shelf and whirled to face him. "There you are. Do you know what you have done?"

"No, Vanessa. Why don't you tell me."

"You've married that . . . that entertainer. Have you no regard for your family name?"

Although his voice remained low, his anger threatened to explode. "Don't ever question *my* regard for my name."

Vanessa blanched, then clasped a hand to her breast. "She is an American. You must have the marriage annulled."

"It's too late for that, Vanessa. She's my wife, and I intend to keep her."

"But she's a common—"

Trevor laughed despite the returning ache in his head. "Common is a word I would never use to describe Eden. You, perhaps, but never her."

Vanessa gasped. "How dare you?"

"Your tirades bore me, Vanessa. My sister has a place in my home, but if you utter one word against my wife, I'll make sure you don't. Good morning." Trevor turned to leave.

"I can see you're not yourself today," mewed Vanessa. "I'll return to visit you and your dear wife some other time."

Without turning back, Trevor said, "That's better." He left the room.

He headed straight for the breakfast room. The sideboard held eggs, pheasant, ham, fruits, and custard, but one glance at them and Trevor left the room again. He asked Finch to bring a pot of coffee to his study.

When Finch arrived with the coffee, Trevor squinted at the butler from the chair in which he slouched. "I am not home for visitors, Finch."

"Yes, sir. Shall I tell Lord Toddington?"

Trevor dropped his head into his hands and groaned. "Why is he here this early?"

"I couldn't say, sir. Shall I send him away, my lord?"

"No. Send him in."

"Very good, sir." Finch left the coffee on the table and left the room.

Toddington came in a moment later. "Good morning, Ryeburn."

Trevor squinted up at him. "I wouldn't know."

Toddington chuckled. "I thought you might feel this way today. Have you tried hair of the dog yet?"

"You're cruel, man. Coffee is enough of a devil's brew this morning." Trevor poured himself a cup of the hot drink.

"Any word on Sterling?"

"None, but it's only been a few days. The runner I hired

promised to report as soon as he learned anything." Trevor sipped from his cup. The liquid burned his mouth, but at least it didn't send him running to the nearest basin.

Toddington cleared his throat. "I'm in need of advice, Ryeburn."

Trevor lifted an eyebrow. "Regarding?"

"Miss Baylor." Toddington flushed bright red. "I realize it's too soon to ask, but can you think of any adverse reaction to marrying an American?"

"You're considering marrying the girl?" His headache forgotten, Trevor stared at his friend. "You've hardly known her."

"I might say the same about yourself."

"That was entirely different."

"Perhaps. I was wondering if I might speak to your wife about her. Find out a little more about her background and such."

"What an idea. Eden is Miss Baylor's friend. She'll be sure to let Miss Baylor know you've inquired about her background."

"Can't you forbid her to talk about it?" Toddington looked surprised.

"Forbid Eden? Can't say that I've ever tried it, but I've given her plenty of advice, every bit of which she's ignored."

"But she's your wife."

"I know."

The two men stared at each other for a moment. Toddington broke the silence. "I've almost forgotten." He tapped his breast pocket and pulled out an envelope.

"What's this?"

"Your award for your countess."

"Award?"

"This is the money I owe you. Circumstances may have

helped, but the outcome is the same. You won the wager." Toddington handed Trevor the envelope.

Trevor pulled out two-hundred pounds. "I wonder where Sterling got the money."

"Probably enlisting the aid of a wife who didn't want her husband to discover her infidelities."

Trevor placed the money on the table. "You're probably right. It feels tainted."

"Buy your wife some trinket with it. She won you the bet, after all. You married her within the month and had time to spare."

"Yes, but I would have won it anyway. I made careful plans."

"I don't doubt it."

"You can have my list of suitable women, if you wish."

Toddington laughed. "Keep it."

Eden hadn't meant to eavesdrop, but as she passed the room on her way to breakfast, she heard the men talk about her. Curiosity had overcome good manners, and now she wished she had heeded her upbringing. She wished she hadn't heard that her husband had wagered on wedding her or any woman within a month. How could he be so callous?

A man who thought marriage a mere inconvenience of time. A man who ranked women according to suitability. A man so arrogant that he'd place a wager on his own nuptials.

How could she have fallen in love with a man without a heart?

Eden gasped. Dear God, it was true. She had fallen in love with Trevor.

Lily was going to laugh at her for this.

CHAPTER TWENTY-ONE

"I won't stay here as if nothing is wrong." Eden stuffed another dress into her valise. She turned back to the armoire.

"You can't just leave. What will people say?" Lily pulled the garment out and folded it before returning it to the case.

"I don't care what people think. I'll let Ryeburn worry about it." She threw another item into the valise and opened the drawers. She knelt and pulled out an armful.

"Where will you go?" Lily removed this item, folded it as well, and replaced it in the bag.

Eden sat back on her heels. "I suppose going home would be impossible. I have married the cad, after all, and I doubt he'll chase me all the way to Massachusetts."

"Are you sure you want him to chase you?"

"Yes, devil take him. How could I have been so stupid

as to fall in love with him?'' Eden dropped the armful and grabbed her handkerchief as tears rolled out of her eyes.

''Don't cry again. Your eyes are red enough.'' Lily began to sniff with her friend. ''I hate to see you so miserable.''

Eden made a valiant attempt to stop the flow of tears. She continued to pack, stopping to brush away a tear between folds.

''Would you like it if I came with you?''

Shaking her head, Eden drew in a ragged breath. ''I want you to stay here and win your Lord Toddington.''

''I would be happy to accompany you.''

''No, Lily. It's enough that one of us is heartbroken.'' Eden put the last item into her bag. ''The coach should be here.''

''You never told me where you are going.''

''Concordia. It's my home now.'' Eden stood and grabbed her valise. ''Finch will send for a coach.''

''Where is Lord Ryeburn?''

''He's visiting Toddington. They had some business to discuss.''

When Eden appeared downstairs. Finch hurried to her with a look of concern on his face. ''Did you wish something, my lady?''

''Yes, Finch. Please order me a coach. I'm returning to Concordia.''

''Does the earl know about this?''

''No, Finch, he doesn't, but you are welcome to inform him *after* you get my coach.''

''Begging your pardon, my lady, but the staff doesn't expect you. Some may be on holiday.''

''That's fine, Finch. In America I often fended for myself. I know that's not how it's done here, but I'm not waiting for the staff to return. I wish to leave.''

''My lady—''

"Finch, I want a coach. Will you please send for one?" Eden crossed her arms and gave him a scolding look.

Finch bowed. "Yes, Lady Ryeburn." The butler hurried off to do her bidding.

Lily looked after the butler. "You do the countess very well."

"I didn't enjoy it. Poor man. Torn between loyalty to the earl and his duty to the countess." Eden sighed. "I'll have the coach drive you home on the way. Mrs. Roberts won't come back for you for another hour."

"No, I think I prefer to walk. I need the fresh air."

"Roberts will scold you for going out without a companion."

"I know, but I'll take that risk." Lily hugged Eden. "Good-bye. Send for me if you get lonely."

"Good-bye, Lily."

Lily pulled on her gloves and swung her shawl around her shoulders. With a final wave, she descended the stairs and started up the street.

Eden waved until Lily disappeared around the corner. Even then, she stood in the doorway, peering after her friend. Now she felt utterly alone, but she wasn't so selfish as to spoil Lily's chance for happiness. Eden just hoped Lily had better luck with her earl.

Toddington's library was smaller than his own, but comfortable nevertheless. Toddington never had been much of a reader, even when they were in school together. Trevor watched while Toddington looked through his books. "He married her and took vows."

"But he is the king." Toddington moved his search to a different shelf.

"He cannot dissolve a marriage on a whim."

"I seriously doubt it is a whim. They haven't lived in the same country for years, and now that she wants to be queen—"

The butler interrupted. "Pardon me, my lord. A Miss Baylor has come to see you." His tone rang with disapproval.

Toddington nearly stumbled. "Miss Baylor? Here?"

"She probably has that Mrs. Roberts in tow," remarked Trevor.

"The young . . . lady is alone." The butler raised his nose a notch.

Toddington sent a glance to Trevor, then turned to his butler. "Show her in."

"Very good, my lord."

Lily entered the room a moment later.

"Miss Baylor, good morning." Toddington smiled at her and went to take her hand. Lily lifted her chin and didn't return his greeting.

"Won't you sit?" Toddington's smile wavered as he indicated a chair.

"No, thank you." She glared at Trevor and Toddington with her lips set in a firm line.

The two men exchanged a look. Toddington asked, "What can I do for you?"

"Nothing." Lily opened her mouth to speak further, then snapped it shut. Her chest heaved with every breath. She began again. "I came to tell you both . . . oh, when I think of poor Eden . . ."

"What about Eden?" Trevor sat up. Fear flashed through him.

"After what you did to her, I wouldn't blame her if she never spoke to you again." Lily burst into tears.

Running to her, Toddington whipped out his handkerchief and handed it to her. "Good heavens, Lily. What has happened?"

"To think you could be a part of it. I never would have believed it of you." She wiped her eyes and blew her nose. She turned her gaze to Toddington, her expression filled with accusation and betrayal.

"Where is Eden?" Trevor bounded from his chair. "Is she hurt?"

"Of course she's hurt. I don't care if you are an earl. You're a pompous oaf." Lily hiccuped.

Trevor grabbed her shoulders. "Tell me what happened."

Toddington pried his hands off Lily. "Ryeburn, calm yourself. We shan't learn anything if you frighten her."

"I'm not frightened. I'm angry and disappointed." Lily sniffed into the handkerchief. "How could you be so cruel?"

"What are you talking about?" Trevor ran his hand through his hair to keep from throttling the girl.

"Eden found out why you married her." Lily glared at him.

"She knows why I married her. She was there. Because of Sterling."

"Because of the wager." Lily hiccuped again, glanced at Toddington, and burst into fresh tears. "How could you?"

"The wager?" repeated Toddington. His face screwed up into an expression of chagrin and disbelief.

"Yes, the wager. What sort of men wager on marriage?"

Trevor wanted to shout at Lily. This talking in circles was making him dizzy. "Is Eden injured?"

"No. Whatever gave you that idea?"

Relief slammed through him . . . "Where is she?"

"I don't know at the moment."

. . . and just as quickly fled. "What do you mean, 'you don't know'?"

"Eden has left your house. She had no desire to stay in London any longer to face the ridicule of society," Lily sniffed.

Toddington patted her hand. "It's not all that bad."

Lily snatched her hand away. "You don't see anything wrong in what you did, do you? If word does get out that Lord Ryeburn married Eden on a bet, she'll be the object of pity or the butt of jokes."

Memories of his father's antics bandied about on the tongues of the *ton* sent a wave of disquiet flooding through Trevor. "No one had better dare make the Countess of Ryeburn the butt of a joke. Besides, no one knows about the wager except Toddington and myself. And Sterling, but he won't dare show his face in London." Trevor paced the room. "The wager wasn't in earnest. It happened on a whim. Eden has to know I didn't marry her to win a mere hundred pounds."

"Two hundred," muttered Toddington.

Trevor glared at him. "It doesn't matter. Do you have any idea where she may have gone?"

Lily nodded. "To Concordia."

Why hadn't the chit said so earlier? "At least she didn't get it into her head to go back to Massachusetts."

"She thought about it."

That information gave him pause. "Why didn't she?"

Lily shrugged. "You'll have to ask her yourself."

When Trevor returned to the townhouse, Finch was waiting for him at the entrance. "Pardon me, my lord. Lady Ryeburn has left."

"I know, Finch. When did she leave?"

"Just over an hour ago. She told me to tell you she went to Concordia."

"I know that also. Pack my things."

"Would you like me to ready the coach, sir?"

"Didn't she take it?"

"No, my lord. She hired one."

"With your help, no doubt."

Finch looked pained. "I warned her the staff will be limited at Concordia. She didn't listen."

"She wouldn't." Trevor shook his head. "I've made arrangements to meet Lord Wellsley at the Greyfolkes' ball to discuss his legislation for Parliament. Damn. I'll have to leave after that. Have my coach ready tomorrow morning."

"Very good, sir. You have a stack of correspondence in your study, sir." Finch bowed and retreated into the house.

As Trevor walked toward the room, he sensed an air of melancholy in the house, as if the house knew she wasn't there. He missed hearing her singing from some corner of the house or other. The ghost of her footsteps haunted him.

What folly. She had only lived in the house for two days. He had hoped his fanciful thoughts would disappear once he wed her. Instead she fascinated him more each day.

Trevor looked at the pile of letters on his desk. He couldn't afford to run after her with so many people wanting his attention. With a sigh, he sat and opened the first letter. It was a congratulatory note from Lord and Lady Lockwood. The second and third were similar. Both congratulated him on his marriage. The fourth wondered if he and the new countess would be able to attend a forthcoming ball.

Each letter contained words of praise for his wife. Pride filled him at her accomplishments. She had only been in England a short time yet had charmed so many of the *ton.*

The newspaper lay open beside the correspondence. A notice about his marriage to the American Nightingale caught his attention. The paper told of their elopement. Trevor waited for the shame of the scandal to hit him. To his shock, he found he didn't care. He read the notice again. From that bold statement in the paper, people would draw the conclusion that he had seduced her and had to marry her. He didn't care.

He rose from the desk. He wasn't quite sure why he didn't care. It didn't matter what people thought. Eden was his wife to honor, protect, and cherish—a duty he realized he would happily perform. And as soon as he could, he would tell her so.

Lighter of heart, Trevor left the rest of the correspondence unread.

Eden stood on the top step, her valise in hand. No wonder the coachman had laughed when she said she was the countess. She felt more like a waif. He waited beside her until someone came to open the door. She wondered if Mrs. Byrd was here, or if she too was on holiday.

The door opened. A footman poked his head out. "Lady Ryeburn," he exclaimed. He threw the door wide. "Forgive me, your ladyship. No one told me of your arrival."

"No one knew."

"She really is the Countess of Ryeburn?" The coachman rubbed his head.

"Of course she is. Now get you to the back. The cook'll give you food, and then you can be on your way." The footman shooed him away from the front door, then took the bag from Eden.

"Thank you. . . . Pardon me, but I don't believe I know your name."

The footman bowed. "John, my lady."

"Thank you, John. Is Mrs. Byrd here?"

"Yes, my lady."

The woman in question appeared in the hall and gasped. "Lady Ryeburn. No one told us of your arrival." The housekeeper hurried to greet her. "Take her ladyship's bags to her room."

"Yes, Mrs. Byrd."

Eden smiled at Mrs. Byrd. "I'm glad you're not on holiday. Finch told me to expect most of the staff to be away." Eden walked past the surprised housekeeper.

"Some have gone, to be sure, but most of the staff is here."

"I hope my arrival won't cause too much trouble."

"Trouble, my lady?"

Eden removed her gloves and shawl "I don't require much. Just a room to sleep in and a piano to sing at. And perhaps a bite to eat now and again."

Mrs. Byrd stared at her. Eden draped her shawl over her arm.

"My goodness." Mrs. Byrd took the wrap and gloves from Eden. "Forgive me, my lady. I'll put these away for you. Will your maid be arriving soon?"

"I don't know. I didn't tell her I was coming."

Eden saw the worried look on the housekeeper's face. "I expect I've flustered you. Not only did I arrive with no warning, but I also don't know how to talk or act like the English."

"No, my lady, I mean, yes . . . oh, dear."

Laughter bubbled up inside her, a welcome feeling after the past few days. "Someday, I shall have to tell you about the housekeeper at Fairlawne, my parents' home."

"I think I should like that, my lady." Mrs. Byrd offered

her a timid smile. "If you'll excuse me, my lady, I'll make sure your room is readied." The woman scuttled off.

Eden glanced around the entrance. Alone again. She was beginning to grow accustomed to the feeling. She wandered down the corridor, poking her head into one room after another. Her previous stay had not left her enough time to familiarize herself with the entire house. Now she was sure she would have ample opportunity to do so.

When she came upon the library, she stepped inside. Shelves covered three of the walls, and books covered every shelf. She gazed upon the titles. Livy, Tacitus, Caesar . . . oh no, Latin did not suit her mood. Further perusal discovered the works of Bacon, Marlowe, and Smith. Then, tucked off in the corner, Eden found the volume she wanted. *Pride and Prejudice* by Jane Austen. She had already read the book, but reading it again would be a pleasure.

Finding a comfortable chair, Eden pulled up her legs in a most unladylike fashion, curled into the cushions, and delved into the book. The words carried her away from her present plight with ease.

Eden didn't know how much time had passed when a prickling on the back of her neck made her look up from the book. In the doorway of the library stood a young girl. Spectacles sat on her nose, and her dark red hair was tied back in a way that looked almost painful. Green eyes peered out from behind the lenses.

"You must be the new countess," she said without preamble.

"I am." Eden set the book aside. "My name is Eden."

"My mother told me about you. She said you were crass and common. And American."

Eden lifted an eyebrow. "Did she now? Who is your mother?"

"The dowager countess. She hates being called that, so I do it whenever possible. But I didn't believe her. I seldom believe anything she says to me."

"What don't you believe?"

"That you're crass and common. Mother tends to exaggerate, and my brother never told me anything. I like to make up my own mind." The child stood back a step and examined her.

Trevor had a sister? He had never mentioned that he had a sister.

"I think you're pretty, but I'll reserve my judgment on the rest until I know you better."

"What is your name?"

"Goodness. I am always forgetting my manners. Miss Dunfield says it is the greatest lack in my education. You won't tell her, will you?"

"Not if you *tell* me your name."

The girl had the grace to blush. "Lorane."

CHAPTER TWENTY-TWO

"A pleasure to meet you, Lorane." Eden shut her book and put it to the side.

Lorane came into the room. She stood in front of Eden and peered into her face. "Miss Dunfield won't let me sit like that."

"Mrs. Roberts didn't let me either, but she's not here now."

"You had a governess, too?"

"Yes. My brother and I shared one for years."

"My brother is too old."

"My brother is my twin."

Lorane's eyes grew wide. "Truly?"

"I'm older by a few minutes."

"It must be nice to have a brother your own age."

"Not always." Eden remembered the many times Nicholas had tried to correct her behavior.

Flopping onto another chair, Lorane said, "I don't like my brother."

That surprised Eden. "Why not?"

"He doesn't like me." No rancor tainted her voice; it was a mere statement of fact.

Eden couldn't deny it. Trevor had never mentioned he had a sister.

"You don't like him much either."

The girl's grown-up tone astonished Eden. "Why do you say that?"

"You ran away from him, didn't you?"

"I ran away, but not because I don't like him." More's the pity.

Lorane shook her head. "Mother has told that me that no one leaves London during the season unless they are running away from something. I've observed enough to know this much is true. During the season, I am pretty much guaranteed the quiet and solitude I enjoy. Except during the weekend of that awful masquerade."

"Where were you during the masquerade?"

"Upstairs. I stayed in the nursery, and Miss Dunfield brought my food."

"Weren't you bored?"

"Oh, no. I had my books." Lorane examined Eden again and pulled up her legs in an imitation of Eden's posture. "This is comfortable. What book are you reading?"

"Pride and Prejudice."

"I thoroughly enjoyed Miss Austen's work."

"Eden looked at the little girl. "How old are you, Lorane?"

"Eleven."

"Does your mother know you've read *Pride and Prejudice?"*

"Of course not. She doesn't supervise my reading habits.

If she did, she'd probably forbid me from reading altogether. Miss Dunfield doesn't know either. She thinks the book is frivolous with no redeeming values. Clearly she hasn't read the novel."

A skinny woman with a stern expression entered the library. "There you are, young lady. You should be upstairs studying your declensions. How are you sitting in that chair?"

Lorane straightened up at once, her back erect, her feet flat on the floor.

"That's better." The woman looked down her nose at Eden. "And who are you?"

Eden suppressed a smile. "Eden St. John, Countess Ryeburn."

The woman's mouth dropped open.

"And you must be Miss Dunfield. Lorane was telling me about you."

"Forgive me, Lady Ryeburn. I had not realized you were visiting us."

"I'm not visiting. This is my home."

"Y-yes, of course." Miss Dunfield's pale face took on a rosy hue.

Eden turned to Lorane. "Have you finished studying your declensions?"

The girl nodded.

"Fine. Miss Dunfield, I'm sure you can excuse her for the rest of the day and give me a chance to know my new sister."

"Of course, Lady Ryeburn." Miss Dunfield left the room, her hurried steps echoing back into the library as her heels clicked down the hall.

"You'd do that for me?" Lorane gazed at her with suspicion.

"I remember when I was your age, I always enjoyed an

unexpected holiday. Eden straightened up. "What would you like to do?"

"I don't know. I've never had anyone ask me before."

Eden fought the pity she felt for the child. Lorane didn't need pity, she needed attention. "Hmmm. Does your head hurt with your hair pulled back like that?"

Lorane touched her hair. "Most definitely."

"Then let's go find a brush and do something about it." Eden held out her hand.

Lorane looked at the outstretched limb as if she didn't know what to do with it. She lifted her own hand and placed it in Eden's palm.

"If I do your hair, you must do mine as well. That's only fair."

"But I'm not sure—"

"Trust me." Eden led the girl from the room.

Half an hour later, they returned downstairs. Lorane's thick red hair fell in a neat braid down her back. Eden's blond hair fell in a braid as well, but it twisted to the side with gaps and tufts not entwined with the rest. Eden didn't care. Lorane's joy at Eden's trust was well worth the messy braid.

Lorane led Eden to the orangery. The room teemed with potted palms and fruit trees. A cheerful fountain bubbled in the center of the room. Fish swam in the pond that formed at the base of the fountain. In the water grew lilies and other aquatic plants. Here and there stood benches and low stone tables. Lorane guided her to the corner of the room. From seven pots grew seven different orchids. Large flowers bloomed on three of them, but the other four were green, healthy plants.

"Those are beautiful." Eden gazed in wonder at the flowers.

"Thank you. I grew them."

"You did?"

"There is something beautiful about plants. I love to sketch them. Don't tell Miss Dunfield, but whenever I have a free moment, I follow the gardener around to learn more about them. Sometimes he lets me care for them myself."

"How wonderful."

"You don't think it's strange that I like plants?"

"Good heavens, no. I think you have a real talent for growing them, and any talent is something to be cherished. If these beautiful blooms prove anything, you are quite a talented botanist."

"Do you really think so?"

"Most definitely. Don't let anyone try to control your talent or change it. Enjoy it as the gift it is."

Lorane cocked her head. She pushed her spectacles higher up on her nose. "You're the American Nightingale, aren't you?"

"How did you hear of that?"

"I steal the paper from Miss Dunfield every morning."

Eden laughed. "You are too clever by half. Come on, show me the rest of the house. I suppose I should learn where everything is if I am to make any sort of a good countess."

When the coach bumped over a rut in the road, Trevor woke. He wanted to stop the coach to stretch his legs, but a glance out the window told him he was almost to Concordia. A sense of eagerness filled him. He would see her soon.

In his imagination, he pictured her greeting him in the entry, throwing her arms around him, kissing him, her breasts pressing against his chest. He groaned. He would have to learn to control his thoughts about her if he didn't want to walk in discomfort. How many men grew hard at the mere thought of their wives? The control he had lived with so long was slipping.

The Greyfolkes' ball had bored him. He'd talked with the men he needed to speak with, and danced with the wives of the men he wanted to influence, but the evening lacked excitement. Even the proposal for Parliament hadn't held his interest. The hostess asked after Eden, and her look of regret when he informed her that Eden wasn't attending gave him pause. Was she sorry Eden wasn't there, or that Eden couldn't sing for her guests? For the first time, he had understood how Eden's talent could be a curse.

Trevor jumped from the coach almost before it had stopped in front of Concordia. Not waiting for the footman, he pushed the door open, almost hitting the man in the head.

The man jumped back. "Pardon me, my lord."

"My fault entirely." Trevor looked for Eden. He couldn't stop the rush of disappointment when she didn't appear. "Where is the countess?"

"She went into the village with Lady Lorane."

Trevor suppressed his groan. He had just come through the village. "Thank you, John. See that my bags are unloaded."

"Yes, my lord."

He would have to change his clothes before he went into the village. His traveling clothes were rumpled and covered with a layer of fine dust.

By the time he reached the village, the day had warmed up enough to make him regret his decision to wear a cravat. He tugged at the offensive cloth and finally removed it altogether. Tucking it into his pocket, he urged his horse forward. As he passed the houses and shops, those villagers who saw him bowed or nodded their heads.

He stopped in front of the baker's shop and dismounted. He had seen no sign of Eden or Lorane. Stepping into the shop, he said, "Good day, Mr. White, Mrs. White."

"And a fine day to you, Lord Ryeburn. 'Tis good to see you."

Trevor nodded. The villagers hadn't trusted him when he first became the earl. His father's practices had harmed them along with himself, but Trevor's efforts to bring prosperity back to his holdings had earned their respect. "Have you seen the countess or my sister? I was told they came to the village today."

"Aye, my lord, they did. Your lady came to introduce herself to us. She is quite lovely, my lord," answered the baker's wife as she measured flour for the next day's baking. "The last I seen of them, your lady held a child by each hand with a host of others behind her, and they was headed for the stream."

"Thank you."

Trevor left the shop and untied his horse. Deciding not to mount, he led the animal down the road, greeting the people he met. At the edge of the village, he left his horse tied near water and grass and proceeded to the stream.

As he neared the water, he heard the giggles and joyful shouts of children.

"Let me try it again, but you must help me." Eden's voice rang out over the noise.

Trevor waited a moment, then heard her sing. The children accompanied her. Her clear, pure voice, buoyed by the exuberance of the children, took his breath away. For a moment he didn't recognize the song. Then he frowned—"Green Bushes," a song about a woman who sings sweetly about meeting her true love, then forsaking him for someone else.

Eden stumbled over the words. The song stopped as the children giggled.

"No, that's not right," she said with a laugh. "Let's try it again." She sang again, and the children sang with her.

Trevor moved closer until he could see her.

Eden stood in the stream. She had drawn her skirt through her legs and hooked the hem into her sash, forming a sort of trousers. Her stockings and shoes lay discarded on the bank. Her hair was in a long, messy braid. She splashed with the children as she sang, and they splashed back. There must have been twelve of them.

Noticing another child sitting on the bank, he turned his gaze to her. Good heavens. She was Lorane, just as barefooted as his wife. Lorane sketched in a book, but she sang and laughed with the others. He stared at his sister. He had never seen her look so happy.

One by one the children grew quiet as they noticed him. They stared, until one remembered to bow. The others followed his example. Eden turned around. The joy fled her face. A guarded wariness covered her features.

"You came."

Trevor didn't like the surprise in her voice. "I did."

The somber expressions of the children surprised her. She glanced at Lorane. Lorane had closed her book and reached for her stockings and shoes. Eden looked at Trevor. Was this the reaction he always received? For the first time, she realized what a burden a title could be. Small wonder he was a stickler for propriety. Small wonder she didn't fit in his life.

"Thank you, children, for teaching me such a lovely song." Eden climbed up the embankment. She unhooked the hem and let it fall down to the ground. "I hope we can do it again sometime."

"Yes, my lady," the children answered as if in chorus.

Eden sighed. She didn't think they would repeat such an event now that they had a reminder of who she was. "Whenever I sing 'Green Bushes,' I shall think of you all and this lovely afternoon. Good-bye."

The children scrambled away as if they couldn't leave fast enough.

Sitting on a grassy knoll, Eden pulled her stockings toward her. Lorane looked at Trevor and blushed.

"Trevor, if you would be so kind as to turn around . . ." Eden motioned for him to turn.

"Why?"

"Because I wish to put my stockings on." She nodded toward Lorane.

"I've seen you with . . . " He stopped and turned away.

Because her feet were still wet, pulling her hose on proved difficult. She decided to pocket the stockings and slip into her shoes without them. "Ready."

"That was fast." Trevor turned back.

Lorane hid a smile.

"Shhh," scolded Eden with a wink.

Trevor looked between them and shrugged. "Shall we return to Concordia?"

"By all means." Eden reached a hand to him, waiting for him to help her up.

"You were able to climb into the water without help."

"Perhaps, but now you're available." She didn't lower her hand.

Trevor grabbed her hand and pulled her up.

"Thank you. Now help your sister up."

"Eden—"

"If someone has to teach you manners, isn't your wife the proper one to do so?"

Trevor glared at her, but Eden didn't shrink back. He crossed to his sister and helped her rise.

"You haven't greeted her properly."

Two could play this game. "Good afternoon, Lorane." Trevor bowed to the girl.

"How lovely to see you, Trevor." Lorane dipped into a curtsey.

"Excellent. Now we can go back to the house." Eden linked arms with Lorane.

"Where is the gig?"

"We didn't bring it."

"How did you get to the village?" His voice almost squeaked with disbelief.

"We walked. Back home—I mean, back in Massachusetts—I often walked such distances. I saw no need to use the gig on such a lovely day."

"You walked?"

Eden just smiled at him. "Since you're here, why don't you carry Lorane's bag?"

Lorane handed the bag that held her book to him. Trevor stared at his sister. It was as if she knew exactly what Eden was doing and enjoying every minute of it. He wished someone would let him in on the secret. "I have my horse."

"It won't hurt you to walk beside him. Perhaps you can hook Lorane's bag over the saddle if it gets too heavy."

Trevor vowed he would carry the bag the entire way even if his arms stretched with the effort.

Half an hour later, Concordia came into view. He was never so happy to see his home as now. Dust had settled over his fresh clothes. He would have to change again. Lorane's bag, although light, had gained weight with every step. Eden had not spared him another glance since they started home. Handing the horse to a groom, he watched Eden and Lorane step inside the house.

He followed them inside. Lorane had disappeared, but Eden stood in the entry. She was speaking with Mrs. Byrd, who nodded at Eden's every word.

When Mrs. Byrd moved off, Eden faced him. "Why are you here?"

"Don't you know?" He stepped closer to her. How could she still smell of lavender after such a long walk?

"I expect you came to bring me back to London. It can't look good for the earl to be missing his countess." Her voice dripped with ice, matching the iciness of her eyes. "I don't want to return."

"As you wish."

That response surprised her. Her face displayed her confusion. She scratched her nose. "Why didn't you tell me you had a sister?"

"I didn't think of it." He shrugged. He wasn't proud of that answer, but it was the truth.

"How could you not remember you had a sister?"

Trevor sighed. "Lorane is nearly twenty years younger than I. My father died just after she was born. I was . . . too busy to worry about my sister."

"She is a young girl neglected by everyone in her life. I can believe it of Vanessa, but I wouldn't have believed it of you."

Trevor's irritation grew. He wasn't used to having his actions questioned. "I've given her a home and security."

"You haven't given her love."

"How could I? I'm not sure she *is* my sister."

Eden paused at that.

"Vanessa was not a faithful wife. She had numerous lovers. Once she tried to seduce me. Father was surprised he could still sire a child, but he was thrilled when Vanessa was expecting." Trevor ran his hand through his hair. "No one in our family has ever had red hair. Just about the time of the conception, Vanessa had taken a Scotsman for her lover. His hair was the same deep red as Lorane's."

Eden gazed at him without blinking. "Does that really matter to a little girl who wants nothing more than attention from the brother she believes doesn't like her?" Eden turned on her heel and fled up the stairs.

Trevor stared after her. Truth was painful. Eden showed him this more often than he cared to acknowledge.

CHAPTER TWENTY-THREE

The sun was at its rosiest, but the encroaching night made its presence known in the east. The shadows lengthened over the country roads as the coach bounced over a rut, eliciting a grunt from the already irritated passenger.

"I never wanted to let her go," grumbled Stuart Grant. "If she had stayed home like I wanted—"

"She needed to go, Stuart." Corinna Grant patted her husband's hand. "Eden is fine."

"How can you say that? Eden is married. I hate the man."

"You haven't even met him."

"I don't need to meet him to know I hate him."

"Be fair." Corinna leaned onto her husband's shoulder and ran her hand down his vest.

"Not this time, Corinna. You won't make me forget how angry I am at that man."

Corinna sighed. "He has a name."

"Early Ryeburn. What kind of name is that?"

She giggled. "Earl, not early."

"I know."

"Don't you think perhaps Eden should have a share of your anger?"

"She does, but it's that man's fault." Stuart moved away from her.

Corinna sidled up to him. Stuart moved to the other seat. Corinna sighed again. "It won't do you any good to remain upset about it."

"And you're not at all upset about this," he accused her, pointing his finger at her. "You expected this."

"Don't be ridiculous."

"You gave her that coin. You were hoping this would happen."

"I thought you didn't believe in the coin."

"That is totally irrelevant. You wanted this to happen." Stuart crossed his arms on his chest and glared at her.

"She's my oldest child. I'm going to miss her, too, Stuart." Corinna blinked rapidly as tears filled her eyes. As they rolled down her cheek, she brushed them aside.

Stuart handed her a handkerchief. His voice was gentle when he spoke again. "I *have* missed her."

He moved back to his wife and took her in his arms. "Who knew when we planned to surprise her, we would end up the ones surprised? Dry your eyes. We should be there soon. You wouldn't want Eden to think something was wrong."

Corinna blew her nose. "Do you promise to behave?"

"I promise to do my best. I cannot promise more."

She thought about how protective he was of his family and smiled. "That's all I ask."

* * *

Eden wrestled with the tangles in her hair. She had allowed Lorane to braid her hair for two days. Unfortunately, Lorane's skill at braiding didn't match her intellectual skills. Eden tugged on another knot and winced. The pain was worth the grin on Lorane's face at her finished handiwork.

With the earl in the house, dinner would be a formal event. It was a little silly to set the long table for only three, but what did she know of the habits of the English nobility? Eden repressed the doubts and fears that raced through her. Perhaps in time she could overcome her inadequacy as a countess.

Twisting her hair into a simple yet elegant chignon, Eden readied herself for dinner. She checked her dress once again, and slipped out of her room. The dinner bell wouldn't ring for another half hour or so, but she couldn't stay in her room any longer. The specter of her failings plagued her too much in there.

She made her way to the library. A few minutes with a book might ease her disquiet. She entered the room and stopped short. Trevor sat in the armchair.

He hadn't noticed her yet. Perhaps if she slipped out the door—

Rising from his chair, he crossed to her. "Good evening. I see we had the same idea."

The faint smell of soap tantalized her. He had bathed before dinner. Immediately a picture of him reclining in a tub appeared in her mind. She imagined herself holding the soap and lathering his back, running her palms over his ribs, down lower to his waist, then lower still . . . Her heart pounded in her chest. Swallowing hard to dispel the image, she lifted her gaze to his. Was he happy to see her? His dark eyes hid his thoughts too well.

"Are you ill? You're flushed." He laid his hand on her forehead.

"I'm fine." Eden tried to keep her voice even.

"You don't look fine, but your head is cool." He removed his hand.

"I didn't mean to disturb you." Eden crossed to the table to put room between her and Trevor.

"You didn't. I was merely passing the time before dinner." He picked up the book he had been reading and placed it back on the shelf. "I've been thinking about Lorane."

"Yes?"

"Does she really think I don't like her?"

Eden nodded.

"Why? I haven't done anything to give her such an idea."

"What have you done?"

"I've given her a home, education, clothes, security . . ."

"What of love? Lorane is a child. She's already lost her father, and she may as well have lost her mother for all that Vanessa sees her. How can you deny her the attention of her brother?"

"I have little in common with her."

"How do you know?"

Silence greeted that question.

Eden placed her hands on her hips. "Did you know she has grown the most beautiful flowers?"

Trevor furrowed his brow. "Flowers? We have a gardener to do that."

"But she likes to grow flowers. She also can draw quite well, and she reads things that a child of her age shouldn't be able to understand. I've never seen a child so intelligent."

"That proves her parentage is questionable," muttered Trevor.

Fury filled Eden. "Why is that important? She isn't the heir. Your father accepted her, and you have acknowledged her to be your sister by giving her a home."

"If I don't produce an heir, and she does, the title will pass to her child." Trevor's gaze never left her face. "And out of the line."

"What makes you think you won't produce an heir?" Eden blushed at her words as the memory of their passion rose in her mind.

"I never said I wouldn't, but I've seen it happen too many times. We could have no sons."

"And how would that look to the *ton?*" Irony gave her tone a sharp edge.

Trevor's eyes narrowed. "What do you mean?"

"I mean, you have no qualms risking my reputation for a wager, but heaven forbid scandal should become attached to your name."

"You have my name now."

"Through no choice of my own."

Just before the sun disappeared, the coach pulled up in front of Concordia. Stuart stepped out, helped his wife from the coach, and turned to examine the building. After a minute's silence, he nodded. "I assume he can provide for Eden. But a building doesn't prove anything."

Corinna shook her head. Holding her skirt in her hands, she mounted the steps without waiting for Stuart. She noticed the well-maintained lawn and carefully planted flower beds. The steps were clean.

As she reached the top, the door opened. A footman in livery stepped out. "May I help you?"

"Yes. I'm here to see my daughter."

"Your daughter, madam?"

Stuart arrived beside her. "Yes, our daughter."

The footman's gaze traveled up to Stuart's face, which towered above him.

"Are you going to announce us?" Stuart peered down his nose at the footman.

"Glaring at the man isn't going to bring you to Eden any faster," Corinna scolded. She sent Stuart a withering glance and then turned to the footman with a smile. "You must forgive my husband. He's far too protective of his children. We were told our daughter lives here. She has married the Earl of Ryeburn."

The footman bent in a deep bow. "Forgive me, madam. I was not aware you are the countess's parents. Lord and Lady Ryeburn are presently in the library. Shall I announce you?"

"Do you think we could surprise her? She didn't know we were coming."

The footman nodded. "I'll see to your bags. The library is the fourth door on the right."

"Thank you so much." Corinna flashed the man a smile.

The footman stared for a moment, then hastily bowed.

Stuart took her arm and led her away. He whispered in her ear, "You don't have to charm him. You got your answers."

"If I didn't know you better, I'd say you were jealous."

Stuart stopped, jerking her back a step. He pulled her into his arms. "I'm only protecting that poor man from your spell. He'll probably never be the same." Stuart kissed her.

A breathless minute later, Corinna lifted her head and gazed into her husband's bright-blue eyes. A blush heated her cheeks.

Stuart chuckled softly. "I can still make you blush." He kissed her again. "I love you."

Corinna leaned against him for strength. "And I love you. Now let's go see our daughter."

Following the corridor, Corinna counted the doors. One, two, three . . . Voices carried into the hallway. She recognized Eden's at once.

"Through no choice of my own."

"It's a little too late to lament the loss of your name," a deep voice responded.

Beside her Stuart stiffened.

"I'm not lamenting the loss of my name." Eden felt the hot sting of tears rising in her eyes. "I lament being used as a token."

Trevor ran his hand through his hair. "I have never—"

"Admit it," she interrupted. "Your pride wouldn't let any sort of scandal taint your name. Better to wed me than let gossip harm your reputation. If I hadn't been thoroughly ruined, you never would have married me."

A movement in the doorway caught her attention. Eden glanced over his shoulder and gasped as her father stormed into the room. "Daddy?"

Trevor turned at her exclamation, just in time to meet Stuart's fist flying into his face. The blow knocked him to the ground.

"Daddy!" screamed Eden and rushed to Trevor. She tried to cradle his head in her lap, but he brushed aside her efforts and rose to his feet. She looked up as her mother entered the room. "Mother, do something."

The two men stared at each other, fists clenched at their sides.

"Stuart, what have you done?" Corinna asked with a frown.

"Is this man really your father?" asked Trevor. His nostrils flared in anger.

"Yes," answered Eden.

"Then I shan't hit him in deference to his age."

"I'd like to see you try, pup. 'Twould give me much pleasure teaching you to respect your elders." Her father's voice sent chills down Eden's spine.

"Daddy, stop it." Eden rushed between the two men. She faced her husband. "Oh, Trevor, your eye."

The skin around Trevor's left eye had already started to redden and swell. "We need to get something cold on it." Eden ran to the bell cord.

"I'm fine, Eden." Trevor never turned from Stuart.

"Don't be stubborn, young man," chimed in her mother.

Mrs. Byrd appeared in the doorway a moment later. "My heavens."

"We need something cold for his lordship's eye, please." Eden said to the startled housekeeper.

"My heavens," repeated the housekeeper, then rushed away.

"Will you two step away from each other? You're acting like dogs staking out a territory." Corinna said.

"Daddy, please?" Eden wheedled.

Stuart stepped away from Trevor. He turned to his daughter and opened his arms to her. Eden stepped into the embrace. She lost the fight against her tears. They rolled down her cheeks in rivulets. Stuart wiped her face. "He's making you cry."

"No—well, yes, but don't worry." Eden burst into fresh tears.

"I will kill him." Stuart turned to Corinna. "You can't tell me now that I was wrong."

"We haven't heard everything," said Corinna.

Mrs. Byrd returned with a basin of water and a cloth. She placed it on a table. Eden moved from her father to the basin. Dipping the cloth in the water, she wiped her own face before wetting the cloth again. She said, "Sit here, Ryeburn."

Trevor clenched his teeth. He had learned that she called him Ryeburn when she was annoyed with him. He took the indicated chair. Eden wrung out the cloth and placed it over his eye. "How is that?"

"It hurts." He looked up at her with his one good eye, then he glanced at her father. He knew where she got her startling blue eyes. "So these are your parents."

"Yes. I told you Daddy tends to protect me overmuch."

"Mmmm." Trevor removed the cloth from his eye. He glared at Stuart. "Trevor St. John, Earl Ryeburn." He didn't extend his hand.

Eden took the cloth from him and dipped it in the water again. "Keep this on."

Corinna crossed to him. Now he knew where Eden got her beauty. "I am Corinna Grant, and this is my husband, Stuart. But you've already met."

Her gaze wasn't friendly. Trevor couldn't blame the woman. Heaven knew how much they had overheard.

Lorane entered the room. She stared at the newcomers and crossed to Eden. "Who are they?"

"My parents," whispered Eden.

Lorane's gaze fell on Trevor. She stared at the cloth until Trevor snatched it off his eye. Lorane's eyes widened. "What happened?"

"I'll tell you later." Eden took the cloth and placed it on his eye again.

He had to admit he liked her ministrations. Tilting his head slightly, he let the cloth slip from his eye. Eden snatched it up, wetted it, and laid it on his injury with care. He almost grinned until he remembered he wasn't alone. Examining his mother-in-law, he noticed that Corinna watched him with a curious expression on her face. She didn't show emotions on her face the way her daughter did.

The footman appeared in the doorway. "Dinner is ready."

From the man's lack of reaction, Trevor was sure news of his mishap had already traveled through the servants' quarters. He removed the cloth from his eye and sat up. "I'm sure Mrs. Byrd has already set two more places. Shall we go in?"

CHAPTER TWENTY-FOUR

Dinner was a silent affair. Stuart glared at Trevor, Trevor glared at Stuart, and Corinna glared at Trevor and Stuart. Eden stared at her plate. The only words spoken were thank-yous to the staff.

When the footmen had cleared the dinner plates, Corinna stood. "Gentlemen, you may go off to drink your brandy. I trust you won't kill each other."

Stuart glanced at her and opened his mouth to speak, but Corinna didn't let him. "I wish to talk to my daughter. I didn't say you had to converse with him, only that you cannot kill him."

Trevor rose. "If you follow me, sir, I shall show you to my study, where we can enjoy our brandy and each other's company."

Eden shot Trevor a cautioning look. The cold irony in his expression didn't reassure her. Her father rose at the silent challenge. He swept his arm in front of him, inviting

Trevor to lead the way. She couldn't help but notice how similar they were in height and stature. The urge to follow them and ensure Trevor's safety rose in her. She knew her father would listen to her mother. If only she could be as sure of Trevor's behavior.

When she turned back to the table, Lorane stared at her. "Did you wish to say something, Lorane?"

The child drew her brows together. "Only that if this is a typical grown-up meal, I'll take my dinners in the nursery with a good book from now on."

Eden laughed. "It'll be better next time."

Lorane twisted her lips to the side. "If you say so. May I be excused?"

"Yes."

The girl skipped out of the room, remembering at the last minute to walk. But from the sound of her footsteps, as soon as she was out of sight, she began to skip again.

"What a bright child," said Corinna. "Who is she?"

"Trevor's sister. Half-sister. She really is a clever girl." Eden crossed to her mother.

Mother and daughter looked at each other for a moment, then Corinna opened her arms and hugged Eden.

Eden felt the burden of loneliness lift from her shoulders. "What are you doing here?"

"We came to accompany you on the last part of your journey. We wanted to surprise you."

"You did that certainly." Eden laughed, but the mirth didn't reach her soul.

"You surprised *us.* Can you imagine your father's face when Mrs. Roberts informed us you had married?"

"I think I'm glad I wasn't there."

"Coward." Corrina laughed at her. "We took a coach here the next day, after poor Mrs. Roberts answered your father's questions."

Eden grimaced. "I can imagine what he thinks of Trevor after hearing the details."

"What details? Mrs. Roberts said only that you eloped." Corinna examined Eden's face. "Is there more to the story?"

"She didn't mention the kidnapping?"

"Kidnapping? Eden Grant, you will tell me right now what happened." Her mother placed her hands on her hips and scowled at her.

"It's Lady Ryeburn now."

"Don't play word games with me, young lady. I'm still your mother."

"Let's go to a more comfortable spot." Eden led her mother to the drawing room. Tea waited for them. Eden silently thanked Mrs. Byrd. "Tea?"

"You're avoiding the subject, Eden."

"I know. Would you like some tea anyway?"

Corinna laughed and took a chair. "You can pour while you explain."

Eden sighed, but knew she couldn't put her mother off any longer. She told Corrina of her success with the *ton* and the many invitations, of Lily's feelings for Toddington, of Sterling's interest in her and how he kidnapped her from Trevor's masquerade. She ended with her marriage in Gretna Green.

Corinna shook her head. "It's hard to believe the earl married you under such circumstances."

"You don't know Trevor. He just wanted to avoid the scandal." Tears stung her eyes, and a hot lump burned in her throat. *I will not cry, I will not cry.*

"You love him, don't you?"

"Oh, Mother, I do." Her resolve broke at her admission, and the tears rushed out. She wiped them away angrily.

"I have never cried this much in my life. Nothing's been the same since I lost the coin."

Corinna froze. "What did you say?"

"I lost the coin. I'm sorry, Mother. It had brought me such good luck."

"It was just a token." Her mother patted Eden's hand. "There was no luck attached to it."

Eden sniffed. "But it belonged to your mother—"

"It's not important. What is important is that you're unhappy." Corinna rose. "I'm going to send your father to see you. He's missed you terribly. But I'd dry your eyes before he comes in. You wouldn't want to give him more reason to dislike your young man."

Eden sniffed. "Where are you going?"

"I have to speak to your husband."

Panic grasped her. "Mother, you can't tell him—"

"I don't intend to. I know better than to mix myself into your problems—unless you want me to." At the door her mother stopped and turned back. "Perhaps you should tell me where the study is."

Trevor stared at his glass with his one good eye. Eden's father possessed good power for a man his age. Trevor didn't doubt his own strength, but he was certain challenging his father-in-law to a brawl wouldn't look right. He looked at the man. Stuart hadn't shifted his gaze since they came into the room. "More brandy?"

"No."

The terse answer didn't surprise Trevor. A thank-you might have.

"Here you are. I found it, after all." His mother-in-law stepped into the room.

Trevor rose and bowed to her. He had never known a

woman to interrupt gentlemen at their brandy, but then again, Eden was her daughter. Unconventional behavior must run in the family. "Mrs. Grant."

A look of concern covered her features. "That eye looks terrible. Honestly, Stuart. You should learn to control that temper of yours. You're lucky the earl restrained himself after you hit him."

"Lucky? That pup—"

"That pup, as you call him, is a full-grown man, and if you haven't noticed, he is easily as big as you."

Mrs. Grant's smile amazed Trevor. More amazing was the way his father-in-law's face mellowed at the sight. No trace of the man's annoyance remained in his expression. Until he turned back to Trevor.

Mrs. Grant continued. "Go see your daughter. I wish to speak to the earl."

Stuart rose and kissed his wife on the cheek. Trevor had the impression that if he were not present, the kiss might have lasted longer than the mere peck it was.

"Where is Eden?"

"In the drawing room. Down this hall, turn right, first door on the right."

"This house is a mausoleum." Stuart left the room.

Trevor set down his glass and glared after the man.

Corinna smiled. "Right now, he wouldn't say anything nice if he met the king."

"I know how he feels."

Her laughter astonished Trevor. He hadn't expected to hear anything pleasant from either of Eden's parents for a while yet. "You wished to speak to me?"

"Eden has told me all about your wedding. That explains much."

"Indeed?"

"Don't sound so skeptical. I'm sure there's much I still

don't know, but I'll leave that for you two to work out. I merely wanted to ask you if you've found anything?"

Eden was definitely her mother's daughter. This jumping from subject to subject was making him dizzy. "Pardon me?"

"Have you found anything recently? A token perhaps?"

What an odd question. "No."

Mrs. Grant's shoulders drooped. "You haven't? I felt so sure—"

"No, wait." He pulled out the coin from his pocket. "I'd almost forgotten about this. I've gotten so used to carrying it around." He handed her the coin.

Mrs. Grant took the coin and examined both sides. The smile on her face baffled him. "I knew it. Where did you find this?"

"In London. It was lying on the street when I picked it up. Do you know what it is?"

"Just a lovely old coin with Venus on the front. Have you read the words on the back?"

"Numquam tuas spes dedisce. Never forget your dreams. A lovely sentiment, but hardly practical."

She fingered the coin almost lovingly. "I'm not sure about that. Don't you have any dreams?"

He hesitated.

"Forgive me. I have no right to ask such a personal question." Her eyes twinkled. "Yet."

Trevor rubbed his forehead, then winced when he brushed his eye. If he wasn't mistaken, Eden's mother had forgiven him, although the reason eluded him. Her attitude perplexed him.

Mrs. Grant handed the coin back to him. "Take care of this coin. I think it's lucky."

He placed the coin on the desk. "I don't believe in lucky talismans."

"Neither do I, but I do believe in destiny." Corinna patted his arm. "You don't have any objections to us staying here, do you?"

"Of course not. You are my wife's parents. Where else would you stay?"

"Not every newly wedded couple wants the bride's father in their house."

I can understand why.

"If you'll excuse me, I'll go back to my daughter. I haven't seen her for several months." Mrs. Grant paused in the doorway. "What shall I call you? Lord Ryeburn is too formal."

Trevor couldn't answer for a moment. His mind whirled from the non-conversation he had just had. "I think perhaps Trevor will suffice."

"Good night, Trevor. I doubt I shall see you again tonight. Take care of that eye." Mrs. Grant waved and left the room.

Trevor stared after her. For a moment, he wondered what her cryptic words meant. How had she known about the coin? His gaze sought out the coin on the table. The words echoed in his mind. *Numquam tuas spes dedisce.* What were his dreams?

Picking up the coin, he flipped it in the palm of his hand. He wanted a family, children, a son who would never have to be ashamed of his father. He wanted to restore his family name with enough dignity that no one would ever recall the transgressions of his father. He wanted . . .

An idea hovered just outside the realm of his consciousness. The harder he tried to fasten onto the concept, the more elusive it became. Frustrated, he pounded his fist on his desk.

"If you're not careful, we'll have to doctor your hand as well."

Trevor spun around. Eden stood in the doorway.

With a gasp, she rushed to him and cupped his face in her hands. "Your eye looks terrible." Dropping her hands, she crossed to the bell pull.

"Don't."

"We must put something cold on your eye."

"Mrs. Byrd has already thought of that." He pointed to a basin of water and a cloth on the corner of a table.

"Then sit, so I can put this on." She brought the water and cloth closer to him. Her foot tapped the ground with impatience until he sat.

Trevor didn't flinch as she laid the cloth over his eye. "Where are your parents?"

"They were tired from the journey. I sent them to bed." Eden lifted the cloth and dipped it in the water again.

"That's different." Trevor chuckled.

"What is?" Eden placed the cloth over his eye again.

"A child sending her parents to bed."

"I suppose that does sound a bit strange." Eden peeked under the cloth and sucked in her breath through her teeth. "This is going to look bad for a while."

"I don't have to be anywhere for a while."

Eden cocked her head. "I thought you'd be in a hurry to get back to London, to Parliament or whatever you need to do there."

In that instant Trevor realized that he had no desire to rush back to London. "I can't go looking like this."

"No. Heaven forbid someone should see Lord Ryeburn with a blemish." Eden snatched the cloth from his eye and dipped it in the water again. She pressed it back with less gentleness.

"Hey. Careful." Trevor jerked his head back.

Chagrin molded her features. "I didn't mean . . . Did I hurt you?"

"Yes." He scowled at her.

"What should I do?"

"Kiss it." Where had that come from?

For a moment, Eden drew back and stared at him. Then she leaned forward and brushed her lips gently against his temple. "Like this?"

"No. Like this." He reached up, swept her into his lap, and claimed her mouth with his. The cloth dropped unheeded to the floor.

His mind whirled anew, but not with confusion. His senses roared. Her lips responded to his demands, sending heat shooting to his loins. He wanted her. He wanted to feel himself buried within her.

Shifting her above him, he pulled back for a moment. Her eyes shone into his. She ran her tongue over her lips, tempting him to touch them with his finger. Her lips parted under his touch, her warm breath blowing against his finger.

He needed more. The low décolletage of her dress offered little impediment to his desire. Freeing her breasts from their constraints, he savored the sight of them exposed for a moment before bending his head to take one rosy peak into his mouth. Her nipple hardened under his tongue.

She arched her back and let loose a low, husky purr. Trevor thought he would spill his seed as the sound washed over him. One hand cradled her back, the other reached for her skirts. He burrowed under the layers of material until he felt the warm, smooth skin of her thigh.

Lifting her skirts higher, Trevor glided his hand through her drawers to her silken wetness. Above him Eden gasped.

"You are ready for me." He withdrew his hand and unfastened his trousers. Freed of the tightness of his trousers, his manhood strained against the cloth that still covered it. Trevor grasped Eden's hand and led her to his shaft. Her touch stopped his breathing. He could hear the thunder of his blood in his ears. "Take me in."

Lifting herself over him, Eden guided him to her softness. He slipped inside, her walls tightening around him in a welcome embrace. He rocked his hips, moving her. She grabbed his shoulders as he increased his movements. Soon she rode him without his encouragement, finding her own rhythm. Trevor met her, thrust for thrust, until he felt ready to explode.

Above him, Eden cried out as she clenched around him in bursts. His release came at her body's encouragement. He rocked under her, sending his seed deep within her feminine sheath.

Eden leaned heavily upon him. Her breathing gave evidence to the effort she had spent. He lifted her from him, letting her garments slip into place as he placed her across his lap.

"That was . . ." She paused, and then she grinned.

Trevor chuckled. "I couldn't agree more." Cradling her in his lap, he waited until her breath, and his own, came more evenly.

Eden lifted her gaze to his. "Perhaps we should blacken the other eye as well."

CHAPTER TWENTY-FIVE

The first one to breakfast the next morning, Eden helped herself to ham and eggs, sat at the table, and pushed the food around on her plate. She was restless and moody. After the passion they had shared, she had hoped to spend the night lying beside her husband, but Trevor had escorted her to her room and left her there. Disappointment had troubled her—until it changed into resentment that he could so easily abandon her. She had tossed about in her big bed all night.

Her mother entered the breakfast room. Crossing to Eden, Corinna kissed the top of her head. "Good morning, Eden." She glanced at Eden's plate, but made no remark.

"Good morning, Mother. Did you sleep well?"

"Quite well, thank you. There's nothing better for a good sleep than having your mind at ease." Corinna dished up some roast pheasant and eggs for herself.

Eden looked at Corrina with bewilderment. Her mother seemed terribly cheery this morning.

"Eat. I don't want to see you get skinny." Corinna lifted a bite of the pheasant to her mouth. "Mmmm. You have an excellent cook."

As she continued to stare at her mother, Eden took a bite of her eggs. She didn't taste them at all. Her mother's demeanor baffled her. After the battle between her father and Trevor, her mother should be concerned, or at least wary. Yet Corrina ate with no apparent loss of appetite and no apparent worries.

Before she could make an appropriate comment, Trevor entered the room. His eye was still swollen, and a range of colors began to accent the skin around it.

"Good morning, ladies." He got himself a dish and approached the sideboard.

"Good morning, Trevor." Corinna greeted him with a smile.

Eden dropped her fork. It clattered against her plate. Trevor and her mother stared at her. "Sorry." She reached absently for the fork. She didn't understand her mother's friendly tone. Her mother looked genuinely pleased to see him.

Her father entered the room, and nodded to them. "Morning."

"Good morning, Daddy."

"Stuart filled his plate and turned to the table. He noticed the empty spot next to Trevor. Glaring at his son-in-law, he moved to the other end of the table and sat in an empty chair at the far end.

Her father's behavior Eden could understand.

Breakfast wasn't as silent as dinner had been. Corinna asked question after question about Concordia, ignoring Stuart's heated glances. Her mother's interest in Trevor's estate perplexed Eden. Trevor, too, looked puzzled at Corinna's amicable mood. As happy as Eden was that her mother made an effort to include Trevor, she also felt betrayed. Hadn't she cried on her mother's shoulder last night? Didn't Mother realize how unhappy she was?

Her father rose from the table first. "I'm going for a walk." He glared at Corinna.

"I'll go with you." Corinna beamed at Trevor. "You've described it so well, I want to see more of the estate."

Stuart cleared his throat. "Are you coming or aren't you?"

Eden had always marveled that her mother wasn't frightened of her father. When he frowned like that, everyone cowered—except Corrina. Eden hated being on the receiving end of that frown, yet it never seemed to bother her mother.

"Coming, my love." Corrina linked her arm in her husband's, and they left the room.

Silence replaced the friendly chatter, much to Eden's relief. She had not realized just how nervous her mother had made her.

"I trust you slept well."

Trevor's voice startled her. "Y-yes, I did, thank you," she lied.

"Your mother has surprised me. I never expected her to warm to me after last night. Your father's reaction I can understand."

Eden looked at him. "Is your eye troubling you?"

"Only when I smile."

"Then it shouldn't hurt you much."

Trevor chuckled at her words. "That was a jest. It only hurts if I touch it." He rose from the table. "I have some business to take care of. Perhaps you should join your parents on their walk. You haven't seen much of the estate yourself."

"I think I shall."

Trevor crossed to her chair and pulled it out from the table. Eden stood.

"If you need anything, ask Finch or Mrs. Byrd."

Eden nodded, his dismissal of her cutting her deep in her heart. It was as if he had forgotten their intimacy last night. No, it was more as if he couldn't face her. Had she done something wrong?

Tears threatened her composure. She rushed from the room without another word to him.

Trevor stared after her. *Her* behavior baffled him as much as her mother's. He ran his hand through his hair. Watching Eden during breakfast had been an exercise in self-control. Each time he looked at her, the image of her limbs entwined with his filled his mind. His response to her last evening frightened him to his core. He hadn't trusted himself enough to spend the night with her. He didn't trust himself now. Thank heavens for Mrs. Grant. Without her constant flow of questions, Trevor couldn't guess what his actions might have been at the table.

Sitting at his desk in his study, Trevor tried to concentrate on the newspaper in front of him. His gaze was drawn time and again to the chair that bore silent witness to their passion of the previous night. Exhaling in a burst of impatience with himself, he rose from the desk and turned the chair around. He returned to his desk and resumed his efforts to concentrate. The newspaper told of the workings of Parliament, but it didn't hold his interest. Pushing the paper aside, he looked at the accounts. Numbers interested him even less. He leaned back in his chair.

His infrequent mistresses had never abandoned themselves as Eden had to him last night. And certainly he had never experienced such a soul-satisfying climax. What was wrong with him? He shouldn't think of his wife in such terms. Most of his colleagues in Parliament had mistresses to satisfy their needs and wives to maintain the line. He had been ready to follow their example. When had he decided Eden was enough?

Trevor stood and paced the room. His thoughts jumbled together, panicking him. His speed increased. At no time in the past had he not known his own convictions. The disorganization of his mind frightened him.

He stopped short. Through the window he spotted Eden walking with her parents. Stuart stood in the middle. On his left walked his wife. On his right was Eden, her arm linked with her father's. The three talked with each other, sometimes cutting the other off, laughing and smiling. A wave of pure jealousy ran through him. He envied the family group he saw. His father had done little but ignore him. When his father *had* paid him attention, it was to belittle or berate him.

He had grown to hate his father.

Another glance outside the window showed him three people who enjoyed each other's company, who respected each other. Even when angered, no one could ever doubt their devotion. And love.

Trevor sat down hard. The panic subsided. His mind cleared, and one thought remained. He wanted the same for his family. He wanted a family that loved one another, that supported one another. Too many of his acquaintances had their heirs, then hired someone to make sure their progeny never bothered them. Too many of their families were groups of strangers, tied together by blood but little else.

He had been ready to embark on just such an existence.

The thought chilled him.

Instead, a woman who smelled of lavender had shaken up his life until he couldn't recognize himself any longer. She took everything he believed true and noble and tossed it in his face. She ignored convention and followed her heart. And he had been lucky enough to catch her.

His breath caught in his throat. A wave of dizziness overcame him.

He loved Eden.

In that first instance when she looked up at him with those accusing, cold blue eyes, she had entered his heart and stayed there until he couldn't imagine existing without her. She was as much a part of him now as his heartbeat.

Trevor looked out the window. He couldn't see her anymore.

His first thought was to search for her, find her, and carry her to his room, keeping her prisoner until she admitted she could feel something for him. He shook his head. He would only frighten her with such behavior. No, it would take careful planning to overcome her pride.

A movement out of the corner of his eye caught his attention. He saw Lorane move to the cool of some trees. She carried a sketchbook under her arm.

Guilt hit him like a blow. His sister suffered far worse than he. He had learned early that his father wasn't fond of him. She was still young enough to hope for affection. Her mother wouldn't provide it, and he had withheld it over something as stupid as her possible illegitimacy. Eden's words echoed in his ears. It didn't matter whether Lorane was his sister by blood or not. She would become the sister of his heart.

Although he wished to see Eden, here was an opportunity to start the repairs to his relationship with Lorane. Eden wouldn't miss him. Her parents occupied her attention at the moment in any case. Trevor stepped through the casement door.

He reached Lorane in a few minutes. She looked up, startled to see him.

He sat beside her on the grass. "May I see what you are sketching?"

Lorane hugged her book close to her chest and squinted her eyes at him. "Why?"

"I should like to see how talented my sister is." He held out his hand.

She peered at him through her spectacles. With some hesitation, she handed her book to him.

Trevor flipped it open. A detailed drawing of an orchid caught his eye. The graceful curves of the flower stood bold on the page, and although the drawing was in charcoal, he could picture the bloom's color. He turned to another page and stopped. The picture was of Eden, up to her calves in the water. Lorane had drawn this the day he surprised Eden and her by the stream. Eden's smile shone on the children around her. Lorane had captured Eden's essence even though the drawing was incomplete.

"Incredible," he whispered.

"That one isn't finished. I know it's not very good—"

"You're wrong."

Lorane furrowed her brow. "I want my book back."

"No, no. You misunderstand me. Your talent is incredible. I never knew you could draw like this." He showed her the picture and pointed to Eden. "See here, how her neck is tilted? You've captured her playfulness exactly. You can feel her happiness and the joy of the children."

"But most of their faces are blank." Doubt tainted Lorane's voice.

"That doesn't matter. If you ever finish it, all that will shine through, because it's already there." Trevor ran his hand through his hair. "I don't believe I'm explaining it at all well, but then again, I'm not an artist. All I know is that you can *feel* this drawing in addition to seeing it."

"Do you really think so?" Lorane's green eyes lit up.

"I really do. I also think I need to hire you a teacher."

Lorane frowned again. "You've already hired Miss Dunfield."

"Can Miss Dunfield teach you to draw?"

"No."

"Then I need to hire someone who can. An art teacher." He grinned at her.

"Do you mean it?" Lorane's upturned face held pure joy in its features.

"Yes, I mean it." Trevor flipped through a few more pages. Her drawings of plants dominated the slim volume. "You seem to like plants."

"Oh, yes." She paused. "Can I tell you something?"

"Please."

"Plants are like my family. I watch them grow. I help them to be strong and bear fruit or flowers. There are so many things one can learn from plants."

"I think that's admirable. But plants are not your family. I am."

Lorane looked at him for a moment, then frowned. "You think I'm silly for having such thoughts."

"Not in the least. In fact, when I was a boy, I couldn't wait to go to school so that I could get back to my books. *They* were my family." Trevor tilted Lorane's chin so that she looked him straight in the eyes. "I haven't been the best of brothers, Lorane, I know that. But I hope, with time, you'll give me a chance to make up for it."

Lorane's eyes filled with tears. "I don't know . . ."

Trevor smiled. "At least promise you will let me try."

Lorane swallowed hard. "That much I can promise."

With a chuckle, Trevor kissed the top of her head. "Eden was right. You are a remarkable child."

"I like Eden." Lorane gave him a tremulous smile. "You picked a good wife."

"I believe I did." Trevor handed her book back to her. "If you are this good now, I shudder to think what will happen after you've had lessons."

"Do you think you could get me a few books on botany as well?"

Trevor winked at her. "I don't see why not."

Lorane opened her mouth again, but Trevor lifted his hand. "I may have a few years of neglect to make up for, but that doesn't mean I shall spoil you."

For a moment, Lorane looked crestfallen; then she laughed. "You're smarter than I thought."

Trevor chuckled with her. "I suppose I will have to be to keep up with you." He rose. "Did you see which way Eden and her parents went? I need to speak with her as well."

Lorane's expression told him she understood him all too well. Trevor realized his little sister wouldn't remain a child for long. He had almost waited too long.

"They went to the garden." She opened her sketchbook and lifted her charcoal.

"Thank you." Trevor took a step in that direction, then stopped again. "Does Miss Dunfield know you're here?"

Lorane flushed. "No."

He grinned. "Well, I'd find a better place to conceal yourself. If she looks out the window, she's sure to spot you."

After her look of surprise subsided, Lorane snatched up her book and retreated farther from the house. "Thank you, Trevor," she called over her shoulder.

"Just don't do it too often," he yelled after her. He

waited until she had disappeared, then turned toward the back of the house.

He heard them before he saw them. Eden was singing, her father was clapping, and her mother leaned against Stuart. The family group looked content, and Trevor knew he couldn't intrude. Not yet, but soon, he promised himself.

Retracing his steps, he went back to his study. The papers interested him as little as before, but he sat down at his desk to finish his business. A slow smile spread over his face. He knew what he wanted, and he knew he had the determination to work for it. Eden's heart would be his, of this he was certain.

CHAPTER TWENTY-SIX

Darkness settled over the estate. It was time.

The bushes near the gates shook as Sterling crawled out from his hiding place. He brushed the dust off himself, then stopped. Soon he would buy new clothes, and he could burn these. The thought cheered him.

Stretching his limbs, Sterling glanced to the left and right. The road was empty, as was the drive to the house. The only lights he saw came from the manor. He took a step onto the estate and gritted his teeth. His legs had fallen asleep during the many hours under the bushes. His limbs prickled and burned him as he moved. Damn Ryeburn. He could blame this on the bastard as well. God, he hated Ryeburn.

His stomach growled. The day in the bushes had taken its toll on his body. He would have to stop at the kitchen first. Another delay, but one he would savor. A good meal at Ryeburn's expense. Perhaps he would steal some brandy as well. Sterling snorted. No need to get too sure of himself. His plan would work better with a clear head. He would have time for brandy later.

Although darkness provided enough cover, and no one prowled the grounds, Sterling darted from tree to tree. Cockiness could cost him his revenge. Better to hide in the shadows than risk discovery and ruin his surprise.

The house loomed ahead of him in the darkness. Its lights spilled onto the lawn. In the window to the study, the draperies weren't closed. Fools. He could see into the room as clear as day. Sterling noticed a figure at the desk. Ryeburn. At work as usual. The man had no right to his fortune if he didn't know how to enjoy it.

Narrowing his eyes, Sterling watched for a moment, then moved on. He wouldn't face Ryeburn yet. His plan was too perfect to spoil with impulse. Besides, Sterling wanted to relish Ryeburn's expression as he gained everything and Ryeburn lost it. Congratulating himself on his patience and wisdom, Sterling chuckled under his breath.

Careful to avoid the puddles of light, he swept to the side in a wide arc. Voices reached his ears. Servants, no doubt, but he increased his distance from the house. At the back of the manor, the garden and maze concealed him better than the darkness. Fewer lights shone here. The bushes and shrubs aided his progress, covering his every step and movement. He reached the orangery. The door swung open with nary a squeak, just as he had remembered from the night of the masquerade. He had chosen the perfect entry.

Sterling stepped inside. The room still retained the heat of the day. The plants and trees gave the air a fresh tang. He inhaled deeply. Wonderful. Exhilaration filled him. Soon his wealth would rival his father's and Ryeburn's combined.

From the hallway the sound of footsteps reached him. Darting behind a palm, he pressed himself against the wall. The footsteps passed. Sterling released the breath he didn't know he was holding.

His stomach growled again. Damn. He would have to take care of that problem right away.

Slipping back into the night, he moved further along the back of the house until he reached the kitchen. With luck the servants would be at their dinner. He peeked into the room. Empty.

His spirits rose. Destiny must be on his side. Despite the discomfort of hiding, despite the dirt he ate during the heat of the day, and despite the protests of his muscles, he had had little difficulty gaining entrance to the grounds of Concordia. His plan would work. Destiny would avenge the injustices he suffered and the trials of the past days. And he'd have a good meal to celebrate.

Roast beef sat on the sideboard. Taking a plate from the shelf, Sterling sliced off two thick slabs. He helped himself to a quail and an apricot tart. To this he added some ham and peas. The fish he left alone. Making room on the plate, he added a handful of strawberries, took a small jug filled with cream, and sneaked out of the kitchen. Finding a hidden bench, he settled upon it and feasted, finishing with the strawberries and cream.

An ale would suit me now, but alas, I have work. I'll have Eden bring me one later. He smirked. He was tempted to smash the plate on the stone bench, but the resulting sound might raise an alarm. Leaving the plate on the bench beside him, he circled back to the conservatory entrance. Inching the door open, he slid inside. Circling the pond in the center, he crossed with soundless steps to the hall.

Ryeburn was in his study, Sterling knew. He tapped his

jacket pocket. The pistol was ready. He just needed to find Eden.

Poking his head into the hall, Sterling saw no one. He slunk into the corridor. He eased down the hallway, listening for any sounds, ready to duck into the next room if necessary.

Where might she be at this hour? It was too early for bed, although he would enjoy finding her there. He was one who learned from his mistakes. He wouldn't wait to mount her this time and claim her as his.

He heard the tones of a pianoforte from the music room. How appropriate. With a crooked smile, he changed direction and returned down the hall. Peering into the room, he saw Eden picking out notes on the instrument. She was alone.

Chest puffed out, Sterling stepped into the room. "Good evening, Lady Ryeburn."

Eden gasped. Her hand dropped to the keys and sounded a discord. "Sterling."

Before she could move, Sterling drew out the pistol. "Do remain quiet, Lady Ryeburn. I shouldn't like to use this on you."

Nodding to show she would obey, Eden stared at the black barrel of the gun. Her heart hammered in her throat, and her legs wobbled beneath her. "What do you want?"

"Nothing that shouldn't have already been mine."

A shiver of revulsion slithered down her spine. "I don't understand."

"You will soon enough."

"Why are you here?"

"To right a wrong. Ryeburn must pay for his actions. You should have been my wife. It would have been much simpler if you had just married me when we had the opportunity. Now Ryeburn will have to die."

Fear threaded its icy fingers around her heart and squeezed. Eden couldn't breathe. Kill Trevor? She had to stop Sterling. Somehow.

He pulled a sheet of paper from his vest. "Take this." He handed it to Eden.

She turned the blank sheet over. "There's nothing on here."

He gave her a look of disgust. "I know that. Here." He handed her a portable writing set. "Write Ryeburn a note."

"What shall I say?" The longer she delayed, the more chance that someone might discover them.

" 'Meet me in the conservatory.' "

Placing the sheet on the pianoforte, Eden wrote out the words with a careful hand. When she finished, she looked up. "I should put a reason. He'll wonder why."

"If he's curious, he'll come." Sterling laughed. "Curiosity killed the cat, you know."

Cold gripped her stomach. Sterling was mad. Perhaps she could write a warning to Trevor—

Snatching the sheet from her, Sterling narrowed his eyes. "You think me mad, but I'm not. I'm desperate, which makes me nearly as dangerous. Don't forget that." He scanned the brief note. "Perfect. I knew you were too smart to try anything."

With one hand Sterling packed up the inkwell and quill. The gun remained pointed at her. Tucking the implements into his jacket pocket, he folded the note and handed it to her. "Ring for a servant and have him deliver this to Ryeburn. Don't let him come into the room, and don't try to warn him. I will shoot if I must, and either you or the servant will die. But so you know, I have the pistol aimed at you."

Sterling stepped behind the door and pointed at the bell pull with the barrel of the pistol.

Her heart raced in her chest. She tried to keep her breathing even, but failed. Pulling the rope, she wondered if she could somehow give a signal to the servant. A quick glance at Sterling squelched that idea. He watched her like a cat waiting for a mouse.

Finch entered the room. Almost too late Eden remembered she wasn't to let the man in. She stepped to him to prevent him from entering further. "Would you deliver this note to Lord Ryeburn, please?"

"As you wish, my lady." Finch bowed and took the note from her.

"Thank you, Finch." Her voice squeaked with fear.

Finch raised his eyebrows at the unusual sound, but said nothing. He left the room.

As soon as Finch disappeared, Sterling leapt out from behind the door. He grabbed her arm and shoved the pistol against her neck. "You almost erred, Lady Ryeburn. Your beautiful voice nearly betrayed you. Let's go."

Pulling her to the doorway, Sterling peeked out. Eden hoped someone lingered in the hall. It was empty. Sterling yanked her beside him. She let out a yelp.

"Quiet," he hissed as he dashed to the conservatory. He pulled her behind him. Eden stumbled, but Sterling never slowed.

The warm air of the room smelled like a garden after a rain, but Eden couldn't enjoy it. Taking her past the fountain, Sterling shoved her onto a bench and took a place opposite her. She faced the rear of the orangery, unable to see if anyone passed in the hall. The pistol remained targeted on her face.

Eden tried to reason with the man. "You can't be sure Trevor will come."

"He will. He can't ignore a lady's request without seeming rude."

"But you don't know how long he shall be." Her mind searched for some weakness in Sterling's plan.

"Lady Ryeburn . . ." He paused. His face took on a look of dissatisfaction. "That won't do at all. You won't be Lady Ryeburn much longer. I shall call you Eden. We shall be husband and wife soon."

"You will have to kill me first." Despite her fear, Eden lifted her chin a notch.

"No. I will kill Ryeburn first. Then I shall marry you."

"I won't marry you."

"Let's not start this again. You won't have the choice."

"You are despicable." Eden fought between rage and terror. She didn't know how long she could keep her wits about her.

Jumping to his feet, Sterling slapped her. "Hold your tongue, bitch. You don't know what it is like to lose everything you have worked for."

Eden cradled her cheek in her hand. "Neither do you. You've never worked for anything in your life."

"Do you know what that bastard Ryeburn has done to my reputation? It's in tatters. No one will take me in. How am I supposed to get money if no one will see me?"

Sterling paced in front of his seat. "Ryeburn even sent Bow Street runners after me. Can you imagine how my father reacted when they knocked on his door? He didn't tell them I was there, but that same night, he turned me out. My own family has disowned me. My father gave me money enough to leave the country and told me to settle modestly somewhere. *Modestly,* when he chooses between three country homes and a city palace. And why?" Sterling pointed the pistol in her face to emphasize his words. "Because I abducted you. As if you were such a significant creature. You're an American."

Eden watched Sterling's growing agitation in horror.

Spittle flew as he talked and flecked his lips. His face grew ruddier and he waved the pistol about.

"It's not too late, though. I realized that when I thought of my plan. You shall be a rich widow, no doubt, and there's still your father. Even if he won't support us, you have your voice. We shall have to move to America, I suppose. Barbaric country, but it can't be helped." Sterling stopped his rampage. He calmed himself in the next instant and sat on the bench. "I get ahead of myself."

Sterling smiled. The sight turned her stomach. He no longer waved the pistol. "I want you to sing."

"Sing?"

"Yes. I wish to hear your voice again. We shall pass the time with your singing. When we are wed, you shall have to learn to obey my commands without question." Sterling's smile held a warning.

Eden tried to breathe, but her throat burned. She couldn't sing for this man. He planned to kill Trevor. How could she sing as if nothing extraordinary . . . ?

Her mind whirled with an idea. Eden eyed the gun, which was still pointed at her. Strength flowed back into her limbs. Her plan could work. She prayed Trevor would remember. And that he would get here in time to hear her.

"You'll forgive me if my voice quivers a little. I'm not used to singing when I'm terrified."

Sterling laughed. "Your mouth is as fresh as ever. I shall enjoy taming you."

"Does your eye still hurt?"

Sterling popped up from his chair. The pistol shook. Eden faced it with a strange calm. If he shot early, Trevor would be safe, and the report would alert the household. *Pull the trigger,* she silently pleaded.

Rage mottled his face, but he sat again. "Yes. Taming you shall be a pleasure. Now sing."

Eden nodded. "You won't mind if I choose one of my favorites? I might sing better if I love the song."

Sterling waved his free hand. "By all means."

Eden drew a deep breath.

> A tree covered a lazy brook
> Its leaves were green and cool,
> And in the pool beneath the limb
> There swam a trout in its school.

CHAPTER TWENTY-SEVEN

"Thank you, Finch." Trevor took the note from the butler. He waited for Finch to leave before he opened it.

Meet me in the conservatory.

Trevor stared at the words for a second. They seemed to shout from the nearly empty page. The note had to be from Eden, but why was she so cryptic? If she needed to talk with him, she could have come to the study. He didn't have the time . . .

He stared at the figures on his desk. A few more minutes, and he would finish the accounts. He glanced at the note.

He pushed himself away from the desk.

Folding the note, he tucked it into his waistcoat. The edge of the paper crimped against the edge of the coin. *Numquam tuas spes dedisce.* Grinning, he left the room. He was about to follow his dreams rather than his head, and his heart soared at the idea.

Still, one thought disturbed him. Why would she need

to send him a note? She could have sent a servant to fetch him just as easily. Shaking his head, he walked down the corridor. He had ceased to try to explain Eden's actions long ago.

As he approached the conservatory, her singing floated into the hall. He smiled. Her voice was glorious. But a few steps later, he stopped.

> My love is like that trout
> Gasping for air in the water.
> Hoping your hook will pull him out
> Sooner not at all later.

The fish song. That atrocious song that even her voice couldn't make beautiful.

> Oh pull me out, dear one,
> Let my fish nourish you.
> For you alone I am meant
> Or I will drown in that cold brook.

Eden hated that song. Why would she sing it?

"Enough," barked a man's voice. "That song is terrible. Sing something worthy of your voice."

Who was with his wife? Trevor almost rushed in, but Eden's next words halted him.

"But I like this song," Eden argued.

She was lying. He knew she hated the song.

"One of my suitors wrote it for me. I have fond memories of him."

More lies.

"All the more reason not to sing it. I won't have you singing ditties from your former lovers."

Trevor froze. He recognized the voice. Sterling.

Damn the bastard. A wave of scorching fury washed over Trevor. He should have realized Sterling would seek revenge. Drawing a deep breath, Trevor strove to keep his emotions under control. He wouldn't let hatred blind him and risk Eden's safety with rash behavior.

"Sing something else."

"No. I want to sing—"

"You will do as I say," Sterling shouted at her.

Creeping to the door, Trevor peered inside. At the far end of the room, he spotted Sterling. And a pistol. Anger roiled within him.

"What is taking Ryeburn so long? I grow tired of waiting." Sterling looked up.

Trevor ducked back into the hall. What did Sterling want of him?

"I told you he might not come." Eden didn't sound frightened.

"He'll come. Sing another song. A better song."

Trevor chanced another look. Just as he poked his head in, Eden twisted to look at the door. Her eyes widened, and then she shook her head.

"Turn around," ordered Sterling. "I can't see the door if you're blocking my view."

Eden turned back.

"Now sing. And no more songs about fish. Don't forget my little friend." Sterling lifted the pistol higher.

"You won't hurt me. You'll never see my money if you shoot me. Besides, if you waste the bullet, how will you shoot Trevor?"

Trevor knew her words were meant for him. She was telling him she was safe for now and warning him that Sterling planned to kill him.

"You are too clever by half. However, if you sing for me now, I promise to be merciful when Ryeburn arrives."

Eden drew a breath audible in the hallway. Without another word she started singing a lovely, long folk song.

His mind seething with fury, Trevor tired to think of some way to save his wife. Sterling wanted to kill him, not Eden, so he didn't fear for her life, but leaving her with that snake took all his discipline. If he ran in now, they might both get hurt. He needed help. And he knew whom he needed to seek out.

Trevor dashed to the library and burst into the room. Corinna sat in Stuart's lap. She hurried to right herself, while Stuart glared at Trevor. "Did you never think to knock?"

"Hush, Stuart. 'Tis his house." Corinna straightened her dress as a blush rose to her cheeks.

Ignoring his mother-in-law, Trevor stood in front of Stuart. "I need your help."

Stuart rose, but said nothing.

Their gazes level, Trevor clenched his fists. "Damn it, man, I don't have the time to beg. Eden needs your help."

Stuart's expression changed immediately. "What about Eden?"

"The man who kidnapped her has returned. He has her trapped in the conservatory."

"Who kidnapped Eden?" Accusation filled Stuart's glare. His eyes grew even colder.

"I don't have time to explain."

"Later, Stuart, I promise," added Corinna.

Trevor shot Stuart an impatient look. The man's glare sent no fear through him. Trevor cared not a whit for what his father-in-law thought. His concern lay with Eden. "As we waste time with our arguments, Sterling is holding a pistol to your daughter's head."

"Oh, Stuart." Corinna voice broke.

"I believe she won't be harmed. He plans to use the

pistol on me. He wants to kill me and marry Eden for her money." Trevor never averted his gaze from Stuart's blue eyes. Eden's eyes.

"Does she love this Sterling?"

"Stuart!" Corinna snapped.

"No." Trevor didn't waver under Stuart's stare.

"If I thought she did, I'd just as soon kill you myself to see her happy."

"I know." Trevor waited for the man's response.

Corinna pulled her husband around to face her. "Eden is in trouble. Our daughter needs you. Her husband needs your help. If your stubbornness kills her, I'll never forgive you."

Trevor turned to Corinna. "Nothing will happen to Eden." It couldn't. He grabbed Stuart's shoulders. "Will you help me?"

"What do you need me to do?"

"The conservatory has a door to the garden. Sterling expects me to enter from the house—which is exactly what I shall do."

Trevor stood outside the entrance to the conservatory once again. Eden had almost finished the folk song. He drew a deep breath and stepped into the room. "You wished to see me?"

Eden gasped. Her hands covered her mouth in horror. Her song stopped in an abrupt death.

Sterling jumped to his feet. "Yes, join us, won't you?" He cackled at his own joke. He grabbed Eden's arm and pulled her to him. He pressed the pistol against her temple.

Eden stiffened, but gave no other sign of discomfort.

Trevor paused for an instant, then continued into the room. He steeled himself against the sight of the gun touching the skin of the woman he loved, thanking his years of rigid behavior for his success at hiding his rage. "Ah, Sterling. I was wondering when you would show yourself again."

Trevor crossed to a refectory table against one wall. A salver with several decanters and glasses sat on the table. "Brandy, Sterling?"

"No."

"As you wish." Trevor poured himself a drink and took a swallow. He continued toward them, passing beside the pond, and then sat on a bench that faced the rear of the conservatory. He had to keep Sterling's focus toward the entrance to the house, not the garden. "How can I help you?"

"Are you blind, man? I have your wife." Sterling pushed Eden forward. Eden winced as her arm wrenched backward in his grip.

"Yes, I see that you do." He took another sip of the brandy, hoping to hide the fury that swelled through him. He would kill Sterling for hurting Eden like that.

Sterling noticed Trevor's eye and laughed. "Who did that to you? I'd like to congratulate the man."

"At least I can claim it was given to me by a man. How are your eyes, Sterling?"

Sterling curled his lip into a snarl. "I shan't miss your clever mouth, Ryeburn. I'm sure many will thank me for ridding them of your caustic wit."

Eden stared at Trevor. What was he doing? Didn't he know Sterling wanted to kill him? Why was he baiting the man? He should have stayed away. Sterling wouldn't hurt her. How could he sit calmly and drink brandy?

"Are you sure you won't have any?" Trevor lifted his glass to Sterling. "It's quite smooth."

"No, damn you." Sterling flung Eden to the ground. She

saw Trevor tense, but he didn't move. He had something planned. She didn't know what it could be, but she saw now that he was quite aware of the danger.

Rising from the ground, Eden moved to one side. If she could slip out . . .

"Don't take another step, Eden."

She froze.

"Sit down." Sterling pushed her.

She landed on the bench. The cold stone knocked the breath out of her for an instant.

Turning to Trevor, Sterling sneered. "Do you know why I am here?"

"I imagine it's to take your revenge against me." Trevor took another sip. He never raised his voice and, in fact, sounded bored. Eden marveled at his control. "In your misguided little mind, you believe me to be the root cause of all your problems. It has never occurred to you that you brought your own ruin upon yourself."

"You arrogant cur. You won't accept your part in the shredding of my reputation?" Sterling shoved the gun into Trevor's face.

Eden let out a scream. Sterling turned to her and gazed at her as if he had forgotten she was still there. He grabbed her and drew her forward. "Perhaps your arrogance would slip a notch if I enjoyed your wife while you watched."

Trevor raised his eyebrows. "Really. It isn't as if you haven't enjoyed her before."

Eden's gaze flew to his face. Trevor knew that was a lie. She searched the darkness of his eyes, but couldn't find a glimmer of compassion in them.

Sterling's mouth dropped open. "I never . . ." He stopped and stared at Trevor. A chortle blasted from his mouth. "You believed her soiled goods, yet you married her? Why? No wait, don't answer. You did it to save her reputation and yours. Oh, ho. This is rich. Either you haven't consummated your marriage or you've discovered she wasn't as innocent as you hoped."

Sterling laughed until tears rolled down his cheeks. "I believe I will take that brandy after all. Your whore can fetch it."

Eden saw Trevor's knuckles turn white as he clenched the glass but his face betrayed no emotion. She hurried to the table and poured a brandy. She didn't want Trevor to lose more of his restraint.

Sterling leaned into Trevor's face. "I did have her, you know. She squirmed so sweetly. I'll take her again, as soon as I rid myself of you."

Bile rose in her throat at the thought of Sterling touching her. She returned with the brandy and passed him the glass. Sterling grabbed her hand and licked the back of it. She snatched her hand away and wiped it on her skirt.

"She *is* my countess, Sterling. I shall have to ask you not to speak of her in such a manner." Only the hard lines around his lips revealed his fury.

"Ever the proper earl, aren't you, Ryeburn? You can't abide your wife, but you'll stand up for her because she is your countess. I shall enjoy stripping you of your dignity piece by piece."

From the corner of her eye, Eden saw a movement from the back of the conservatory. She shot a glance to the spot. Her father stood with his finger to his lips. Stuart took another step toward the men.

Eden looked at Sterling. He faced away from her father.

"And I shall start by cuckolding you to your face." Sterling threw his glass at the wall. He sneered at Eden. "Come here, harlot."

"Don't speak to my daughter that way." Stuart stepped up behind Sterling.

As Sterling's shocked gaze darted to the second man, Trevor lunged from his chair. He seized Sterling around the middle and shoved him to the side. With a deafening explosion, the pistol released its shot as Sterling fell to the ground. Trevor fell on top of him, pounding the man's face and gut with punches filled with all the fury, rage, and fear Trevor had pent up for the past endless minutes.

Sterling managed to toss Trevor off and scramble to his feet, but he had taken only two steps before Trevor jumped him from behind. Sterling crashed face first into the fish pond. He came up sputtering.

With no care for his boots, Trevor waded into the pond and pulled Sterling upright. "Come, man. Let's see the lesson you would teach me." Trevor dodged a blow, then landed his fist on Sterling's nose.

Sterling covered his nose with his hands. Blood squirted from between his fingers.

"If my fish die from your blood, I'll see you hanged. I might just see you hanged for the fun of it." Trevor hoisted Sterling none too gently over the rim of the pond and threw him to the ground.

Stuart stepped up to him. "Nicely done, Early. Here's the rope you asked me to bring. May I assist you in tying up the worm?"

"I would be delighted."

"You fight very well. I think I'm glad you decided not to strike me back after our initial meeting."

Trevor touched his eye. It still hurt. "I think I could learn a thing or two from you, sir."

Stuart brought both of Sterling's hands together behind the man's back and secured them. "Would you like to finish?"

"No, you may have the honor. I wish to see my wife."

Trevor turned back to Eden, who sat on a bench with her hands clenched around her middle. He hurried to her.

"I'm sorry you had to see that."

"You're safe." Her voice wavered, and her smile waned. Tears slipped from her eyes.

"Thanks to you. Very clever of you to sing the trout song." Trevor wiped a tear from her cheek. Her skin felt cold to his touch. "You're cold. Let me get you a brandy."

"No," she whispered. "Hold me."

Trevor wrapped his arms around her. She trembled in his embrace. "We need to get you warm."

"Don't let me go." She drew in a ragged breath. "I think I'm hurt, Trevor."

Trevor pulled back to look at her. "It's the shock. You were very brave and now the terror of the events has you in its grip."

She shook her head and closed her eyes. "No. The gun . . ."

Eden's hands fell from her stomach.

Trevor's gaze followed her hands. Red covered her palms. He glanced up in horror. A red spot stained the ivory material of her gown and grew larger even as he watched.

"Dear God, no."

CHAPTER TWENTY-EIGHT

"Eden." Trevor stared into the pale face. "Eden!"

The sound of the report brought most of the household to the conservatory. The footmen rushed in to help with Sterling, while the maids gathered in the doorway. A low buzz of voices hummed through the room.

Trevor didn't notice the commotion. He lifted Eden in his arms. She groaned.

"Finch," he shouted. "Finch!"

Finch appeared at his elbow. The butler saw the mistress in the master's arms. "Oh, sir."

"Fetch the surgeon, Finch. Hurry."

Stuart lifted his gaze from Sterling and jumped to his feet. "Eden."

Trevor carried her past Sterling, who gazed up from his bonds in panic. "I didn't shoot her! I wouldn't hurt her. You can't blame me for this."

Trevor ignored the man as he swept by him.

"I won't hang for her death, Ryeburn. I didn't mean to shoot her!" Sterling yelled after him.

Stuart knelt beside Sterling. The prisoner squirmed as he saw vengeance in the man's eyes. Stuart's hand shot out and grabbed Sterling's throat.

"You'd better pray she doesn't die, worm, or I will kill you myself." Stuart released the man's throat.

Sterling coughed and sputtered. A clear red handprint remained on his neck.

"Get the authorities. Lock this creature somewhere far away, before I tear his heart out." Stuart dashed after Trevor.

Corinna stood in the entrance to the conservatory. As Trevor approached her, her hand covered her mouth. "Eden. My baby," she whispered.

"Give her to me, man." Stuart blocked Trevor's path.

"Get out of my way." Trevor stepped to the side.

"She's my daughter." Stuart stopped him again.

Trevor's gaze narrowed. "She's *my* wife." He stepped around Stuart and started for the stairs.

Corinna put her hand on Stuart's chest. "Continue your argument later. Let him get her to a bed." She picked up her skirts and ran after Trevor.

Hurrying as best he could without jarring her, Trevor cradled her next to his heart. *Don't die. You can't die.*

Trevor kicked open the door to his room. He did the same to the door to the bedchamber. He placed Eden on his bed and took her hand. Her eyes didn't open, and she didn't make a sound. She was so pale, her hand so cold. The red was so bright against her, the spot so big.

His chest constricted as if a stone pressed the life out of him. With trembling fingers, he unfastened the sash around her chest. He couldn't reach the buttons in the back without moving her, so he grabbed the material in each fist and rent the dress down the front. The stain on her chemise was larger than the one on her dress.

Despair clenched at his soul. Helplessness washed over him like the waves of a storm. He could do no more than watch the life slip from the woman he loved. He could feel no more than his own life slipping into a deep crevice of his heart, never to see the light again.

Letting out a scream of anguish, he wadded up the sheet from his bed and pressed it into her wound, hoping to stop the flow of blood.

Corinna stole up next to him. "Dear God." She stroked Eden's forehead and lifted Eden's hand in her own. "Eden, can you hear me?" Her voice broke with the onslaught of tears.

Eden didn't stir.

Trevor's knuckles turned white as he held the sheet. The door opened again. His gaze flew to the entrance. Mrs. Byrd came in. Dismay pierced his heart. Where was the damn surgeon?

Mrs. Byrd carried a bowl and several cloths. "We'll need to remove her chemise."

Trevor didn't hesitate. The material of the chemise split with an easy tear. The hole in his wife's side looked obscene against the perfection of her skin. Mrs. Byrd dipped a cloth in water and wiped the blood from her skin. "Go now, sir. 'Tis unseemly you should be here."

"I am her husband."

"Yes, sir." Mrs. Byrd didn't lift her gaze from Eden's side.

Corinna touched him on the arm. "Trevor, please. Stuart is alone."

"Then go to him, madam, for I will not leave my wife." Trevor bent over the bed and brushed Eden's hair from her face.

Mrs. Byrd laid a cloth over the wound and pulled a blanket over Eden. "I cannot do more."

The door opened again. Through the portal, Trevor caught a glimpse of Stuart. The man seemed to have aged in the past hour, but Stuart disappeared from his view in the next instant. The surgeon strode in and pulled the door shut. He hurried to the bed and dropped his black bag to the floor.

Pulling back the covers, the man asked, "What happened?"

"She's been shot." Trevor couldn't prevent the rush of irritation he felt at the man as the surgeon gazed upon Eden.

The man pointed to Mrs. Byrd. "I'll need clean water and plenty of it. Some towels and clean sheets ripped into bandages. Start a fire in here. This room needs to be warm."

Mrs. Byrd rushed out of the room.

The surgeon bent over his patient and uncovered the wound. "Everyone must leave."

"No." Trevor remained by the bed.

"I cannot help her with you hovering and blocking my light. Get out. If I need help, I'll call." The man probed the skin at Eden's side.

"Come, Trevor." Corinna led him away, and this time he made no protest. He had heard the anxiety in the surgeon's voice.

In the outer chamber, Stuart paced the floor until he saw his wife. He stopped. "Eden?"

Corinna shook her head. "We don't know yet." She closed the door behind them.

Trevor stared at the wood keeping him from his wife. The door seemed impenetrable, closing out all warmth.

Finch crossed to him. "Begging your pardon, sir, but I

have a clean shirt and trousers waiting for you in the next room. Why don't you clean up a little? You wouldn't want to frighten the mistress with your appearance when she awakens."

For the first time, Trevor looked down at himself. He lifted his hands in front of him. Eden's blood covered his fingers and wrists. Red striped his waistcoat and shirt. Trevor closed his eyes. *Eden. Oh, God. Eden.*

"This way, sir." Finch opened the door for him.

As if in a trance, Trevor followed the butler to the next room. Eden's room. A basin of water waited for him. His fingers didn't feel the buttons of his waistcoat or shirt as he unfastened them. He dropped them to the floor. As Finch picked up the soiled articles, something fell from the pocket with a clink. Finch retrieved the coin and placed it beside the basin.

Trevor washed himself as if he were an automaton. He knew the water was warm, yet he didn't feel its heat. The soap slipped from his fingers time and again. He scrubbed his skin with a brush until he knew it was raw, yet he felt no pain. The water turned pink in the basin.

His gaze fell upon the coin. He reached for it. Why had he expected Venus to be weeping? On the reverse, that damn swan swam in its tarnished pond. The words echoed in his mind. *Numquam tuas spes dedisce.*

His dreams were dying in the next room.

With a shout of anger, Trevor hurled the coin across the room. It hit a vase upon the mantle. The resounding clang deafened him. The coin was no harbinger of good fortune. It had cursed him since the day he found it.

Turning his back upon the talisman, he dressed himself and returned to his own room to wait.

* * *

As the surgeon came out, he wiped his hands on a towel. Trevor rose, but said nothing.

Corinna groped in the air for Stuart's hand, but she didn't find her husband. Neither Stuart nor Corinna turned their gaze from the surgeon.

"I have done all I can." The surgeon faced Trevor. "The bullet entered near the bottom of her ribs. As far as I can tell, it bounced off the bone and exited without damaging her lung or stomach. I have cleaned the wound and stitched it as best I can."

"Does this mean she will live?" Corinna's voice was hardly above a whisper.

"It's too soon to tell. She lost a lot of blood, and her pulse is weak. She's in shock. Keep her warm. She could recover from the loss of blood, but frankly I'm worried about infection. Try to keep the wound clean. I cannot say more."

"Is there nothing else we can do?" Corinna's voice grew even quieter.

"Wait. And pray." The surgeon raised his hand to Trevor's shoulder and left it there for a moment. With a nod that conveyed his sympathy, the surgeon left the room.

Trevor sank into his chair. His head dropped into his hands. No thoughts entered his mind. A numbness enveloped him like a cloud, obscuring him from everything—feelings, sound, sight.

He didn't know how long he sat there, head in hands. At some point he was aware of Corinna rising to check on Eden, only to return to the room shaking her head. Mrs. Byrd came in with food, which congealed on the table beside him.

Toward dawn the room grew lighter, but Trevor remained in the chair. He didn't know what he waited for. The two times he had checked on Eden had given him no hope for her recovery, yet waiting for the alternative was unthinkable. His mother-in-law had moved her vigil to Eden's side. His father-in-law stayed in the outer chamber with him. They exchanged no words. Trevor saw the accusation in Stuart's eyes, yet he made no move to defend himself, for the man was right. He had failed his wife. If she died, it was his own fault.

The door to the hall creaked open. Lorane poked her head in, her red hair still tousled with sleep. "Trevor?" She ran to her brother.

Trevor gazed down at the child. Tears shimmered in her green eyes.

"Is it true? Miss Dunfield told me Eden was shot. Is it true?"

Trevor swallowed hard. He nodded.

Lorane burst into tears. She flung her arms around his neck and sobbed with the abandoned, uncontrolled grief of a child. For the first time, he realized that others were hurting as much as he. His arms reached up to hug his sister.

"Shh, little one." His voice came out gravely from the night of silent tension.

"She can't die. I love her." Lorane looked at him for his reassurance.

"And she loves you. You can always be sure of that." He remembered Eden's fury at his treatment of Lorane. Eden had broken down the wall between his sister and himself. She had broken down the wall between his heart and himself as well.

"Would you like to see her?" Trevor wasn't sure if he

should allow Lorane in to visit Eden, but he could think of nothing else to offer the child.

Lorane nodded. Trevor took her hand and led her to the bed.

Eden had not stirred since he had laid her on the mattress. Her breathing was even, but she still lacked color in her cheeks.

His mother-in-law lifted her head from the bed. Red rimmed her eyes, but she made no protest as they approached.

"She looks like she's sleeping," Lorane whispered.

"I know." Trevor looked at the woman he loved. The pain washed over him anew, and this time he didn't try to prevent the tears in his eyes. He knelt beside the bed.

Two small hands cradled his cheeks. Lorane turned his face to hers. "You can cry, Trevor. I always feel better if I cry."

Trevor hugged his sister to him as the tears rolled down his cheeks. "Thank you, Lorane. I needed someone to tell me that."

Corinna held her hand out to Lorane. "Come with me, Lorane. I think Trevor needs some time alone with Eden."

Lorane slipped her hand into Corinna's. "You're her mother."

"Yes, and I love her very much."

"She's very lucky." The pair left the room as Trevor marveled at Lorane's statement.

Eden lucky? He examined her face. The pale cheeks gave no hint to the life within. But Lorane was right. She knew the love of her family, the admiration of strangers, and the freedom of spirit. And with luck, she would know the love of one man. If she recovered, he would spend the rest of his life showing her how he loved her.

As he stood, he backed into Stuart. Trevor faced the man. An ominous expression covered Stuart's face.

"I'm taking her home."

"She is home."

"It's clear you don't deserve her, and you've proven you can't take care of her. She's coming home with us."

Trevor straightened to his full height. "You can't take her."

Stuart poked him in the chest with one finger. "Watch me."

"You'll have to kill me first."

"Don't tempt me, Early."

"She is my wife."

"That doesn't matter. Marriages have been dissolved before."

"Not in my family."

"Your reputation means so much to you that you'd ruin her life?" Stuart narrowed his eyes.

Trevor's hands balled into fists. "My reputation be damned. She is my wife, and she will remain my wife."

"She is my daughter, and I will do what I think is best for her."

"Her welfare is no longer your concern."

"It is when you are incompetent."

"If you try to take her from me, you will regret it." Trevor spoke through clenched teeth.

"Are you threatening me?"

"Most definitely."

"I'd like to see you try to stop me."

Before Trevor could respond, a faint rustling reached his ears. He whirled toward the bed. Eden's blue eyes fluttered open. A grimace twisted her lips as she tried to scowl.

"Will you two please stop arguing? I am trying to sleep."

CHAPTER TWENTY-NINE

Trevor stared at her for a moment, then dropped to his knees beside the bed. "Eden? Can you hear me?"

"Of course I can hear you. You're loud enough to wake the dead. Now may I please go to sleep?"

Trevor threw his head back and let out a whoop. He grabbed Eden's hand. "Do you remember what happened?"

"Yes. Sterling shot me." Eden's eyes opened fully. She gave up the battle to return to sleep. "Good morning, Daddy."

"Good morning, Angel." Stuart bent to kiss her forehead.

Eden looked up at her father in surprise. "Daddy, you're crying."

"Yes, I am. You had us worried." The false irritation in his voice erased the tears. "How else would you expect me to react?"

"I love you, too, Daddy." Eden tried to sit up, but fell back. The ache in her side stole her breath. Her face grew cold as color drained from it.

At once Trevor caught her and eased her onto the pillows. "Don't move yet. Your wounds might open."

"I didn't realize it would hurt so much. I won't try that again for a while. Trust me."

"And when you're better, we'll take you home." Her father smiled down at her.

"Home?" Eden repeated without understanding.

"To Fairlawne. Where we can take care of you."

"Is Trevor coming?"

Stuart glared at Trevor. "He's staying here."

"I understand." Eden drew a deep breath. The pain in her side didn't hurt nearly as much as the pain in her soul. Before she could say anything else, her mother entered the room.

"Eden." Corinna ran to the bed and cupped Eden's face in her hands. "How are you feeling?"

"Terrible." Tears flowed from her eyes in hot rivulets into her hair.

Corinna stood from the bed. She wagged her finger at the men. "Both of you, get out."

Trevor rose to his feet and faced his mother-in-law. "Madam, I—"

"Out." Corinna pointed to the door.

Stuart crossed his arms. "Corinna—"

"You, too, Stuart. I won't have you in here when Eden needs quiet. Go."

"I know better than to argue with you." Stuart kissed Eden and left.

Corinna's foot tapped the ground as she gazed at Trevor. "What are you waiting for?"

"I haven't learned yet *not* to argue with you." Trevor

smiled at Corinna. "I intend to stay with my wife. We have much to discuss."

"Indeed?" Corinna turned to the bed. "Do you wish him to stay?"

"No," whispered Eden.

Triumph in her visage, Corinna faced Trevor again.

Trevor spoke before Corinna could. "I haven't learned yet to give in to her either." He walked around his mother-in-law and pulled a chair up to the bed. He took Eden's hand. "Are you in much pain?"

His hand warmed her more than the blankets. How could he cause such a reaction in her when she knew he didn't want her to stay with him? She squinted up at him. "I think I feel worse than you look." With a careful motion, she reached up and touched his eye.

"It doesn't hurt anymore." He turned his head and touched his lips to her palm.

She dropped her hand to the bed. "Is Sterling . . . ?"

"The justice of the peace is holding him until a Bow Street runner can fetch him back to London. The villagers are quite incensed that he dared harm you." Trevor paused and stroked the back of her hand. "Your visit with the children won them over. They've grown fond of you."

Eden didn't know how to respond. Why did it matter if an entire town admired her when the one man whose love she wanted didn't care for her? How did one ask one's husband to grow fond of his wife? "I'm sure they'll recover fast enough when I'm gone."

Corinna frowned. "Where are you going? You're not strong enough to go anywhere, and I won't hear of you not recovering."

"Daddy explained to me that you're taking me home when I'm well."

"He did what?" Corinna shouted.

"It's for the best, Mother."

Trevor released her hand and gazed into her eyes. "Is that what you want?"

She swallowed the bitter lump of anguish in her throat. Thinking back to the attention she had garnered from the *ton,* she sighed. After only a few weeks in London, the *ton* knew of her and her escapades. He didn't need a wife who couldn't behave with decorum. "Yes," she whispered.

Trevor stood and paced the room.

"You can't mean it!" Corinna exclaimed. "Your father doesn't have the right to take you from your husband."

Eden's eyes filled with tears. The image of her mother blurred. "You don't understand. I'm sure it's not too late to have the marriage annulled, and then Trevor can find himself a proper wife."

Stopping in mid-stride, Trevor turned back to the bed. "On what grounds? The marriage has been consummated."

Eden shook her head. "Nobody need know."

"And if there is a babe?"

Closing her eyes, Eden felt tears slip through her lids, burning their trails down her cheek. "I'll be gone long before anyone would notice I am with child."

"You would raise my child without a father?"

She could feel the heat of his gaze. "Don't yell at me. It's not something we need to worry about yet in any case."

"Have you considered what your reputation would be if you returned to America *enceinte?*"

"My reputation again." Anger combined with the pain in her heart, giving her words strength. "I don't give a fig for my reputation."

"Perhaps, but how will your indifference affect our child? He will inherit your reputation." The cold fury in Trevor's voice sent shivers down her spine.

Eden understood Trevor's hostility. The little she had heard about his father was appalling, and she knew Trevor had struggled hard to overcome his father's unwanted legacy. But that didn't lessen her wrath at him. "If I carry your child, I'll happily love him and try not to teach him to hate the father who didn't care for his mother."

"Don't tell me whom I do or do not care for, damn it. I happen to love you," Trevor shouted.

"Well, that's fine, because I love you also," she shouted back.

Laughter burst from Corinna's lips. When she had regained her control, she crossed to the door and opened it. "I think I'll leave you two alone." She slipped from the room.

Eden stared at Trevor. "You love me?" She gazed into his dark eyes—eyes that now welcomed her—and saw the tears form in them.

Trevor sat on the edge of the bed beside her, careful not to rock the mattress too much. "You mustn't leave me." He lifted her hand to his lips. "You mustn't ever leave me."

"Never," she whispered. In awe, she wiped away the tear that escaped his eye. "You really love me?"

"I love you." Trevor kissed her forehead. "I love your frightening blue eyes"—he kissed her lids—"the curve of your mouth"—he kissed her lips—"the voice that comes from your throat." He kissed her neck, then looked up with a wicked smile. "The rest I'll have to show you later, when you've recovered."

Eden caught her breath, which had grown ragged with desire.

"But more than all that, I love *you,* this part of you deep inside." Trevor placed his forefinger over her heart. "I need you. You have shaken me out of my boring existence and brought me back to life."

"I have?" She choked the words past the lump in her throat. "I thought I was a hoyden."

"You are." Trevor gave her that wicked smile that stole her breath again. "And if you ever stop racing horses, or wading barefooted in the stream with the village children, or beating the duke at whist, I shall never forgive you."

"But what of your reputation?"

"What of it? I deluded myself into thinking I was an honorable man. What sort of honorable man would let his sister never know the warmth of a family? What sort of honorable man would let the dictates of society rule him? What sort of honorable man would let the woman he loved leave him?"

"Oh, Trevor" The hot lump rose, and tears spilled from her eyes. "I swear I don't usually cry this much." She lifted her arms to embrace him, then grimaced and dropped her arms. "It hurts too much to touch you."

"We'll have the time when you are well." Trevor ran his hand down her cheek, wiping the tears away with his caress. "But recover quickly. Seeing you in my bed and knowing I cannot lie with you causes an ache of my own."

"I know."

Trevor sat back and gave her a curious look.

"I feel that same ache." Heat rushed into her cheeks at her admission.

He smiled, but a puzzled look soon covered his face. "Would you have really raised my child alone?"

She nodded. "I loved you long before today. If I had to leave you, I would want your child."

"You really are remarkable."

"We've never talked about children . . ."

"And now isn't the time."

A shiver of uncertainty passed through her. "Don't you want children?"

Trevor let out a low moan. "Yes, but if we talk about it much longer, I won't be able to face your parents." He leaned closer and whispered in her ear. "Until we can do something about it, I prefer to keep my thoughts away from your bed."

Trevor slipped from the room half an hour later. Eden slept once again, a true sleep. His relief overwhelmed him. He had watched her as she slept. Her even breathing sounded like music to him. As he shut the door behind him, a smile played at his lips.

Corinna and a glowering Stuart waited in the outer room.

Grinning at his father-in-law, Trevor said, "She's staying."

"I heard, Early." With a cold gaze, Stuart glared at him. "My daughter nearly died last night. Why should I think you can take care of her?"

"Because I love her." No trace of embarrassment accompanied his admission. He crossed to his father-in-law and stopped in front of the man. "I love her more than my own life, and if I am any judge of character, I'd wager you know exactly how I feel."

Stuart's gaze slipped to his wife. For an instant his features softened, but when he faced Trevor again, the hardness had returned. "What of Eden? Does she love you?"

"That's what she claims." Elation surged anew in him at that thought.

"She might be delirious." Stuart stroked his chin.

"Stuart, leave Trevor alone," scolded Corinna. "Your daughter loves him, and he loves her."

"She's too young to know what she wants."

Trevor's eyes narrowed. He grew tired of sparring with the man. "With all due respect, sir, you won't win this argument. If by some outrageous turn of fortune, you succeed in taking her to Massachusetts, I will follow you and bring her home. She belongs at my side. I almost lost her, and I guarantee I will never come close to losing her again."

For the first time, the coldness left Stuart's eyes. A half smile spread over his lips. "Glad to hear it, Early. I know all too well what it feels like to believe you've lost the woman you love." He shot a glance at Corinna. "I'll have to tell you about it someday."

The sudden change in Stuart perplexed Trevor.

"Don't look so puzzled, Early. I still don't like you, but Eden has made her choice. I expect I'll have to live with it, if I want her or her mother to speak to me again."

Corinna beamed at her husband. "I always knew you were intelligent." She slipped her arm into Stuart's. "Take me to our room, Stuart. Now that I know Eden is better, I need some sleep."

Trevor raised a hand. "I do have one request, Mr. Grant."

The frown returned to Stuart's face. "What is it?"

"Would you cease calling me by that ridiculous name? You may call me Ryeburn, or Trevor, if you wish, but I can't abide 'Early'."

Stuart furrowed his brow as if contemplating the request. Then he nodded. "I can understand your feelings about that, but I'm afraid I can't see myself doing that any time soon, Early."

Trevor joined in the laughter.

CHAPTER THIRTY

Trevor sat in the study, trying in vain to finish some work. Eden had rested peacefully through the night, unlike himself. The image of Sterling holding the gun wouldn't leave his mind. The echo of the shot repeated itself in his ears.

He was glad Sterling was locked away, for Trevor would surely kill the man if he saw him.

Each time Trevor thought of how Sterling had nearly cost him Eden, a cold shudder shook him. He had three cups of coffee in an attempt to warm himself, but the beverage gave only temporary relief.

But when he saw Eden, the warmth returned to his soul. Eden would recover. The color in her cheeks bloomed this morning, and her eyes glowed with love for him. It had taken all his strength to leave her side, but he knew her parents wanted to spend some time with her.

Finch appeared in the doorway. "Forgive me, sir."

Trevor was grateful for the interruption. "What is it, Finch?"

"You have visitors."

"Visitors? Send them away. I don't want guests at this time."

"I tried, sir."

That response surprised Trevor. He knew Finch to be a model of efficiency. Who could have defeated Finch?

"Who are they?"

"Lord Toddington, Mrs. Roberts, and Miss Baylor."

Trevor nodded and rose from his desk. "I'll see to them. Where did you put them?"

"In the drawing room, my lord." Finch bowed and exited.

When Trevor saw the visitors, he understood Finch's retreat. Lily paced the room, worrying a handkerchief in her hands. When she looked up at him, the concern that covered her features would have weakened the hardest man. He bowed to Lily and Mrs. Roberts. Toddington hovered behind them.

"Good afternoon, ladies."

Lily rushed to him. She grabbed his arm. "How is Eden? No one would tell me anything. We came as soon as we heard—"

"Eden is recovering." Trevor tried to reassure the girl, but found it difficult when his own efforts to comfort himself had failed.

"The papers say Sterling shot her," said Toddington.

"He did."

Trevor didn't miss the narrowing of Toddington's eyes. He knew the man blamed himself for letting Sterling get close to the ladies. Just as Trevor blamed himself.

"I can't believe someone would hurt Eden," Lily said with a tremor in her voice.

"Try not to worry, Miss Baylor. Sterling is in custody, and Eden is growing stronger by the hour."

Mrs. Roberts touched a handkerchief to her eyes. "This is excellent news."

"May I see her?" asked Lily.

"I think she would like that." Trevor rang for Mrs. Byrd. When the housekeeper appeared, Trevor said, "Please take the ladies to see Eden. Toddington, I would like a word with you."

Toddington looked surprised, but nodded.

As soon as Lily and Mrs. Roberts had left, Trevor faced Toddington. "Do you love her?"

Toddington blinked rapidly. "I say, Ryeburn, what sort of—"

"Do you love Miss Baylor?"

Opening and closing his mouth a few times, Toddington finally stammered, "Y-yes, I do."

"Marry her, Toddington, and thank providence every day that you have found someone to love. Don't wait until it is too late. I almost did, and I would have regretted it with all my soul for the rest of my days."

"But what of the *ton?* What will they say?"

"To hell with what they say."

Toddington looked stunned. "But she's an American with no family to speak of."

"Does that matter?"

"I don't know. The *ton*—"

"Would you rather spend your life with some female who suits the *ton*'s needs or yours?"

Toddington paused. "By God, Ryeburn, I never thought of it in that way."

Trevor smiled. "We can be the two most unconventional men in Parliament—the two who love their wives, not their mistresses."

"I'll do it." Toddington grinned.

"Good man." Trevor clapped his friend on the back. "If I'm to be unconventional, I'm glad I have a friend to share in the experience."

In a matter of days, Eden was fit enough to sit up and move about, although her gait had a stiffness to it. Eden rejoiced at the news of Lily's engagement, which had surprised everyone except Trevor. Eden suspected he knew more about the announcement than he revealed. Visits from Lorane and her parents made her confinement easier, but she waited each day for Trevor's appearance in the room. When he was with her, her aches disappeared, and she felt able to fly. The giddiness he caused made it seem so.

She moved back into her room—until she was recovered enough to spend the nights with him. The surgeon came, checked her wounds, and reported them well healed. Trevor's relief brought a smile to her face. She had known all along that she was fine.

Two weeks later, she was ready to join the family at dinner. Over the protests of her mother, father, and husband, she dressed in her favorite green gown. In front of the mirror, she brushed her hair until it shone, and pulled it back with a ribbon.

A glint reflected off the mirror into Eden's eyes. Eden turned her head. Furrowing her brow, she crossed to the mantle and squatted down to search for the source. There. Lodged between the andiron and the wall, where the maid couldn't sweep it out, rested a coin. She pulled it from the fireplace.

The coin had a fine coating of ashes. Eden blew on the coin, then gasped. The image of Venus, a little soot-covered, stared back at her. She flipped the coin in her hand. On the reverse of the coin, the swan glided in its tarnished pond as the words *numquam tuas spes dedisce* circled around the bird.

Eden picked up a cloth and rubbed the coin. Soot soiled the cloth, but each wipe revealed more of the coin. Eden sat on the edge of the bed.

How was this possible?

She turned the coin over in her hand, again and again. This was her coin, she knew it, but how had it gotten here?

Trevor appeared in the doorway. "I've come to escort you to dinner."

Eden said nothing, never lifting her gaze from her hand.

Trevor rushed to her. "Eden, are you ill? I knew it was too soon for you to be up. Lie back." He placed his arms around her to lay her back on the mattress.

Shaking her head, Eden pushed his arms away. "No, I'm fine."

"You're sure?"

"Trevor, I'm fine." She held out the coin. "Do you know what this is?"

Taking the token from her hand, Trevor glanced at it and smiled. "Yes. It's my good-luck charm. I threw it across the room the night you were shot. I guess it did bring me luck after all." He kissed her forehead.

"How long have you had it?"

"Not long. I found it lying on the street in London."

Eden took the token from him. "When?"

Trevor grew pensive. "Several weeks back. Ah, yes, I remember now. It was the night I first met you."

"And you found it in front of the theater."

"Yes." Trevor wrinkled his brow. "How did you know?"

"Because I lost it."

"What?"

"My mother gave me this coin before I started on my journey."

"Impossible."

"I know. Mother said it was a good-luck charm. She also mentioned something about losing it and Daddy finding it." Her eyes grew wide as she stared at the silver circle. "Just as I lost it and you found it."

Trevor was now staring at the coin with the same intensity as she. "The night your parents arrived, your mother came to the study. I thought it was to see what sort of man you had married. But rather than throw blame at me, she asked me if I had found anything. When she saw the coin, she didn't seem at all surprised."

"You've shown this to Mother?"

"Yes. She asked me about my dreams, but somehow I don't think she really wanted to know. It was as if she already knew."

Eden shook her head. "She never mentioned it." She stood and grabbed his hand. "Come on. Let's go ask her about it."

Pulling him behind her, Eden led him from her room. She heard him chuckle, but she paid him no heed. She wanted to know about the coin. With a giant stride, he reached her side and took her arm.

"At least let me walk beside you."

She laughed at herself. "Only if you don't slow me down."

Her mother wasn't in the drawing room yet, but her father sat in the armchair by the fireplace. He held an aperitif in his hand. He stood as soon as he saw Eden.

"Why are you running? Slow down. You've just gotten out of bed."

"I won't break, Daddy. Where is Mother?"

"She isn't dressed yet."

Eden frowned.

"Is something wrong?" asked Stuart.

"No. I merely have a question for her." Eden crossed to her father and showed him the coin. "Do you remember this?"

"Of course. Your mother gave it to you before you left." Stuart glanced between Eden and Trevor. "What happened?"

"I lost this coin in London," began Eden.

"And Trevor found it," finished her father. Stuart sank back into the chair.

"Yes. How did you know?"

"Because that is the way the coin works." Her mother's voice came from the doorway. Corinna breezed into the room. A gentle smile graced her visage. She kissed her husband, then faced Trevor and Eden.

"My mother gave me that coin just before she died. She had received it from her aunt, who told her an outrageous story connected with it, a legend about the coin bringing two people who were destined for a great love together. My mother died before she could tell me the story, but my father told it to me later."

Eden stared at the coin. "But how . . . I mean, what—?"

Corinna took the talisman from her daughter. "The legend says when a woman loses the coin, her true love will find it. It happened to my mother, and it certainly happened to me." She gazed at Stuart with such love that Trevor could almost touch the connection between the wedded couple.

"And now it has happened to us." Awe filled Eden's voice.

"Coincidence," muttered Stuart.

"It is hard to believe," acknowledged Trevor. "How could a coin—"

"I didn't say it did. I only said it was a legend." Corinna gave Trevor an enigmatic smile. "But Eden did lose it and you did find it."

"No one will believe it." Trevor shook his head. The silver circle in Corinna's palm flashed up at him. He didn't understand why, but he did believe the coin had worked some sort of magic.

He looked back at the coin and blinked. From this distance, he would have sworn Venus winked at him.

"What will you do with the coin now, Mother?"

"Oh, no. The coin is yours." Corinna handed the token back to her daughter. "You'll know what to do with it."

Trevor opened his mouth to protest, but Lorane appeared in the doorway.

"What are you talking about?" The girl looked from one face to the other.

Trevor turned to Eden. "Don't you dare."

EPILOG

Four months later, Eden cried as Lily spoke her vows to Toddington. Her husband handed her a handkerchief.

"This is a happy occasion," Trevor reminded her.

"I am happy. Just because I am crying doesn't mean I am not happy." Eden blew her nose.

"You won't be able to sing if you continue to cry."

"Don't remind me." Eden blew her nose again. She wiped away the tears and inhaled deeply.

The ceremony ended. Lily looked at her. Eden nodded and stood, taking a place at the front of the church. Organ music filled the nave. The rich notes reverberated through her. Eden began.

The words of Goethe hung in the air, and even if the congregation didn't understand the German, the joy in Eden's voice told them it was a song of celebration. Her voice placed the high notes like fragile porcelain for all to admire, yet with enough life and shine that the very air seemed to glitter with her song. By the end of the first line, many cried with the happiness she expressed in her voice. The organ's robust tone was the perfect accent to Eden's ethereal singing. When the organ played the final notes, the pews looked as if white flags fluttered in every row as the ladies and gentlemen wiped their tears with their handkerchiefs.

Eden returned to her seat.

"They're going to pester you with even more demands to perform after this." But Trevor's eyes gleamed with pride.

"I know, but how could I refuse to sing at Lily's wedding?"

"If I remember correctly, you offered to sing."

"A gentleman wouldn't throw a lady's words back at her."

"Are you trying to correct my behavior?" Trevor's face took on a look of exaggerated surprise.

Eden laughed at his expression. "*I* would never do such a thing."

The wedded pair finished signing their names and headed out of the church. As the rows emptied, Trevor took Eden's arm. "It's too bad your parents couldn't stay for the wedding."

"I didn't think you would miss my father."

Trevor chuckled. "I don't."

Eden frowned at him.

"Let's just say that your father and I came to understand each other before he left. And if *we* ever have a daughter, I'll probably act exactly like him toward her husband."

A portly woman waved at them. "Lady Ryeburn, Lady Ryeburn."

Trevor and Eden stopped and waited for the woman to reach them.

Panting and fanning herself with her handkerchief, the woman jiggled as she tried to catch her breath. "So good of you to wait, Lady Ryeburn."

"Of course, Lady Feathering. We met at the ball last evening."

"I'm so pleased you remember me. You sang so beautifully this morning. I was quite moved to tears."

"Thank you, Lady Feathering."

"Might I ask if you'd be willing to sing at my daughter's wedding?"

Trevor's shoulders shook with silent laughter. Eden nudged him with her foot. "I hope your daughter's wedding is soon, for I shan't be able to sing in a short while."

Trevor's gaze shot to her. Eden ignored the question in his eyes.

"Next month," responded Lady Feathering.

"Then I think I shall be happy to sing at your daughter's wedding. Do call on me and we can discuss it." Eden smiled at the woman.

"Oh, I am so pleased. I shall call on you next week."

"I look forward to your visit."

The woman moved off, waving again.

Trevor handed Eden into their coach. He took a seat beside her. "Just what did you mean by you won't be able to sing in a while?"

Eden smoothed her dress, then patted his arm. "Just that. In a few months I shan't be able to sing for anyone—except you, of course."

"You're not making any sense." Trevor glared at her.

With a bright grin, Eden stroked his cheek. "I hadn't planned on telling you in the coach, but in a few months, I shall be in confinement. After all, we can't have the *ton* talking about the scandalous behavior of Lady Ryeburn, can we?"

"Confinement?" Trevor stared at her.

"Certainly. In my delicate condition, you can't expect me to entertain all your friends." Eden watched as his expression changed from puzzlement to wonder to joy.

Trevor cupped her face in his hands, pulled her to him and kissed her. The welcoming tightening in her stomach sent sparks of pleasure flashing through her. All of a sudden, Trevor released her.

"How are you feeling? We should get you home. You shouldn't be out." Trevor reached his hand up to knock on the top of the coach, but Eden pulled his hand down.

"The baby won't come for months yet. I am strong and healthy. At all events, I'm not missing Lily's wedding breakfast."

Trevor gave her a look filled with doubt. "Are you sure?"

Eden gave him a mischief-filled grin. "Trust me."

About the Author

Gabriella Anderson makes her home in Albuquerque, New Mexico, with her husband, three daughters, two dogs, and assorted fish. When she's not writing romance, she volunteers at her daughters' school library, plays volleyball, and tries to avoid cooking and housekeeping. Fluent in English, Hungarian, and German, as well as knowing Latin, Gabriella loves the way language works, especially when she can use it to put a story on paper.

If you liked Gabriella Anderson's A MATTER OF CONVENIENCE and A MATTER OF PRIDE, be sure to get the third installment of The Destiny Coin series, A MATTER OF HONOR, available March 2001 wherever books are sold!

Eden has obtained happiness and feels she can now pass the destiny coin on to her new sister, whom she has grown fond of. In A MATTER OF HONOR, Lorane St. John is entering her third season and is expected to wed, but she has different plans. Eager to flee London, she stows away on board a ship bound for America. However, the dashing captain Nicholas Grant discovers her and is determined to send Lorane home as soon as they reach shore. He has plans of retiring and taking a wife to build a home. Nicholas's vision of a peaceful summer is suddenly interrupted as Lorane stirs up trouble in Boston society. But both soon find that they're destined for each other.

BOOK YOUR PLACE ON OUR WEBSITE AND MAKE THE READING CONNECTION!

We've created a customized website just for our very special readers, where you can get the inside scoop on everything that's going on with Zebra, Pinnacle and Kensington books.

When you come online, you'll have the exciting opportunity to:

- View covers of upcoming books
- Read sample chapters
- Learn about our future publishing schedule (listed by publication month *and author*)
- Find out when your favorite authors will be visiting a city near you
- Search for and order backlist books from our online catalog
- Check out author bios and background information
- Send e-mail to your favorite authors
- Meet the Kensington staff online
- Join us in weekly chats with authors, readers and other guests
- Get writing guidelines
- AND MUCH MORE!

Visit our website at
http://www.zebrabooks.com